ALSO BY ROBERT GAGE EVANS

FICTION

OTHER BOOKS OF THE SOJOURNER SERIES

Book One
YOKUTS WARRIOR
SPRING
1792

Book Two
SUTTER'S FORT
ALTA CALIFORNIA
1838

Book Four
JAMES CATHCART
SLAVE TO THE DEY OF ALGIERS
1785

NONFICTION

PINE FLAT: A QUICKSILVER BOOMTOWN (2005)
PINE FLAT: FAMILIES OF THE MODINI PRESERVE (2016)

OMROD SMYTH

A COD FISHERMAN FROM BRISTOL TOWN

1579 - 1634

A NOVEL

ROBERT GAGE EVANS

THE SOJOURNER SERIES
BOOK THREE

OMROD SMYTH - A COD FISHERMAN FROM BRISTOL TOWN, 1579–1634
by Robert Gage Evans
Book One of the Sojourner Series

Edited by Jocelyne Thomas, Branwen Books Editing Services
Cover design and interior layout by Ellie Searl, Publishista®

ISBN-10: 0998342505
ISBN-13: 9780998342504
LCCN: 2016958538

PINE FLAT EDITIONS
Sebastopol, CA

For Christine

CHAPTER ONE

1579
Bristol, England

T HE LAST SNOW melted in mid-February and the fruit trees finally bloomed in late April. When the apples were the size of my little fingernail, Da stopped shoeing horses, cleaned and ordered his tools, oiled the leather of his bellows, and repaired the brickwork on his kiln. When all about the workshop was suitable to his eyes, my Da got ready to leave our cottage in Bristol to go fish for the cod of New Founde Land. I knew from past years that the Gravenstein apples would be sweet when Da returned with his share of the profits earned from selling salt cod.

For the five years past my older brother, Jeremy, joined Da to learn how to fish for the cod in New Founde Land; he also started his apprenticeship as a smyth. We call ourselves the Smyth family because that was the truth of the matter. The men of our family had always learned, father to son, how to pound hot metal into nails or horseshoes or anchors, and as it happened with many families of no wealth whatsoever, the craft or trade of a man also became our name of record.

I was proud of Da, for he was the best smyth in our part of Bristol, and me and Jeremy never tolerated a hint from those who were inclined to think otherwise. "You take the big one with the smart mouth," he'd whisper. "I'll take the other two peckerwoods."

It was all in play—the fighting part. So we said, anyway. Even so, with the neighborhood clans and families the way they were, sensitive to their own lineage, it was simple to find a vulnerable spot to touch if I was inclined for a little action. I knew for a fact that one playful comment about a certain sister of the Brown family would lead inevitably to a brawl. Of course, any comment regarding a man's ability to walk home unaided from the tavern, or a woman's propensity to smile in a certain fashion at strangers, was an invitation to battle.

There were well-established rules to fair fighting in our part of Bristol: no weapons of any sort, no fingers to the eyes, and no chewing on a handy nose or ear. Still, all were bloody battles, much encouraged by the spectators who inevitably gathered. Victory was claimed only by the last standing participant, that being usually Jeremy, and it was he who always dragged me from the pile to stand at his side.

Jeremy added his share of silver coins from fishing and shoeing to the family welfare, as was also natural and expected. I'd recently turned thirteen years of age, and it was my time to join in the annual trip to New Founde Land. I readily admitted that last year, when Da and Jeremy left me with the children, I was in a bad mood the whole time they were away.

"Stop pouting," Ma said, a million times or so. "Naa, naa on little Omrod," sister Ruby said, about two million times before I gave her a backhand that brought blood to her nose. I helped stop the bleeding and held her close to whisper "I'm sorry" enough times for her to promise not telling Ma about the backhand. For a girl, and a sister to boot, Ruby was usually a good person to have on your side, and the backhand was a mistake I'd never make again.

I was big for my age, with black hair between my legs even last year at age twelve. There was the hint of a moustache now, and I was near as tall as Da and within a stone of Jeremy's weight. Even so, my stomach hurt all day, and I didn't sleep a wink on our last night of waiting. Jeremy wasn't much better with his constant rolling about and hogging the blanket to hisself and getting all riled up over nothing at all. With not a whisper, both of us stood packed and ready to go with dawn a bare hint in the east.

We were all three at the front door inside our cottage. Da looked me in the eyes and said, "Just keep your mouth shut and do what I say." He added, "The back of my hand if ya don't."

"Yes sir," I said. The chances of a backhand from Da were always pretty good, mouth shut or not. His left hand alongside of my head was worth a pause, but the right hand always meant gushing blood and blackened eyes. Ruby was in her glory whenever she saw the black and purple around both my eyes. "Naw, naw," she'd chortle. "Omrod's a nitwit! A nitwit." Over and over until Ma or Da told her to shut her lips and give us some peace and quiet.

Da pulled the latch string and walked out into the first touch of dawn.

"Just keep away from Da and watch what I do with any job," Jeremy whispered. "The work is hard, but give it the best you can and it will all work out."

"Thanks," I said. "If a tin whistle such as yourself can keep free from Da's backhand, I should think there's no fear for me."

Jeremy winked his left eye at me but said not another word—not while we were in front of Ma and the children. My brother was taller than Da and nearly as strong, but slow to burn—not like Da at all. I liked Jeremy, and I knew he liked me.

Jeremy stayed for the moment and put a hand on Ma's shoulder. "I'll give the boy a hand where I can," he said.

"Good fishing," said Ma. "Do what your Da expects, now. The both of you."

We three walked from our far south end of Bristol City over to Bristol Harbor in less than half a day. "Here we be," said Da, and then led us onto a ship tied at the end of a long wharf. Da went to find the captain, and Jeremy led me stem to stern and explained the how and why of everything. I heard a lot of words from Jeremy, but all the strange sights and smell swirled around in such a manner that not one sound got past the wax in my ear.

"Omrod! Are you listening to what I have to say?"

"Sure, Jeremy. Sure."

"Tell me then; what did I say is the name of our ship?"

"*Mosquito*! You said the damned ship was called *Mosquito*."

The captain of the ship was named Gilbert Pike, and it took thirty-eight men and boys to sail the *Mosquito*. There were some for the sails and some to manage the ten large cannon and four swivel guns. We were still tied to shore when all of us were assigned to guns or sails by a man everyone called Bosun.

"The sea's got more pirates than a Bristol dog has fleas," Bosun said.

"One look at the lot of us," I whispered to Jeremy, "and any pirate would die from laughing."

"Quiet down! Damn your hide!" yelled Bosun.

"Shush!" whispered Jeremy.

Da stared straight ahead.

I'd never heard Da make any comments about pirates one way or another, so when we finally had a moment alone, and after he'd swatted me first left-hand and then right- hand, each with the force needed to kill a fly, I asked him about pirates.

"Well," said Da, "I never met a pirate up close and personal, but you've got to know that even the smallest ship of the cod fleet is fit with at least a few cannon or swivel guns."

"Pirates want gold and silver, not a bunch of salt cod," I proclaimed.

"Now listen here, sonny-boy—a shipload of dried and salted cod might sell for a thousand pounds." Da looked me in the eye. "Can you picture in your miserable little mind a thousand pounds?"

"I've seen ten pennies once," I said.

Da gave me the back of his left hand, but more in his idea of play—not for drawing blood. "If we get any pirates this trip, I'll have Cap'n Pike send you over to them, private-like, to talk 'em to death."

After six straight meals aboard the Mosquito, I looked over at Jeremy and whispered, "How come you never told me about all the food?"

Jeremy was growing a beard, and he scratched dandruff flakes all over the table before answering my question. "Just think a bit and it'll break clear for your pathetic little brain," he said.

"At home we're always on one meal a day from when the snow falls until late spring, then maybe there's enough food for two meals in one summer day to the next," I said.

"And how would Ma and Ruby and the other kids feel about their empty bellies when we're filling ours every single morning, noon, and evening?" Jeremy winked his left eye. "We don't want the women and children to know how much we suffer aboard ship, do we?"

"Ma would tell Da to stay home with the kids while she suffered through a season of cod fishing," I said. "She'd like this life of the gentry." I tried to wink an eye but failed. "Maybe she'll try her hand at shoeing horses and put Da in the kitchen to cook the soup and wipe shit from a baby's bottom."

Jeremy winked his right eye, the damned show-off. "Just keep your mouth shut when we get back to Bristol. You know how Da gets when he's upset with someone."

"Three meals a day. Salt meats cooked up hot and with gravy. Biscuits and sauerkraut and all the beer a stomach can hold. Damn! All this and over an hour each meal to chew and drink and shoot the breeze with one another. Damn!"

"Captain Pike's a good man, no lie, but he must figure that a fat and sassy crew will end up catching more cod than a skinny and pissed-off crew. He's no saint, just damned smart gentry."

I sipped my beer from a battered tin tankard and felt the comfortable roll of the *Mosquito*. It was only two days at sea before my feet were spread wide and there was no dip or roll that impeded my way around the deck. My jobs were varied, but all were simpleminded tasks of lifting boxes or pulling ropes and following the orders issued by the able or ordinary seamen. Da was rated able seaman, a small notch below the bosun. He and six other able seamen sat together each meal, and they always had first choice of food and drink, with rum added to the beer as a special treat, and unavailable to the "waisters" who were my companions.

The bosun and Captain Pike had women as companions—wife for the bosun but not for the captain. When I got Da alone and asked him if perhaps Ma could join him on the next voyage, he made himself as big as two men and yelled at me to fetch a bucket and brush and commence cleaning the dining area until the cook himself judged the task complete to his satisfaction.

The trip from Bristol took five weeks with no big storms or pirates either. Some of the crew were sick the first few days, but not me.

When we sailed into St. John's Harbor, New Founde Land, I stared at maybe three hundred merchant ships at anchor, all about our size and all packed like berries in a basket. "Stick close to me and Jeremy when we go ashore," Da said. "It's worse than a summer fair in Bristol." We had some fishhooks and lead sinkers to sell or trade, so Da put me on his shoulders to wave the hooks with one hand and sinkers in the other.

Jeremy kept his eyes out for any slippery cutpurse that might lurk in our shadow, and Da made what deals he could make. When I came to ground, we had no fishing tackle remaining to trade, but we had pants and boots for me and three heavy wool blankets to divide.

"Those Basque folks and most of the Portuguese people will make you a fair deal," said Da. "Just stay clear of the damn Frenchmen and those Spanish devils."

"How can you tell one from the other?" I asked.

"Well, now, the Basque talk sounds like surf on a beach that rolls boulders as big as your head, and the Portuguese mostly smiles into your face. The others you've heard talk before, so stand clear of 'em."

"I know *parley vous* and *hola*, I guess."

Da gave me the grimace he made for a smile and led us back to the *Mosquito*.

At dawn we made our way out of St. John's Harbor and north for half a day. The wind was fair, with only a few clouds scudding along the horizon. There were no sand beaches that I could see. Mostly there were steep stone beaches backed by rising hills filled with green softwood—fir and spruce—but a scatter of oak could be seen on the hills, and willow near the shore. There was nary a sign of people on beach or hills but always at least one ship of the cod fleet in sight until we turned west around the horn of a big peninsula and into Conception Bay. We traveled a bit further west with a failing wind and turned in to Mosquito Cove at dusk. It took a while to set the anchor and store the sails, so it was full dark when Captain Pike told us that we would spend the night shipboard and get to work at first light.

I didn't do much more than take a small nap once in a while. For the rest of the time, I stared into stars that never seemed closer to the touch and heard nothing but the regular beat of surf on the nearby shore of large boulders. I wasn't worried in any way, and certainly there was no fear of failing at any task that I might be assigned, but there was a touch of wonder at the adventure of it all. New Founde Land! The end of the world, for all I knew, and here we were: me and Jeremy and Da.

Da and Jeremy had told me that our captain was a gentleman of substance and that he owned a plantation on the Cove of Mosquitoes in New Founde Land. I knew, of course, that a planter on New Founde Land was not a farmer of wheat or cabbage but a planter of some business in the colony of New Founde Land. Pike owned fishing grounds and fishing boats and employed servants or sharemen in his business of cod fishing.

"Here's the way of it," said Da. "We catch and salt the cod here at the cove every summer for eight weeks or so. There're three men in a boat to catch the buggers and two men on shore to cut and salt them. It's a team of five that sleep and eat together."

"One drafty shack per team," Jeremy added. "Fresh cod or salt cod to eat."

Da nodded to support his eldest son's comments, and added, "In the end, Pike sells the cod when we return to Bristol. Pike tells what he paid in expenses, subtracts all of his expenses from the price received for the cod, and puts half the remaining amount in his pocket."

"The sharemen get to divide up what's left," said Jeremy.

Da looked at me in a way that gave his permission for me to ask a question.

"How about the servants to Pike—how are they paid?"

"Taken from our end," Da said. "Expenses, he calls it."

"Is Captain Pike an honest man?"

"Don't waste your time looking for an honest man, my boy. Pike steals just enough from us Bristol men to make us come back with him the next year. Mostly we end the summer with more in our pockets than if we stayed ta'home."

"Am I a shareman?"

"All the boat captains get double shares, crew gets one share, and the boy gets half share," said Da.

"A half to start, anyway," said Jeremy.

"What about the other two on our team?"

"The splitter gets one full share, and his boy gets the same as you—half a share." Da paused to make sure I was paying attention. "The boys get to keep what's left over after they pay your da for all the good things he had to buy so that both you snot-noses could enjoy your visit to New Founde Land."

Ma always said that I took after Da for telling jokes and all. Hot or cold—back of the hand, or a pathetic joke—that was my Da.

The first week on shore at Mosquito Cove, Da and Jeremy had a forge going full blast to turn out nails and spikes. I worked with a gang of men and boys to drop and limb spruce trees and drag the trunks to a pit in the ground. A boy stood at the bottom to pull the whipsaw down while the man on top pulled the whipsaw up. Up and down, up and down, sawdust in my eyes and nose, red pain in both arms, and a raggedy plank of twelve feet or so as our reward. We hammered together seven tiny cabins for five men each. I'd say they were designed and built to keep most of the wind and rain from both men and boys, but not much more. There were two more of the same for servants of the captain, and one for the captain himself. Captain Pike had two separate rooms and caulking of moss and mud to keep him warm and dry for his stay in New Founde Land. It took better than four weeks for us to finish the cabins, build tables to process the cod, racks to dry the cod, and covered sheds to store the slabs of salted cod.

During those days of construction, and after all five of our crew had consumed what was called cod stew or cod chowder or cod shit for our dinner, Da or Jeremy or both took me in hand to climb the nearby hills to study where the best mushrooms and red berries grew. We ate our dessert of the evening in silent appreciation of something sweet, talked meagerly of the day's activities, then drifted back to our palatial quarters to drop quickly onto our bunks of wood covered with grass and brush and down into a black hole of sleep.

On the fifth week of my time at Mosquito Cove, and the first year of my life with the cod, I finally got to go fishing. I sat in the bow to tend the anchor, bait hooks, and kill the fish brought on board by my Da and Jeremy. Some of the fish were as long and heavy as me. The first cod I grabbed stared his bug eyes at me as I tried to lift him into the boat. Twice he got the better of me and fought his way back into the black water.

"Bring the bugger up, damn you," yelled Da.

"We'll have hooks in our butts if he gets the best of you," yelled Jeremy.

Hand over hand, I pulled the monster and finally yanked him over the gunnel of our boat with every muscle of my arms and legs. I landed on my back with the fish flapping like a sweaty prizefighter on my stomach.

"Roll over and gut the bugger," yelled Da.

"This is no time to fall in love," called Jeremy. "We're in a good spot for fishing, not fucking."

I learned how to hold them by a gill with one hand and cut their throat with the other. Soon I was skilled and fast enough with killing the fish that Da and Jeremy brought into the boat that Da gave me the gear to drop a line of my own over the side. Now we three fisherman landed our own fish, but I still killed and gutted the lot. Each new day I managed to add a few more fish to the total, and each night I had visions of new boots with my half share in the fall. New boots for me, a wool shawl for Ma, and a bucket of candy for all the kids except Ruby.

On my second year with the cod, we three fished, killed, and gutted our own fish, and it got so we filled the boat with cod to the gunnels lickety-split. Often enough, we were first on shore to run the wheelbarrow filled with cod to the two men who split and salted our cod.

On the second day of my second year of fishing at Mosquito Cove, I made the childish mistake of sniggering at the three fishermen from another boat that followed us to shore. Those other fishermen gave me a black look for my error of manners, and Da gave me the back of his right hand. Lights flashed through my head. Blood dripped from my nose.

"Git to work, you damned fool," Da told me, and then he moved up the hill with his barrow full of dead cod. That evening Da took me for a long walk up a steep hill and sat me down with my back against a big fir tree. "Don't you ever embarrass me like that again, sonny-boy," he said.

"Yes sir," I said.

Da's black eyes were submerged in deep holes topped by bushy eyebrows and were held in place with cheekbones made of chiseled oak wood. A fearsome face. A hard face, with no sign of weakness.

"Yes sir," I repeated.

At the end of the second year, Captain Pike took Da and me aside, where no one could hear what was said. "Tell me, Eldad, what shall I put for a family name on my records?"

Pike and the other men who worked for double share—the fishing boat captains, that is—called Da by the name Eldad, while all the rest of Mosquito Cove called him Da, related by blood or not.

"After all these years, Captain, why do you need another name to call me?"

"For the new records I have to give the investors," Pike said. "My records of sharemen and servants must show a given name and a family name—no exceptions."

Da said, "Smyth," without raising his eyes.

Pike smiled. "What about the young'un here, the one called Omrod. Is he a smithy as well?"

"Soon enough," Da said.

"Make it sooner than later, Eldad. I've my eyes on that boy of yours."

"He'll be ready when you are, sir."

A shiver went down my back. Da and Captain Pike with a plan for me? Maybe Jeremy could whisper in my ear about what to expect.

At our little holdings on the edge of Bristol, Da had a forge in a small shack made of wood and thatch that he called his shop. There was a thicket of trees and forty paces from house to forge, so the smoke and sound were not a bother to Ma and the kids. On the first fall season after returning from New Founde Land, I watched as Da hammered away on his iron anvil from dawn to dusk. He beat that hammer with strokes so fast they blurred my eyes. I knew that the red-hot metal was usable only for a few blinks, so it had to be bent and hammered into perfect shape with great passion. I was especially aware that a mistake could not be corrected and that one of aim or timing resulted in both wasted time and metal.

"Waste not, want not," Da was always telling me at the forge.

Da never gave lessons or made any comments about his craft as a blacksmyth, but I knew from the days when Jeremy was learning the craft that soon I would be waved forward to work the bellows.

That was my favorite part of Da's shop—the bellows. They were shaped like a flat accordion—a button accordion, with two handles attached. This set of bellows that Da used was made of slats of wood with leather overlaid, and it had all sorts of valves, pipes, and levers hanging here and there. When Da wanted to pump the fire up to full blast, he worked one handle by hand with his foot securing the other handle of the bellows to the ground. There he was, pumping up and down with one hand, and holding the long-handled clamp with the item to be forged deep into the fire with his other hand. When the wooden shed was desert hot and Da was red-faced, we listened as the bellows worked through a series of hoots, honks, and blares, all the while climbing up the musical scale. Finally, when we heard this whistle of a very particular tone, Da always said, "Now!" and he then immediately removed the molten iron from his fire to forge a nail or shoe or whatever was required by a customer.

Eventually, after that first summer in New Founde Land and during the cold winter of Bristol, I was allowed the opportunity to work the forge while Da managed the long-handled clamp with the item to be forged. It was two weeks on the bellows before Da gave me a chance to produce a single nail.

Da was the best blacksmyth in all of Bristol, of course, and it was he who provided shoes for the horses of the landed gentry and anchors for the best fishermen. When Da removed a molten bit from the furnace and immersed it in the vat of water, he performed a special magic that could not be taught.

On a very special day, Da said, "Come here," and then he handed over the long-handled clamp.

I moved quickly, with no hesitation, to douse the hot metal in the water. A sudden hiss brought the water to a boil, and a cloud of steam obscured the light in our wooden shed. I could feel the transformation of red ember to something solid and useful and quickly removed the horseshoe from the water for Da to examine.

"Remove the shoe from the clamp," Da said.

I trusted Da, but even so, I was surprised that the horseshoe was cool to the touch.

"It gets cold real fast," Da said.

"Not just cold," I said.

Da made that grimace I knew for a smile. "Cold and hard," he said.

Without another word, I dropped the shoe into the briny slop of the slack tub and returned the long-handled clamp to its proper place. After a slow count of twenty—under my breath, of course—I returned to the tub and fished out the shoe to hang and dry. "No rust will find that shoe," I said.

The grimace was gone, and Da was on to his next task.

At the end of my third year of fishing with Da and Jeremy, and also my sixteenth year after birth, Captain Pike called me and Da into his New Founde Land office. Books filled shelves, and rugs covered the floor. "Sit," he said and waved us to the two vacant chairs. "Is he ready, Eldad?"

"Yes sir," said Da.

"Omrod Smyth, is it?"

"Yes sir," I said.

"Listen to me, Omrod Smyth. You must realize by now that each fall season, when we return to Bristol, the savages arrive in Mosquito Cove to burn our boats and cabins."

"Yes sir."

"I'm going to leave both of you here on the cove while the rest of us return to Bristol."

"Yes sir," Da said.

"Jeremy can take care of the Smyth family in your absence, can he not?"

"That he can, sir," said Da. "He's a married man now and knows the ways of Bristol as well as me."

Captain Pike held both of us in his gaze. "When I return next spring, I want all the boats and all my plantation cabins ready for use on the first day of my arrival."

"Yes sir," said Da.

"I'll also need two additional boats ready-built—whaleboats that can hold ten people and sail or row in a moderate sea." Pike leaned forward in his chair. "Do you understand me, Eldad, or not?"

"Yes sir, every word," said Da.

"Good, because I also want you two to put up a good supply of hooks and sinkers for all my Bristol men so they can start their fishing a good month before all the rest on the New Founde Land coast."

Da was not to be pushed beyond his point of tolerance. "That'll be at the standard fee, sir. Five pounds per boat and a ha'penny per hook or sinker."

"Agreed," said Captain Pike. "Of course I'll add the sum total of your costs as expenses for the sharemen to pay."

Da's pause was a mere half beat. "I'd expect that half of my costs and expenses would come from your share of the profit and the other half from the Bristol men, sir."

I watched the silent conversation between Da and Captain Pike. Sparks erupted from the eyes of both men, but not a word was exchanged. Finally, Pike shrugged his shoulders and said, "Done."

"Yes sir," said Da.

Pike and Jeremy were packed and ready to leave.

"The savages burn the boats and the buildings and retrieve nails from the ruins," Da said.

Jeremy asked, "For what purpose, sir?"

"To make metal tips for their arrows and spears."

"Ahhh," said Jeremy.

Da spoke to Jeremy, but Pike was the intended audience. "The savages paint themselves with red ochre to make themselves appear more dangerous than they are."

Captain Pike smiled. "Our ancestors painted themselves blue when preparing for battle."

"So it seems." Da pulled a new indigo-blue shirt from his pack. "I'll put this to good use," he said.

With no additional words, Da and I moved toward the cabins of Mosquito Cove while the captain and Jeremy moved to board the waiting ship.

"Weigh anchor," yelled Bosun.

"Off to Bristol Town," yelled Captain Gilbert Pike.

Chapter Two

Winter 1582–83
The Beothic

THE STERN OF PIKE'S SHIP was still in sight.

"Fetch two axes and a hatchet," said Da.

We dropped and limbed four spruce trees before lunch, and in the afternoon we worked the whipsaw to make a couple of dozen high-quality planks that ranged from four to twelve feet long. At dusk we set out six snares each; Da went east up a nearby ridge, and I put mine west along a damp gully. Da brought back a hat full of berries, and he made a very tasty chowder of fresh cod, salted water, and berries. At dawn we checked our trap lines, with Da netting a good-sized rabbit, and I found two partridge in my snares. During the second day we built a door frame for our cabin with a door that swung into the cabin. We also erected two pair of beds, with a large lower bed and a smaller upper bed, as well as a separate and spacious bed for Da.

"That'll do 'er," said Da. "Men with feet on the floor, boys or monkeys up top."

I was pleased with the changes in our cabin. Solid beds and substantial door—it looked almost homey.

Da looked around the cabin and nodded his head a few times. "She'll look good enough for gentry when we finish with her."

That night we had a stew of rabbit and partridge cooked in saltwater with some greens that Da found near the top of his trapline ridge. We ate the lot to the last bit and had a short fart contest that Da claimed winner for both sound and smell. I was one to never ever debate Da in the wonders of his farts.

"Da," I said. "Can I ask a question?"

"Try me," he answered.

"Is there a god that I should pay attention to?" It was a subject of little interest to me, but I was tired of farts as a source of debate and pulled the god question out of the smelly air.

"You just run like hell at first mention of any god, my boy." Da sat back in his chair, comfortable and full of good food. "Gods are for the gentry to discuss, not us poor folks."

Da was having a good time with me, and that was fine, but I responded in a manner that would keep him talking to me. "We've had a full stomach for two days running," I said, "and there's something about the light in this place that makes me smile."

Da waved his right hand at me with a playful backhand swing but remained silent.

"I'll tell you, Da"—I waved an arm toward our new door—"with the beach up against the spruce trees at sunset, there's something I can't put into words but can feel in my stomach."

Da had a coughing spell that caused him to spit huge globs of phlegm into a bucket. After he settled, he looked me in the eye. "Look here, Omrod."

My name! In all my life Da had never said my name aloud. *Boy* or *son* or the back of his hand, but never Omrod.

"This god business gets real tricky, so I'll give you what I've figured out. Just once, now, and then I'll leave you on your own two feet." Da took a deep breath. "Here's the way of it for me. If you've got a man standing in front of the crowd, with him saying he and some god-or-other have a special connection, you've got to turn around and get away. If you hesitate even a wink, that man will have his hand in your pocket for whatever he can find. If you hesitate two winks, then the god-man and the gentry will tap you for everything you own."

Da moved his body a bit closer to mine. "More times than I can count, the god-men and the gentry have figured ways to work together, with their collections on the plate and their taxes." Da looked me in the eyes. "It's always us poor folks that get to bleed blood in the constant wars the lords and god-men invent. It's always us poor folks that stand to lose the few pennies we've hid under the bed to taxes and collection plates. You've got to make yourself damn well scarce from both."

Tonight, Da had a face that looked carved in wood. Maple or oak—certainly not spruce or willow. There were a bunch of small curves on his cheeks and a nose that brooked no argument from man or beast. An ugly face to some, but more handsome and strong to me. "We've got one gentleman here on the cove in Captain Pike," I said, "but none of your god-people."

"Well now, Omrod my boy, to tell the truth of the matter, I'd say that the Bristol gentry generally stay clear of churches and lords in the same way as do us poor folks."

"Why's that?"

"It's because the Bristol gentry have got the same opinion as I do about taxes and tithes." Da was getting blood up into his eyes. "Just look at St. John's Harbor. Not a tax collector in sight, and us fishermen from a whole mess of places are free to trade this for that without a lord or pope to say otherwise. In the whole of New Founde Land, as far as I can see, there's not much use for the god-men and their fancy-dress partners."

"Da, I like the feeling of you and me here on the cove." He had his eyes on me but kept quiet. "Is there any chance of bringing Ma and the family here to live?"

"Listen close, Omrod."

I leaned forward over the table because Da was speaking in a near whisper.

"Me and Captain Pike is together on this scheme. We both like Bristol the way it is, and we both like this here island as it is. What we're about doing this winter is trying to figure the best way of keeping everything like it is in both Bristol and New Founde Land."

It was nice talking with Da. Here he was dropping more words on me than ever before. Plus, now he was giving me a big secret.

"Okay, Da, you tell me what to do, and I'll do it."

We dangled nails that were sharpened to a point from low branches of trees. Da had picked a sheltered glen an easy day's march through the woods from Pike's plantation. North by northwest was the line we took on Da's best guess, with the sun and all.

"Put some rocks in a big circle, son, and build a fire that will burn with lots of smoke," Da said.

We retreated in an easterly direction from dusk to darkness, then pulled blankets over our shoulders and dozed against the same tree until dawn. It was cold enough to shiver but not yet cold enough to freeze.

When we checked the next day, all the nails were gone.

After three days passed, we hung more sharpened nails and a few long spikes from the same trees and bushes. I built the fire as before, and Da returned to Mosquito Cove while I spent a long night watching Venus traverse the sky.

When I checked the next day at Da's sheltered cove in the deep woods, all the nails and spikes had been collected.

After another three days passed, and with dawn a rosy hint on the horizon, Da poured boiled water over the indigo shirt and stirred the mess until a syrup of dark-blue dye remained. I covered my naked body with the dye until there emerged a ferocious-enough warrior to repel Viking pirates or Norman invaders. I carried a big handful of nails in a backpack, while Da carried a small steel knife, a packet of steel needles with eyes, and a ball of cotton thread. I was bare-ass blue, and Da was dressed as a Bristol fisherman.

We force-marched to our chosen glen and arrived midafternoon. I started a fire, organized the gifts at Da's direction, and then we sat erect and still in front of my fire.

The day was nearly at dusk before he appeared at the edge of our glen. The apparition moved quickly to sit opposite me across the small fire. The two of us studied the other with patient attention: his skin near vermillion, mine indigo blue. I think that he smiled first, but likely we moved on the same beat. Da made no sound, and his expression was solid maple.

The circle filled twice over with red warriors, and all remained quiet until I held out my left arm and pointed at it with the right hand and yelled, "Blue!"

My age mate on the opposite side of the fire mimicked my action and yelled, "Tisquantum!"

Da stood, touched my shoulder to stand, and led me around the fire to stand in front of Tisquantum. All remained still until Da motioned for the red boy to stand and for me to sit in his stead. Without a word, Da returned to his original spot and signaled for the red warrior to sit at his side.

The savages remained silent until dusk was upon us, and then a tall elderly warrior stepped forward to raise both hands and flash his fingers and thumbs.

Da nodded, both he and Tisquantum stood, and they walked down the faint path toward our Mosquito Cove cabin. I knew that a half-moon and Venus provided ample light for them to stay on the correct path and out of the brambles.

I sat alone among the savages. The evening slowly grew darker and colder. Someone put a soft blanket over my shoulders, and another savage motioned for me to stand and follow the lot of them. So far, Da was right as rain. I was still alive and on my way to a new home. All I had to do now was stay alive and fit in with the savages and their savage ways. Da would teach his new son the ways of civilized folks, and I'd learn how to be mean and sneaky like savage demons.

A passel of children was assigned to teach me what I should know. The eldest, a girl who appeared to be about twelve years old, embraced a small tree, looked up into the branches, and made an unintelligible hash of whispers, croaks, and peeps. After her fifth repetition, given in a slow, tedious beat, my rendition of her words brought the tribe of youngsters to their knees with shouts of ridicule and expressions of contempt. The day quickly turned into my worst ever on this earth. The children were merciless in their demands of perfection. At the twenty-third effort to correct my interpretation of her original phrase, my chief interrogator gave me a meager smile. The gesture was more insult than a token of comfort and brought little relief from the worry I felt.

The second scramble of words the girl offered for my memory was worse than the first, and only the diversion of a tag game, followed by slabs of smoked salmon furnished by two indulgent mothers, saved me from killing my female opponent. Could Da be treating Tisquantum in the same fashion? Would the red boy have even redder cheeks from a backhand or two? The possibility, even the likelihood, of such an event, gave this blue boy little comfort.

"Mamateek," she said and "mamateek" I repeated without flaw. That much I had on rote memory: mamateek was the Beothic dwelling, and a fine house it was. It seemed larger and warmer than our Bristol cottage and with added amenities that went way beyond the primitive shacks at Mosquito Cove. There were long poles tied together at the top, and the lower ends spread in a circle around the inside edge of a thigh-deep pit. Small trees were bent into hoops at different heights to keep the poles in position; then the whole frame was covered with birch bark and caribou hides, starting at the bottom and working upward, like tiles. A smoke hole was left open at the top.

The owner of my assigned mamateek was a widow who seemed a bit younger than my real ma. This savage woman had two children, and since the boy considered himself a warrior, he treated me with the aloof loathing necessary for our relationship. His name was Wasamook, which, according to his sister, was also the word for salmon. The girl was Oubee, and she was my primary instructor in the Beothic language. Oubee was much like my sister Ruby; both girls gathered attention to themselves with persistent contrary opinions and the steady refusal to accept tasks not of their own choice. Both were smarter than what was good for them, pleasant to look upon, and better ally than enemy.

Every warrior, especially Wasamook, ignored me for the first two weeks. I slept with a ragged caribou hide at the remote edge of our mamateek, while the other occupants slept close to the fire, spooned together in warm comfort under a pile of blankets. At the point when I could follow very simple directions and greet my hosts with appropriate gender and status, nine young men took me on my first hunt for osweet.

Finally! I was given something to learn from sensible men—not from a demented girl and her mob of vindictive children.

It was still early fall, with frosty nights but as yet no snow of any consequence. When I was shown the selected animal of our hunt, I knew the large stag as a caribou and the meat as a delicacy for gentry. There was a small herd of twenty or so of the osweet, and I was assigned with two of the youngest warriors to drive the animals toward a large river. So it was that we three warriors forced the beasts to jog between fences that had been built by the Beothic villagers over the years. Eventually we forced them into the river just north of the village, and very quickly men in two canoes began to chase and kill the osweet with their long spears. I gathered that this strategy was easier than spearing them on land, as the osweet could not swim as fast as the savages could paddle. Our little troop of warriors killed and butchered two of the huge deer, and on returning to the village we were met with smiles of the most modest sort.

Oubee and her impatient mob of children took immediate command of my life again. They told me in the most patronizing manner imaginable that my hunt was an opportunity designed especially for me to learn the very simple elements of a caribou hunt. Those strategies and tactics of the hunt were, of course, the skills that every child understood very soon after taking their first ten steps. Further, they managed to explain to me, that in a few days the entire village would conduct the essential hunt that would furnish meat for the entire winter.

Through each and every moment of daylight, Oubee remained an acerbic fiend and persistent in the manner of a single vicious mosquito.

"Silly child," she admonished me, for the tenth time of the morning.

"Not child!" I protested in my best Beothic words.

With vicious use of sarcasm—always the weapon developed to a high standard by younger sisters—Oubee directed a combination of sign and slowly enunciated Beothic words toward me. "You," she said, with her right hand pointed directly at me, "learn . . . like . . . a . . . child . . . still . . . in . . . the . . . cradle."

"You"—I pointed directly at her with my right hand—"teach as my enemy, not as my friend."

Oubee looked at me, head aslant like a bird listening for movement of a worm. "Good," she said. "I understood both your words and the meaning of those words."

"More friend, less enemy," I said.

She picked up a fir bough and swept clean a stretch of dirt, threw down the bough, and picked up a long stick. At one edge of her smooth surface she drew a circle and said, "Rising sun." Oubee then stepped six paces to the other side, drew a circle, and said, "Setting sun."

I smiled, stepped forward to take her stick, and then marked the north and south poles. In the next few moments we bantered back and forth until we could quickly exchange the English and Beothic words for the cardinal directions, and then I returned the teaching stick to the rightful owner.

Still no smile as she carved an indentation and said, "Mosquito Cove" in both languages. Then, for a good long while, Oubee drew the rough outline of New Founde Land, with the clear representation of both the northern peninsulas. All the other children removed themselves from such a tiresome activity, so when she finished we sat and silently contemplated her stunning creation.

Oubee pulled a large piece of smoked salmon from a pocket of her jacket, and we shared the entire stick in a slow companionable moment before she stood to continue my lesson. Oubee quickly sketched a lake with a river wandering northeast to reach what I knew as Notre Dame Bay. We taught each other the proper names for lake, river, and bay, and I was able to accurately place our village at the southeast edge of Beothic Lake.

Still no smile, and it was midafternoon.

Oubee stabbed her stick into a point near the middle of the northern peninsula. "Here, in five days, the scout team will begin moving a large herd of osweet south, toward our river. Do you understand me, Blue?"

"Yes, I understand you, Oubee."

"You will join the scout warriors, and they leave tomorrow at dawn."

"I understand."

There were six of us, and the sun was blood-red as we left our village. Clouds quickly covered the sky as we climbed the first ridge of hills north of Beothic Lake, and snow began falling in tentative large flakes at the second ridge. It seemed as though each step forward caused a lower jolt of cold and an increased density of falling snow. When I could barely see the man a few steps in front of me, he stopped, and the remaining four circled around us in a protective ring.

"Stop and listen," our leader yelled. He rummaged through his pack to withdraw a long rope with knots bulged at arm's length from beginning to end. "Follow me," he yelled, and each warrior secured the rope in hand until we were stumbling in an awkward dance through a white blast of snow that would not tolerate an open eye. After an interminable duration, I felt the terrain change from up to down, and the wind increased to an even greater velocity.

I was number five in line and stumbled over some hidden obstacle. The rope disappeared, and in an instant I was buried in snow. It was very quiet and much warmer. A sharp spasm of pain shot through my left leg, but the absence of wind and the quiet and warmth combined to mitigate the pain. Sleep seemed a lovely option.

My snow cave collapsed, and two voices kept yelling, "Blue! Blue! Get up!"

Back into the blizzard—fifth in line and counting each step down the precipitous slope. Somewhere above three hundred, the numbers muddled until they stuck at three seventy and the wind disappeared.

"Blue, here is the cave. Blue, open your eyes."

The five young Beothic warriors smiled at me as if they had told a magnificent joke at my expense—a joke so foreign to one of my lineage that it would remain unintelligible to me forever and a day. I returned a very feeble smile in their direction, and all burst into loud guffaws with much pounding of one on the other until, finally, the leader pulled a long face and in quick order had the rest building a fire, exploring the cave, and checking my leg for serious injury.

When the fire was roaring and nothing found to worry about from the black end of the cave or my intact leg, we pulled hunks of smoked osweet from our packs and chewed silently until our leader pulled a blanket around his shoulders, leaned against the wall, and fell asleep. We all quickly followed suit.

My clothes were part of the equipment given to me in preparation for the excursion with the scout team. The soft, light osweet hide was a marvel to wear, with two hides sewed together to form a shawl that covered the arms and hung to my knees. It featured a belt at the waist, otter fur around the neck, and a wide collar at the rear that could be pulled up to form a tight hood when necessary. Osweet fur lined the inside, and the outside skin was covered with a mixture of grease and red ochre to make it waterproof. It was much better apparel than the grease and black tar of Bristol jackets, by a long shot.

Of course we all wore leggings and mittens and shin-high moccasins, so with our additional blankets we could snooze through the night, as comfortable as six bears in a cave. Dawn arrived with quiet stealth, and we all stared from the cave at deep snow and sun glinting off every surface in a sharp blaze.

Erdu was the leader of our squad. Quick and smooth as his namesake, the otter, he dug through first his backpack to pull out a small wooden device, and then pulled the same item from my pack. "For the sun and snow," he said.

I watched as he placed the wooden eyepieces over his eyes and tied two cords together behind his head. They sat neatly on the nose, and two very narrow slits gave each eye a view of the world. "For the sun and snow," he repeated. The eyepieces fit tightly against my face so that the only light that could enter my eyes came from the slits. As we moved away from the cave into the bright sun, my vision seemed enhanced. I could see snow-covered trees in the far distance and could also follow a slow-moving raven from one horizon to the next.

"From the Kivalliq," Erdu shouted. "The Kivalliq people."

We struggled through the snow until the stars appeared and we could remove our eyepieces. Venus popped above the southeastern horizon, but we continued slogging until both Venus and a slender moon could be seen well above and behind our left shoulders. We merely excavated a hole in the snow large enough for six warriors, sheltered together as spoons covered with blankets, and moved on again at first light. Near dusk on the fourth day of our trek, Erdu stopped, pointed to a hillside, and said, "Osweet."

The entire hillside seemed alive with black specks that moved in slow progression toward us. The huge stags could soon be observed as distinct from the females and their calves. Hundreds and hundreds, all moving at a steady pace through a large valley.

The task was simple. We had to keep the main herd of osweet moving in a generally southern direction without disturbing their sensitive temper—and with only six warriors.

This is how Erdu assigned us our tasks: "Manshet, Bidisoni, and Blue, you three warriors must stop any drifting of the herd down the creeks and rivers that flow west into the ocean." He gave a slight turn of his head. "Bebadrook and Gobidin, you two will stop any drifting of the herd to the east, down the streams that lead to White Bay. I will gently push all from the rear."

There were remnant fences from previous years that were designed to facilitate the success of our hunt and that of every late fall hunt by the Beothic people. Some sections were still effective, while many swaths of fence had been removed by the vicious New Founde Land seasons. At the first spot of a missing fence on our side of the approaching herd, Bidisoni pulled a long rope from his pack, climbed a tall spruce, and then from near the top quarter of the tree he tossed one end of a rope down to me. He made two loops of rope around the tree and then scampered down to the ground.

We pulled the rope taut and moved backward to give Manshet room to begin beating on the tree with a stone ax at about shoulder height. When Manshet was more than halfway through the trunk of the tree, he stopped, jogged twenty paces south, and began beating on another tree. Bidisoni and I pulled our end of the rope in a rocking motion until eventually the tree fell over but remained connected to the stump, thus forming a triangle with the ground.

For the rest of the day I was given the task of climbing wounded trees, securing the rope near the top, and returning to ground so that

Bidisoni and I could pull down tree after tree to form an effective fence that the osweet could neither jump over nor push through. If there were not trees enough for a fence, we stuck poles in the ground and tied birch bark tassels to their tops. As unlikely as it seemed to me, the tassels that flapped in the wind apparently frightened the osweet into moving ever southward as a cohesive herd.

When it came time to turn the mob of osweet to the east and force them to cross the river flowing north into White Bay, we had dozens of villagers up from the lake to assist us with loud noises and waving flags. The fence on both sides was tight, and now the osweet were in a steady run that in the course of one day took the leaders to the river close to our village. A flotilla of canoes waited in the wide river with one warrior guiding a canoe and the bowman holding a long spear. Those osweet that survived slaughter on the river were forced to move down a fenced shooting gallery, where they were showered with arrows and spears. The women skinned and quartered the large deer, then carried the flesh on their shoulders through the snow and back to the village near Beothic Lake.

Everyone shared in the distribution of meat and skins, and Oubee finally smiled at me. "Now the north winds can blow how they will, and snow can cover the earth, but the Beothic will laugh at the tedious gods."

I returned her smile with both my eyes and lips.

It seemed to me, when we finally settled in our homes, that most of the people of my village were happy. The elders told stories that were filled with endless variations, some of which I understood up to the fine details. But most were epics of war with one belligerent opponent or the other, and the tales were always finished to the great satisfaction of the Beothic villagers.

I took the time to observe the challenge of one neighbor against another as they embarked on serious gambling games. Oubee taught me that I could try my hand in mastering the games of holding sticks behind my back, or small stones in my hand, but I could never, ever, achieve a single victory over her. She was correct in her prediction, of course—during that first month of winter, in any event.

Birds and rabbit and smoked fish supplemented the huge cache of frozen osweet meat, and I was not the only warrior who packed meat on his bones. I was happy to spoon through each cold night with my family. I was happy to hear the stories of the elders and participate in the daily check of snares and traps. I was happy to live in my village next to the large and beautiful lake.

Da and Tisquantum appeared in our village on the evening of the third full moon after the osweet hunt. They placed their snowshoes against the mamateek, brushed snow from head and shoulders, and ducked through the supple leather door.

"Omrod, my boy," Da said, "How be ya?"

"Fine, Da, and you?"

He looked around the large and comfortable house. "A bit warmer here than in my place," he said. His grimace told me that he was happy to see me alive and that his scraggly house on the cove was colder than a witch's teat during the full moon of March.

"The shack with the kiln is warm enough," said Tisquantum. "That's where we spend most of our time, in any event."

I noticed that Tisquantum spoke with a fine Bristol accent that was more compatible to a Bristol gentleman than a Bristol fisherman.

"The boy has something to show his folks," Da said.

Tisquantum placed a pile of fishhooks, a metal hatchet head, a metal knife, and a book at the knees of his father. In attendance of Da and his adopted son was my family, plus Tisquantum's father and a few close neighbors. Oubee was front and center. When all were settled and quiet, Tisquantum started to speak. "These metal items I have learned to make under the tutelage of Master Smyth," he said. He smiled at Da. "I call my father Da in the same manner that my brother Blue calls him Da."

The Beothic villagers smiled and nodded their approval of the arrangement that apparently was working well for both the Beothic people and the Bristol fishermen.

Tisquantum's father leaned toward his son and asked a simple question. "Is he treating you as a Beothic warrior?"

"This Bristol fisherman shows his respect for me in every possible way," he said.

Tisquantum's mother smiled and asked, "Are you happy with your adopted father?"

"I understand that Blue is happy in his new home, and I must report that I have a similar attitude of warmth toward my new da."

Oubee interrupted the exchange of pleasantries and shouted, "What is the other thing in the pile?"

Tisquantum held the item up in the air. "It is a book, and Master Smyth has provided the necessary instruction for me to decipher what is contained in this book." The savage flipped through the pages as if performing a trick of magic. "I can now tell you what ancient people of Europe said to one another, what they thought about important events of the time, and where they traveled with their ships and armies." He flipped the pages again, and yet one more time.

Oubee moved away from our mother and brother and around the sputtering fire to sit close to her cousin. She smiled her unpleasant younger sister smile up into his face. "I thought you were taught by the People to show a modest demeanor and not to sing like a silly crow."

The gathered Beothic smiled and tittered at the wit of Oubee. I had no idea what she was implying about modesty or crows, but what was certainly clear to all observers—especially to me—was that their son had achieved a dramatic victory for their side. It was patently clear that Tisquantum could speak Bristol English better than Da, and I was still fumbling with the likes of Oubee and her six-year-old allies. Tisquantum could also apparently decipher words from the squiggles made on paper. Neither Da nor I had the least idea about reading from books.

Oubee was not to be ignored by Tisquantum, nor diverted by the smiles of her neighbors. "I care nothing for tales from foreign lands, but I do care if you abandon the way of your very own people."

Da stood to stem this intrusion into his plans. A young girl, Ruby's age or so, was drawing the savages away from his plan to develop an alliance with the Bristol fishermen and the savages. Da gave Tisquantum a larger grimace than usual and then looked at me. "Well, now, I hope that my boy Omrod hasn't been too much of a bother for you folks." He waited for Tisquantum to translate to the People's language what he had said in Bristol English, and then Da nodded at the recitation of my modest contributions to life in the village.

"Well, now," said Da. "I believe that we have developed some trust between those that live here in this beautiful land and those who visit the same land during the long days of summer." The cycle of translation and discussion ran its course before Da continued. "Here's what I propose for out next step. How about if you folks send four more of your boys to me for the rest of the winter?" Once again there was a swell of murmurs, eventually followed by silence. "I'll teach the boys how to build and sail a boat that can carry ten to twelve people in a moderate sea. We'll also burn the Portuguese and Spanish summer camps and collect all the metal items from the mess." Da waited for another long interruption, and finally, when none of the Beothic people said a word, he finished his proposal. "The thing is, my friends, next spring after the ice breaks up we can all use the new boats to hunt the small whales and seals that run close to shore. Also, your boys will also get to use the forge and learn how to make some useful metal items that will forever serve the families of this village."

Now smiles matched the eager discussion that erupted around the fire. Finally, there was a short period of silence, followed by a statement from Tisquantum's father. "I will speak to the Council of Elders tonight," he said. "We will consider your request for the four additional warriors."

"That's real fine of you folks," said Da. "I want to make sure that everything is fair and square with you people and us Bristol fishermen. If there's any hint of worry about anything at all, just go ahead and tell my son Tisquantum what you have in mind."

There was a long silent period before Tisquantum's father spoke. "What else will you have the Beothuk do for you, Master Smyth? After the new boats and capture of whales, that is." Tisquantum's blood father gave Da a very small smile and then listened for any response in respectful silence.

"Well, now, nothing much at all. I'd just like for you folks to call my boy by his true name, which is Omrod."

Oubee again interrupted the negotiations of her elders. "Blue! Blue is a much better name than one that breaks your lips!"

Oubee's mother smiled and patted her daughter on the knee.

"Blue is a name that we are all comfortable with, Master Smyth," Tisquantum's father said. "Perhaps I can promise to use his foreign name while others of our village may choose one name or the other as they wish?"

The nods and chuckles affirmed the sensible proposal, and Da said, "Agreed. Good enough for me."

After another bout of silence, Da started up again. "I was thinking, if it is not too much bother, maybe you could have someone teach me and Omrod how to build one of those odd-looking canoes of yours?"

"Done," said Tisquantum's father.

"No need for talk with any council," said Oubee. "Done with the name and done with our beautiful canoe!"

She was answered with a rollicking chorus of cheers from the Beothuk villagers. "Blue! Blue! Blue!" they shouted.

A few women brought additional wood to stoke the fire, and some other women produced birch bark trays filled with smoked fish, and also bark cups filled with melted snow. Two men brought a hindquarter of osweet from their storage shed and set it to roast on a metal spit. Food and people swirled about the lodge, and laughter echoed from every quarter.

The haunch of osweet was thawed and cooked sufficiently to produce constant attention from an appreciative audience. Sharp knives sliced dark-brown curves from the shoulder, and hefty sticks served to roll the meat over to the flames. I cut three generous slices, placed them on a platter, and found Tisquantum and Oubee engrossed in conversation.

Oubee looked at me with her nice smile—not the little-sister smile. It was a rare treat on this wonderful day. I handed the plate to her and sat between the cousins. We three were stuffed chock-a-block on the edge of the crowd and removed from the fire by twenty paces. Oubee dropped her smile and said to me, "Are all Bristol sailors as attendant on their masters as our blue servant?"

"Only when our Beothuk hosts provide such generous delights for us to eat," I said.

Oubee laughed and nudged her brother in the ribs. "See! What did I tell you? Our blue vassal speaks his new language with all the wit and grace of a trained crow!"

"No! Cousin-mine," said Tisquantum, "I could understand the word *eat* with great clarity. Much better than any crow that I've ever heard."

We laughed together at my expense for a bit, finished eating the meat, and licked our fingers clean. "Tell me, Tisquantum, where did you get the book?"

"From a dwelling at your Mosquito Cove."

"Da claims that you can read the book, yet I know for a fact that Da cannot read a book in Bristol English or in any language known to man."

"Ha!" said Oubee. "My cousin sucks foreign words from the air and understands their meaning with no effort that I can see." She moved closer and beamed a huge smile into my face. "On a certain occasion my brother spent one day with a Micmac trader who traveled here from a neutral tribe. In one single day he progressed in conversation with the visitor from that of an infant to honored elder."

"But, Oubee, the Micmac was a most helpful man. He was filled with benign patience and cunning intelligence. We became friends and remain so to this day." Tisquantum shrugged his shoulders. "I was able to breathe without thought and learn the Micmac words in a manner for which I have no understanding."

"How do you credit such a gift?" I asked.

"I admit to having given some thought to the process." Tisquantum moved closer so that we three were sitting shoulder to shoulder. "In the case of the Micmac trader, I believe that it helped that we shared some common words and common activities in our villages. I found that if I listened carefully for similarities and put new words quickly into the play of our conversation, I was able to learn very quickly. In fact, it seemed then, as now, that the faster I learn, the easier I learn." Tisquantum looked up into the smoky ceiling and then back toward me. "My teacher knew the rules of our game, and he was willing to participate without reservation, but, in sum, it took in fact only one day for me to gain a certain proficiency in the Micmac language."

"See?" said Oubee. "I told you he was a wonder to all."

Tisquantum smiled at me. "I honor my Micmac teacher by accepting the name he gave to me."

"What?" I thought my hearing was off. "Tisquantum is a Micmac name?"

"I will use no other name."

Oubee jumped into the discussion. "Everyone in the village hated the foreign name at first. Especially me!"

"What was your name before Tisquantum?"

"I will not say the old name, and no one in the village will violate my explicit wish in this matter." Tisquantum flashed a grin at his favorite cousin. "Am I correct to say that *no one* in the village will retrieve my discarded name?"

Oubee made a quick nod and returned to chewing a large hunk of meat.

"But explain this to me, Tisquantum. Da does not read a word in any language, so what or who taught you to read and speak Bristol English?"

"I found a book that showed detailed drawings of how to contrive various knots used by men aboard your large boats." He answered my unasked question. "Da and I found the book among many others in a cottage where Captain Pike dwelled last summer."

"Captain Pike, yes."

Tisquantum settled into a more comfortable position. "It was a simple matter to have Master Smyth remember the name of each knot, and there beneath the drawing of each knot was the written word for that particular knot. We matched Master Smyth's verbal name and the written name in a rapid manner. We then progressed from knots to sails and the various and sundry parts of various ships, all explicitly named in this beautiful book. With such a large stock of words I was able to make meaning from similar words in the context with those known words, and in some magical fashion I was soon able to read Bristol English."

"All in one day, I presume?"

No, Brother Blue. I must admit that the struggle continues with your tricky language, but I am looking forward to some significant help from you."

"I'm as dumb as Da with the reading business."

"Then we will both learn from the other to our mutual advantage."

I had the gut feeling that I was having a conversation with a Bristol gentleman, someone more esteemed in the ways of the world than even Captain Pike. Here was a savage in front of me, offering to teach me how to read my own language and already speaking many of the English words with instinctive poise. Even so, the response fell with ease from my mouth. "It would be a pleasure to work with you on any task you may request," I said.

"Me too!" said Oubee. "I want to play with both of you."

Da and his son and their four new students disappeared into the white desert, and life settled into a comfortable routine. When I made the first effort to kiss Oubee, she screamed like six jays in distress, and our mother pointed for her three children to sit by the fire: two warriors and one noisy brat. Our mother sat very still and allowed the silence to build for what was certainly an eternity. Finally, she nodded her head and spoke to each of us in patient, warm words.

"Oubee," she said, "you are nearly a woman and must relinquish the games of children. Do you understand, my daughter?"

"Should I let Blue kiss me?"

"No," she said. "When you feel yourself as a woman, then you will have the confidence to tell any warrior that he may or may not kiss you. You are now a strong, healthy, and smart child. Soon you will show the same qualities as a woman. For now you must be patient, but with the absolute rejection of your persistent suitors."

Oubee gave her mother a quizzical expression, as if the thought that anything could change in her life was impossible. "What must I do, Mother?"

"There must be no kissing or fondling or intercourse permitted between you and some eager warrior of your acquaintance. None."

Oubee gave her mother a tentative smile. "What is it called when we four spoon together on cold nights?"

"It is called 'keeping warm' and nothing else."

"Oh," said Oubee.

The little brat turned her head in slow rotation to study my eyes and finally show me her most mischievous smile. "It is called 'keeping warm,' Blue," she hissed. "Nothing else."

The three stared at me in silence. I could feel sweat down my back and saw sharp red flashes in my blind eyes. "Play," I muttered. "Just fooling around."

The fire burned in tortured spurts, but eventually the calm silence of our home returned. Our mother studied us all before saying, "I will not presume to tell my warriors what to think or how to behave. I can only caution you to protect my daughter from the world until she can manage the job on her own."

Now she stared at me. "Blue," she said, "I am honored to have you as my adopted son. In two years I would be honored to have you as my son-in law, but you must be patient and kind to Oubee and honest with me. You must also expect to compete with many suitors for my daughter. They will appear like magic from Beothic villages scattered throughout our homeland. Honor them as fellow Beothic warriors, all with a keen eye for beauty, and not as a challenge to your status as a warrior. The decision of who eventually marries my daughter resides solely with Oubee and no one else."

I didn't hesitate a moment. "You have my word as a Beothic warrior, my mother. I will honor you in word and deed."

"Thank you, my son." There was an uncomfortable pause until our mother completed her message to her family. "For the remaining nights of the cold seasons I will have Oubee facing the fire, then me, and followed by my first son and finally the second son."

"Poor Blue," Oubee said. "He'll have a blue butt all winter—a perfect match with his ridiculous name." My sister squinted her eyes at me. "What is an Omrod, if you can say?"

"An Omrod is a magnificent blue eagle," I said. "Strong and ferocious."

"Ha!" Oubee said. "You never could tell a good lie, Omrod!"

When there was more sun than snow, and green leaves appeared on east-facing slopes, Da sent a messenger for me to bring the additional four warriors to Mosquito Cove.

The Council of Elders chose four warriors, and Oubee chose herself for the overnight trek.

It was a miracle! All the cottages were framed with new lumber and made secure with a mixture of moss and clay applied to every corner and knothole. The interiors had two pairs of upper/lower framed beds and a single extra-large bed for the captain of each boat. A stove and chimney of Da's design stood in an alcove of each cottage, and I quickly observed that when the oven baked bread, it also maintained a comfortable temperature for the men. Now the Bristol fishermen could relax in the new chairs scattered about and chat with one another as if they were gentry.

Captain Pike's cottage was large and grand with a book-lined office, a large meeting room, a bed surrounded with Bristol-made mosquito netting, and a cooking alcove large enough to prepare food for a princely number of guests.

Tisquantum gave me a tour of the new wharf, processing tables, and storage sheds. "Better than Bristol," he said.

"Is that what Da says, that Mosquito Cove is 'better than Bristol'?"

"That's what all of us say whenever we finish a task."

"Are all the warriors able to saw lumber and build a square corner?"

"We do whatever it takes to satisfy Master Smyth."

"Do all the warriors call my father Master Smyth?"

"You and I are permitted to call him Da. For the rest it is 'Master Smyth.'"

I smiled and nodded with affection at my father's new son. "Why were we called?" I asked.

Tisquantum led me to a sheltered spot not far from the whipsaw pit. Here on an elevated platform were two whaleboats, both designed for four men to row, plus two at the bow to handle a harpoon, a man at the tiller, and one for the sail. The workmanship was magnificent.

"Better than Bristol," I said.

"Welcome back to Mosquito Cove," Tisquantum said. "Now we can get back to work."

At dawn, Da supervised as the first whaleboat was skidded downslope and into the water. All of us watched as he carried a tub full of rope and a harpoon into the bow. I could see that the forward end of the harpoon was a long wooden spear with a large metal point.

The tail end of the harpoon was tied to the rope coiled in the bow of the boat.

"Listen up, my boys," said Da. "Today and tomorrow we will begin teaching you how to manage the whaleboats. All of you will have practice in all of the positions necessary for sailing and rowing and capturing the seals and small whales. On the third day, I propose to kill our first seal."

"Better than Bristol! Better than Bristol," the warriors chanted.

"Quiet down, you lot. Pay attention." Seabirds, shorebirds, and tiny tree birds could all be heard. There was a slight wind and overcast sky. "Here's the way of it for the first boat. I'll take the tiller, with Blue and Tisquantum on the sail."

Da quickly named the rowers and bowmen, and we shoved off into a calm inviting sea.

The oarsmen quickly proceeded to flail at the water in pathetic fashion, and the bowmen prepared to jump into the sea and swim to shore.

"Stop! Stop! All sit still and be quiet." The boat drifted in a circular fashion until the warriors could listen. He pointed to a young man on the forward port oar. "You! Come to the stern and sit with me." Da waved and coaxed the youngster to sit next to him. "Blue, take his place, and all of you watch as he handles his oar."

I took a grip and moved my hands forward with the oar just above the water. When my arms were stretched to the stern, I dropped the oar into the water and pulled until my hands were on my chest and raised the oar out of the water. I continued with the rowing, causing the boat to move slowly in a large circle. Most of the crew made an effort to mimic my technique, and after a long while Da called to the warrior sitting next to me on the port side to "Join with Blue, my lad. Grab hold of the oar and join with Blue."

"Ready now, drop the oar, and puuuull, my lads. Up and forward; drop the oar and puuuull."

It took a while, but eventually, with the two warriors at the separate port-side and lee-side oars, and with a little help from the tiller, we went along at the rate of a slow walk and in a generally straight line.

"Okay now, my lads—listen up." Tisquantum took my seat, and my partner stayed on his seat. Da called for the forward lee-side rower to sit with him while I took his place. In that fashion all had the opportunity to row with a partner who had some skills to teach each innocent victim. It was a long day for me because as soon as Da considered that he had four Beothuk warriors as adequate oarsmen, he returned to the wharf and replaced them with four new recruits.

During the following day, every man handled the tiller, harpoon, and every position in the boat. A seal was killed on the third day, and within a few weeks both boats were afloat and bloody with a dozen or so seals at the end of each day. Twice we harassed a small whale into the cove and onto a stone beach, where each time we killed and butchered the beast with much laughter and sampling of bloody meat.

"Better than Bristol by a bloody lot," said Da.

"Better than Bristol!" we all cheered, like the bloody lot we were.

CHAPTER THREE

Spring 1583
Tisquantum

C APTAIN PIKE CLEARED HIS BUSINESS in St. John's City in two days, and then sailed his ship around the eastern horn of the large peninsula, across Conception Bay, and tied up to his spanking-new wharf on Mosquito Cove. He was first to shore, of course, and welcomed by me, Da, and Tisquantum. I was dyed blue, my brother in gorgeous red, with Da standing at attention in his best Bristol cod-fishing gear.

"What in hell's blazes have we here?"

Tisquantum stepped forward. "Please, sir, excuse our intrusion on this inopportune moment, but we would like to schedule a meeting with you at your most convenient time and place."

Pike peered at the apparition as if viewing a talking fish. "For what purpose?" he finally managed. "This meeting of yours?"

"We need to report our activities since you left Mosquito Cove last year."

Captain Pike looked over our shoulders to survey what he could see from the wharf. "I see two new whaleboats together with all the cod fishing boats from last year." He paused and took a dozen steps toward shore. "I'll be damned. Every structure that we left here last fall is clearly intact and apparently refurbished."

"The current status of your plantation will be explained in the first part of our report," said Tisquantum.

"Who will tell me what in hell has been going on around here?" Pike took two large and deliberate steps toward Da. "Master Smyth?"

"Sir, that'll be the red-colored savage, Tisquantum. Making the report, that is."

Pike grinned. "After dusk, then. This evening, in my cottage."

Captain Pike sat us down to table and smiled at one and all. "I've saved a few surprises for this meal." He gave a special smile to Da. "Please join me with consuming the bounty from our Bristol home." A servant and cook brought us separate plates filled with lamb roast, new potatoes, and carrots, together with schooners of Bristol beer.

There was no talking at all, other than Pike seeking assurance that his guests were served all the food or beverage they craved. After coffee, with both cream and sugar and wedges of still-hot spice cake, he called for the servant to clear the table and bring the rum. Pike's constant smile indicated that he was pleased to see our reception of his gift, but his eyes, bright and unblinking, revealed the joy of success we had all achieved.

Captain Pike swallowed his first tot of rum, and after a decent moment of silence he spoke. "Master Smyth, I have to inform you that the men who came with me from Bristol this year have given the word that they think they've died and gone to heaven. Every man and boy praises the condition of their boats and sheds and swoons at their comfortable cottages."

"I've also talked with all the men," said Da, "and they're most happy with conditions here on the plantation. All to a man say they are ready to start fishing at your command, sir."

"I am most impressed with what you have accomplished on the cove, Master Smyth, and you can expect a tidy bonus in your hand when next we dock in Bristol."

"I had some mighty good help from the boys here at the table, and they'll be telling you more of what happened over the winter."

Pike sipped his second tot of rum with one hand and tapped a finger on the table with the other hand. I couldn't hold his eyes, but it seemed that he was not only mightily satisfied with what we had already done for him, but now he was scheming for what would come next.

The captain cleared his throat. "So there it is, Master Smyth. Instead of four weeks of brutal work just to get the plantation ready to fish, the three of you have us ready to pull the first cod at dawn tomorrow."

Tisquantum smiled through his mask of red ochre. "It was Master Smyth who had the order of things, sir. Blue and I merely did as we were told."

Captain Pike kept his eyes on Da. "The blue one is your boy Omrod, I believe."

"Yes sir, that is he for certain," said Da.

"And the red apparition—what might his name be?"

"Tisquantum, sir."

"An awkward name, to be sure," said Captain Pike. "Can we invent some name for him that can fall with ease from our lips?"

"No sir." Da was not apologetic with his answer. "He'll go by no other name, and we've all come to see him as Tisquantum, and nothing less will serve for us, either."

"Tisquantum. It does seem to have a pleasant ripple of the tongue. Fine. Good. So it shall be: Tisquantum."

Da neither smiled nor frowned. "Yes sir, so it is: Tisquantum."

Pike showed his first full smile. "My cook says his new stove is better than most in Bristol, and that his very own bed is turned out for a queen."

"Master Smyth repaired your stove and added a few inventions of his own to the new stove," said Tisquantum. "Indeed, Master Smyth set us to building every bed on the cove, square and solid with pine lumber and strung with a mattress of osweet leather, all according to his specifications."

"Osweet?"

"Caribou, Captain Pike," I said.

"Indeed."

"There's also closets in every cottage to hang wet clothes," I added.

Captain Pike put his hand up for silence. "Enough of all this good news. I believe it is time for Mister Tisquantum to give us the full report of what has been happening here on my plantation." Pike made a motion as if to lift my red brother from his chair. "You have the stage, sir, and I will study what you say."

Tisquantum did stand, and he presented his practiced oration with relaxed ease. He was entertaining, with both glib anecdotes and the serious facts of first meeting between Bristol fishermen and Beothic savages. He described the village osweet hunt and managed a laugh from Pike over my struggles to learn the Beothic language. My red brother described his cousin Oubee as a smart and even-tempered creature, but then reported in unnecessary detail that she had been held responsible for teaching the dullest of Bristol fishermen the Beothic language. Even with the silly tale of Oubee's sweet disposition, the story was wonderful in every respect.

When Tisquantum finally returned to his seat, we all sat quietly until our cups were empty and Da's head was bouncing near his chest. Captain Pike stood from his chair and stared at each of us in turn. "Magnificent!" he said. "As unbelievable and dramatic as any story that I've ever heard tell."

"These are two valuable young men," Da said. "Best I've ever worked with, and that's no lie."

"Correct you are, Master Smyth, and I aim to take advantage of your brilliant work in training them in such an admirable fashion."

"And how might that be?" said Da.

"I'll pay a triple share of the profit this fall for you, good sir, and give a double share for Omrod."

Da gave his quick grimace to Captain Pike and then looked at Tisquantum. "What of the red savage?"

"Beginning tomorrow he will work as my secretary at one and a half shares of our Bristol profit."

I jumped in with my suggestion. "The girl is qualified to serve as captain of a whaleboat, sir; you might consider one-half share as a reasonable remuneration for her services. There's plenty of seals hereabout," I said, "and the skins are good for trade in St. John's."

Captain Pike shook his head. "A girl telling men where and when to hunt? Never in this world." He gave a smile to Tisquantum. "If she's clever and comely, I'll take her in hand as a house servant for room and board."

"Oubee will return to our village in the morning." There was no doubting Tisquantum's decision. His voice was sharp. Combative.

"That's the better of it, Captain," said Da. "A woman about always disturbs the men from their fishing, I'd say."

We all stood, and Captain Pike ushered us through the door into cold night air. "Fishermen to their boats at dawn," he said. "Secretary to his desk at the same time," he added.

Da and I were captains of separate boats, and each of us took two Beothic warriors as our fishermen. They were fast learners and already skilled with rowing and with their own fishing from a canoe. They had, of course, served an apprenticeship of sorts with Da during the spring. Although we were not the first boats unloading a full quota of cod at the wharf on the first day, within a week it was either Da or me who would cheer on the other as commanding the second fastest boat ashore.

Tisquantum and I, plus Oubee, developed a system to pay for the fresh supplies of food provided by the Beothic. We three convinced some of the villagers to leave their mamateeks alongside the big lake and establish a summer camp close to our plantation. In fact, Da and Oubee took a whaleboat over to St. John's City and returned with a load of metal hoes and shovels, plus seed for growing corn, squash, and potatoes in this new summertime village of the Beothic people.

Da sent his own cod boat out to fish with a red savage captain and crew for two weeks running. He and Oubee worked those same two weeks to show those Beothic who were interested how to plant and fertilize and grow a crop of foreign plants. Captain Pike made his visit to the new village every other day or so, and he had Oubee explain to her friends and neighbors that this was how red and blue and white people could work together for the good of all. Those were his words, in both Bristol English and Beothic: "…work together for the good of all."

Pike put one hand in the pocket of his dress uniform and raised his voice to Tisquantum. "Tell your people that we Bristol fishermen will visit their land for a short spell every summer and then return to our own home. We Bristol fishermen will trade whatever the Beothic want in exchange for the food that you provide to the cod fishermen."

"What if the Bristol people stay through all the seasons?" Oubee asked. "Where will we all live? How can we find enough food to eat for that many people?"

"Look around, Oubee—what do you see?" Pike was puffed up, like a turkey gobbler in heat. "Wild land with hills and forest and no people at all, that's what I see. The Beothic need never worry about too many people on their land." Captain Pike smiled at the beautiful young woman. "I promise you, my dear. You have nothing to fear from Bristol men."

My ability with the Beothic language continued to improve, and four additional savages became acquainted with Bristol English. I noticed the constant smiles every evening with the steady deliveries of osweet steaks to the cod fishermen. The daily menu included freshly caught trout, plus berries and greens in magnificent variety for the tables in each cottage, all from Oubee's hunters and gatherers.

"Nothin' but cod to eat in past years," said Da. "It was always salt cod boiled or fresh cod boiled—take your pick."

Captain Pike's cook was favored with the same expanded culinary supplies, and the captain, with his now-constant smile, was no exception to the rest of us who worked on his Mosquito Cove plantation. Pike had a secretary now, one who quickly learned to keep exact and useful records. In this particular year, we Bristol men noticed that Pike smiled in a constant beam, whereas in the past years he had carried a dour expression from dawn to bedtime and spoke frequently to his minions with spiteful excess.

Tisquantum needed only pen and ink to compile neat lists of supplies available or needed, all in a clear hand. Tisquantum had a separate ledger in which he made a list of the cod caught and salted every day. He was ordered by Captain Pike to write the weekly exchanges of correspondence between Pike and the Bristol investors. It was six to eight weeks for the round trip of such letters to complete their journey, but such were the responsibilities of competent secretaries at both Bristol and Mosquito Bay. Plus, my red brother became a frequent communicant with the English plantation owners scattered about the coast of New Founde Land. All were keenly interested in an accurate reporting of fishing conditions or problems with savages or pirates. Captain Pike's very own Mosquito Cove plantation became the center for the exchange of information among all the English-speaking fishermen.

In a very short while the foreign plants began to show leaves of green, and vigorous stalks grew to knee height. Even though the calendar said that it was the fifteenth day of the month of May, 1583, a sharp frost during the night tuned all the foreign plants into black jelly. Da was busy with fishing and could take no time to seek additional seeds, and Oubee was counseled by her mother and aunts to learn the merit of green leaves and tubers and mushrooms that had served the People from beyond memory and to forget her failure with the invaders' plants. "A lesson well learned," said one of her aunts.

Still, there was ample food, freely exchanged with the Bristol fishermen for useful items such as metal ax heads and pretty baubles such as beads and ivory dice. Both Bristol fishermen and Beothic savages were comfortable with the whims of New Founde Land weather, and all smiled at the knowledge of their superior trading skills—talent inherent to their race, so it seemed to one and all.. There were smiles everywhere, good food at the evening table, and huge piles of lightly salted cod in the new storage sheds.

Beyond giving rise to a secretary of constant genius, the captain gained a chess partner. Of even happier coincidence, Pike now had someone who was capable of discussing the content of books in his library and the politics of war and peace, as reported in fine detail by the sundry pamphlets sent to Captain Pike by his Bristol secretary for his edification and entertainment. As a matter of policy for the Mosquito Cove side of Pike's business, it was Tisquantum's duty to filter the dross of letters and odd items, such as discarding some of the more outrageous pamphlets written by one Puritan cleric or another.

"Amazing," said Tisquantum. "I have in hand a story that tells of bears fighting bulls at a place called the Paris Garden. Into the waste bin?"

"In London Town is this sport provided?" asked Captain Pike.

"Yes, according to the author, one John Stow."

"John Stow! A friend of mine from our school days at Oxford. He is always my host whenever I visit London."

"Would you care to read the entire pamphlet, sir? It seems a most frivolous use of your time."

"Ha! I could likely tell you the content of John's little story. We've paid visits to the Paris Garden at least a dozen times." Pike held his hand in the air as a signal to silence Tisquantum. "Let's see, does John tell of spies and foreign ambassadors frequenting the Bear Garden?"

"Mmm, yes, here on page one."

"What about the eight people killed and many others injured?"

"Page two, Captain Pike."

"Tisquantum, you may use the paper for kindling, but please write a note to John and thank him for sending us such an entertaining pamphlet."

"Yes sir."

All three of us smiled, but it seemed to me that both Pike and Tisquantum were most pleased with the verbal dance they performed so well. I enjoyed watching each of them appreciate the other in their uncommon partnership.

It came to be that I was a frequent guest in the captain's quarters each evening. The sitting room was cozy on cold nights, with comfortable chairs arranged in front of a large stone fireplace. Hot coffee or tea was served by our amiable host, and there was an easy atmosphere that encouraged reading or discussion, at the discretion of those in attendance. My own reading lessons were normally offered before dusk, with Tisquantum first reviewing the new words I was learning. Then he followed with a tedious session of oral reading from a book of his choice. He'd read a paragraph and then require first my explanation of what I heard as the purpose or meaning of the text, and then my reading of the same passage until it matched his pace and perfection.

It was an unusually windy June night. I was studying my assignment of reading twenty pages aloud, plus compiling a list of words I could not decipher from either context or memory. I was feeling a bit annoyed with the jarring noise of pinecones bombing the roof of Pike's study. "Tisquantum," I said, "can you appreciate the fact that only an unusually mean-spirited savage could demand this brutally boring and repetitive task of his true brother?"

With no smile, and not even looking in my direction, he responded, "It seems that this format is the only viable system that I can conceive of, given that the civilized people of my acquaintance are unable to learn at the sensible rate of red savages."

"Grrr," I answered.

"Ah!" said Tisquantum. "A comment worthy of Socrates. Such magnificent progress you are making, my blue friend."

Captain Pike gave a muffled cough but added nothing in my favor.

While I struggled with strange words, the savage himself was reading a file of pamphlets from last year, all six dated from the later months of 1582. There were occasional comments from his reading that I assumed were meant as supplementary instruction for both me and Pike. Tisquantum shook his paper with a vigorous rattle as a way of getting our attention.

"Pray tell," he said. "Why is this Admiral Drake called a 'sea dog'? And please explain what a 'letter of marque' is."

Pike looked up from a book of poems at Tisquantum. "You have posed two questions, and the first has a simple answer." He pushed the book from his sight. "Drake is a damned clever sailor with excellent ships and determined sailors under his command. He brings captured ships and their gold for his queen, just as a good setter can retrieve a wounded duck for his owner." Pike smiled. "There, you have the 'sea dog' appellation."

Tisquantum returned his captain's smile but remained silent.

"Now then, Queen Elizabeth, God bless her soul, has issued to her favorite admiral a letter that authorizes him to attack and capture all enemy ships at sea. Drake is not the only mariner to receive such a trust from his queen, but as you may surmise, it is a clever device designed to weaken an enemy, strengthen a network of powerful friends, and bring vast sums of gold into the queen's treasury."

"Good," said Tisquantum, "as I surmised." My brother shook his paper again in an apparent strategy to continue his thoughts. "Do you hold a letter of marque from Queen Elizabeth, my captain?

"As a matter of fact, I do hold such a document in my file; it is also true that as yet I have not made good use of the letter."

"Another query, sir. Is not England currently at peace with most the world, including Spain?"

"Indeed," said Captain Pike.

"According to the pamphlet here at hand, and reports that I hear from ship captains here on New Founde Land, there are numerous examples of English ships attacking and often capturing ships flying the flags of peaceful nations, including Spain. How do you explain such a confusing situation, sir?"

Our captain cleared his throat and sipped his cup of tea empty before providing his response to Tisquantum's interrogation. "The queen knows full well that the Spanish king plans war against us in the near future." He paused to give a bold scowl at my red brother before continuing. "Everyone knows that the Spanish king and his pope are assembling a huge fleet to attack England. We can also see from our own eyes that the Spanish have over six hundred sailors that reside as our neighbors in the New Founde Land fishing fleet."

"Are you inferring, sir, that Spanish cod boats will be recruited into a war flotilla for the Spanish king?"

"Merely consider the facts, my secretary. The Spanish transport ships are the same as mine. They carry forty or so fishermen and all necessary supplies for eight weeks of the cod fishing season. Just as with my ship, they carry cannon plus some swivel guns; I am certain that all of the Spanish cod fishing fleet will inevitably be conscripted by their king to move against our nation."

"But legally we are still at peace," said Tisquantum.

"In which particular court would you bring a case against Admiral Drake or the most august Queen Elizabeth?" Captain Pike shook his head in a weary fashion and without permitting an interruption continued. "It is enough for you to know that Queen Elizabeth has whispered into the ears of her sea dogs, and they have listened to her, as they should."

"Pray tell, Captain Pike—what are the whispered words to her salty retrievers?"

"She says, very simply, that she would look favorably on the issue of 'annoying' our future enemy, the Spanish."

"Annoy?"

"In plain Bristol English, she means that Drake and his compatriots are encouraged to capture and plunder the Spanish ships—especially those treasure ships that sail annually from the Caribbean Sea to Spain."

"So," said my red brother, "when the sea dogs display the results of their authorized actions to their queen"—Tisquantum smiled— "what is the split: fifty-fifty?"

Pike seemed amused with his secretary's wit and responded in the same humorous vein. "Well, my savage friend, I'm not privy to each venture, but I believe that fifty-fifty is a good place to begin any negotiation."

Tisquantum returned his batch of pamphlets to their proper file, finished his coffee and spice cake, and stood from his chair. "I am suddenly quite tired and wish to retire to my room, Captain Pike."

"Yes, indeed. Enough of this idle chitchat; you are both dismissed," the captain said.

There were two Portuguese plantation owners who were neighbors of Captain Pike. Each had a cove within walking distance of our Mosquito Cove, yet the three plantation owners never exchanged social visits from one year to the next.

"Tisquantum," Captain Pike called.

"Yes sir?"

"How did our neighbors from Portugal fare in the recent winter?"

"Their buildings and boats were burned to ash," said Tisquantum.

"I will invite them over for coffee and spice cake this Sunday," said Captain Pike.

"Who else here at Mosquito Cove will you have in welcoming our neighbors?"

"You and Blue—no others."

"As you wish." Tisquantum paused. "What instructions regarding this visit do you have for your servants?"

"Make them feel welcome," Captain Pike told me and Tisquantum.

On their first visit, Diogode Sousa and José Maria Agonia were clumsy in a discussion of European art and architecture that Tisquantum had introduced as the likely interest of two educated Europeans. They struggled with the English language; Captain Pike was clearly void of any interest in art of any sort, and, most certainly, the Portuguese language was of little use to Bristol gentry. I watched as the two visitors helped Tisquantum develop the foundation skills of their language and also kept an eye on Captain Pike, who became more and more a morbid drunk with each additional tot of rum.

I made every effort to understand the jest of the Portuguese-English conversation. Apparently, the discussion had something to do with the merits of ancient Roman contributions to English architecture, and the evening of welcome was dying an ugly death. The visitors were soon out of their seats and making toward the door, all the while uttering pleasant words and showing gestures of gratitude for the invitation of a visit.

Captain Pike interrupted the charade with a sudden show of a gracious host. "We're having a side of caribou ribs for our dinner this evening," he said. "What would my neighbors say about having some delicious red meat and a decent red wine?"

There was a brief hesitation, then, "Yes, indeed," they both said in Portuguese.

"What about some chess or cards into the evening?"

The two readily agreed to the evening entertainment and to spending the night at Mosquito Cove as Captain Pike's guest.

Tisquantum gave the pair a long tour of Pike's plantation, and at the same time I plied my captain with coffee and suggested a walk down to the wharf as a way of clearing his head. The plantation secretary continued to talk with the two guests at dinner, and then he engaged Master Sousa in a long chess match that included more discussion than action. Master Agonia and Tisquantum enjoyed a hearty debate over the viability of adding a sideline venture of seal fur sales to the traditional salt cod sales. "Beaver also!" said Diogode Sousa. "There is an excellent market in Amsterdam and Paris for seal and beaver fur both!" he exclaimed.

Then, over a cup of coffee and warm spice cake, a game of Ruff and Honours was suggested by Pike. "It is a simple game, played by children if they can secure a deck of cards."

"Well, then, go ahead and deal the cards and explain the rules as needed." Diogode smiled at one and all with benign regard. "If children can manage, there is hope for us."

Pike dealt four hands, excluding me. "There are fifty-two cards in the deck, and each player receives twelve cards dealt four at a time. The remaining four become the stock with the top card turned up to determine the trump suit."

"Ahh, said Diogode, it is the game we call Triumph. Does the holder of the ace of trump play first, and he collects all four of the stock cards?"

"Indeed, my friend; so we have the same game by two names," said Pike.

Tisquantum matched the benign smile of Diogode. "Could we begin by playing a few games so that the civilized men are free to explain their actions, and therefore permit us two savages to participate as your students?"

"Well," said Pike, "it is clearly a game for four players, so you and I shall be partners while Blue sits at your shoulder."

"Good," said Diogode. "Deal the cards."

I watched the play of hands for a while, and the two Portuguese gentlemen were the persistent winners of each game. My savage blood could easy note the stream of silent messages that passed between the Portuguese partners, and more than once Tisquantum exchanged winks with me.

"Ha! The gods of luck are serving me tonight," said José Maria.

Tisquantum nodded to each of the other players at the table. "Do you gentlemen know the English poet named Shakespeare?"

"Yes," all three responded.

"Diogode and I served as actors in three of his early plays during our college years," said José Maria.

"My goodness," said Tisquantum, "Tell me of the poet—what kind of man is he?"

"No, no. We had copies of his work, not the man himself." Diogode shrugged his shoulders. "It is a small college in the north of our country, and we merely read the various parts for our joy in the effort."

"Even so, gentlemen, possibly you will recognize the following passage." Tisquantum looked at the ceiling as if reading the words he spoke. "She has packed cards with Cesare and false-played my glory; unto an enemies' triumph."

"*Anthony and Cleopatra*," Diogode called.

"I detect a note of savage cunning," said José Maria.

"We were a bit clumsy, maybe," said Diogode.

"Out of practice," said José Maria.

"It is a good game," said Tisquantum. "Shall we play again on another evening'?"

"Certainly," said Diogode.

Tisquantum smiled. "Well, Senor Sousa, I would be honored if you and I could play as partners on our next effort with Ruff and Honors. Perhaps you can accept the indignity of playing with an ignorant Beothic savage?"

Diogode and José Maria laughed and beat the table with joy. "Only if you stop citing English poets as your source for inspiration for playing the game," said Diogode.

On the next day, well after dawn, our neighbors returned to their plantation. Captain Pike had a word us. "Very clever of you both, last night. Well done, my lads."

"What is our goal with these two?" said Tisquantum.

"I want the Portuguese indebted to you; that is what I seek."

"For what purpose?"

"I want you to gain information of Spanish military intentions, for these two must be under the command of the Spanish king in some way."

"But the two are allies, are they not?" I asked. "Spain and Portugal are allies, I'm told."

"Allies under great duress, my blue friend. The Portuguese are only recently conquered by their much stronger neighbor, so there is little blood connection between the two nations."

Tisquantum turned his head slightly, to better hear his master's response. "It is my understanding, sir, that the Spanish and Portuguese people are subservient to the Roman pope. Is that not true?"

"Most assuredly true."

"Are both nations currently allied against the English queen?"

"Of course. The two Catholic nations are united against our Protestant queen. Plus, for your information, they have the current pope as their ally and the agreement that all of his troops will join in a confederation against our Protestant queen." Pike made an appearance of anger, but it was a poor act. "Don't attempt the feebleminded-fool act with me, my red savage. You know exactly what I want."

Tisquantum smiled. "You want them in your debt."

"No, no, no! I want them in *your* debt. I want them beholden to you and to the Beothic people, not to the English people. Think of these two men as honest merchants, not as religious fanatics holding some ephemeral ghost as their savior."

"What an interesting mind you have, Captain Pike." Tisquantum nodded his entire upper body up and down, like an anchored buoy guarding a shallow reef. "Good," he said. "No more with the questions and answers between us. From now on I will handle our guests to our mutual satisfaction."

"Of course," said Captain Pike.

The two Portuguese plantation owners lived within half a mile of Captain Pike's property. They quickly became our frequent evening visitors. Ruff and Honors was a favorite competition, and an ongoing chess tournament took place night after night, with ferocious dedication between all participants.

I was in attendance most evenings and eventually managed the game of Ruff at a competitive level. As for chess, I learned to move the pieces as required by the rules, but I was clearly an inadequate opponent for the lot. Each evening there were conversations and games, followed by the inevitable coffee and spice cake. The dessert marked the end of each evening; our visitors from Portugal went to their separate guest bedrooms, while I returned to my upper bunk and joined with Da's snores and farts in assaulting our three resident Beothic fishermen.

It turned out that Diogode Sousa was the youngest son of large family from Afife, which in turn was close to the important fishing village of Viana de Castelo. José Maria Agonia, on the other hand, was the only child of a family from Chafe, which was very close to the important fishing village of Viana de Castelo as well. The two men were schoolmates and second cousins, but it was Diogode who did most of the talking, and he was certainly the best cook. To the great satisfaction of all, Captain Pike's amiable cook was a ready pupil of Diogode's lessons.

"What is this concoction called?" asked Captain Pike. "It is from my very own kitchen, yet I'm certain that no cook from Bristol has ever produced such a delicious repast."

"Ahhh," said Diogode Sousa, "this is one of the many variations of our *Robalo com Algas*." He looked over his shoulder toward the kitchen. "*Saluda* to your cook, my captain—he is an able student. This *algas* and the lovely sweet *Arroz Doce de Afife* remind me of home."

"Salt cod never tasted better," Captain Pike said.

"Quickly done on a hot grill," said Tisquantum. "There's garlic and olive oil, and spices that I do not recognize. What are the mystery spices?"

"They are my secret—and safe with me forever simply because I do not know their names or derivation." Sousa smiled. "A small tub of spices was given to me from the cook at our home in Portugal, and I have shared a portion with your cook here at Mosquito Cove. Delicious, are they not?"

"Wonderful," I responded, with a chorus of "Yes, yes" from Pike and Tisquantum.

Later in the same evening, I overheard Tisquantum and Diogode in conversation. "Your village is in the very north of your country, am I not correct?"

"Yes sir, we have many vineyards on the hills, olive trees in the glens, and a constant blessing of wind that pours a lovely scent of the sea over our entire domain."

"You have neighbors who are of the Basque nation?"

"Now, now, good sir. There are many Basque people that I know and love, but there is no Basque nation under the sun. There are Basque people who pay taxes to the Spanish king and also Basque people who pay taxes to the French king, but none to a Basque king."

"Tell me, sir—are the Basque people comfortable with their diverse loyalties, to your knowledge?"

Diogode was silent a long moment before answering the question. He had a lovely nose of gigantic proportion and a high forehead, which in combination gave me an impression of studious intelligence. It was clear that Tisquantum and Diogode were comfortable discussing all issues under the sun in peaceful harmony.

The Portuguese don nodded to his savage friend. "I cannot say one way or the other if they are happy or are not happy, but it is my observation that no family of substance gains much pleasure from paying taxes."

"My question, sir, is more about the treatment of the Basque people and your Portuguese families under Spanish rule. Is the Spanish rule equitable for all?"

"It does seem that my family, and that of José Maria—in the matter of taxes, in any event—that the Portuguese families pay less in the amount of taxes than our neighbors who are of the Basque persuasion." Diogode held up his hand to stop any question. "I make that determination of tax differential based upon the intimate knowledge of the families involved, one or the other, and know for a fact that we all have about the same resources of land and the equal production of goods or services."

"Ahh, I see." Tisquantum cleaned his plate of spice cake. "And now, shall we have another game of chess?"

"No, no, good sir. Tonight we must follow our well-marked paths back to our own plantations. Tomorrow we must encourage our fishermen, and then we will sail over to St. John's City for some supplies."

"Are you still able to exchange mail with your families, Diogode? After the recent trouble with the English admiral?"

"Certainly, Spanish and Portuguese ships arrive in St. John's Harbor on a regular basis, and I would be very surprised not to hear from my friends and family."

The guests at Captain Pike's cottage willingly discussed the merits of the various Catholic and Protestant theologies with little rancor and to the satisfaction of none. It was my clear observation that Tisquantum had by then digested all available Portuguese dictionaries, poems, and assorted histories and was most fluent in the language. On his own initiative, he began taking each cousin on separate tours of the Pike plantation, and each in his separate way took notice of the fine cottages, fishing boats, whaleboats, and weatherproof storage sheds.

Diogode could restrain himself for the first tour but not the second. "Tisquantum, my friend. Tell me how I may gain your pleasure in protecting my plantation in the same manner as Mosquito Cove?" He paused for a theatrical shrug. "My plantation continues to suffer the winter ravages of both savages and weather."

"What is your offer?"

"Will Captain Pike know of our conversation?"

"Well, sir, it is my captain's pleasure that you and the Beothic people reach an agreement similar to his. Captain Pike believes that the English, Portuguese, and Beothic people have more to gain from a pact of mutual assistance than from what exists at this time."

"My, what a progressive man you have as your champion. I hope that I can serve you in a similar manner."

"As my champion?"

"Certainly."

"Good. Now here is what you must do when you depart for Portugal this fall."

"Tell me."

"Leave all of your books and maps and equipment for my use. I promise not to damage a single item."

Diogode let the silence spin until he said, "That's all?"

"I would appreciate the presentation to me next fishing season of dictionaries and translations of English books to Spanish and Spanish books to Portuguese."

"Ahh, you are such a linguist, Tisquantum. Of course, I will help you in studying the Spanish language."

"I'll try my best with the language, good friend. Thank you. Thank you." Tisquantum waited a beat. "Provide me with newspapers, my friend, in both your language and that of the Spanish aggressors."

"I will do what I can, Tisquantum." He shrugged his shoulders. "You shall receive all newspapers that are delivered to me in their original casings."

José Maria took a few additional weeks to begin negotiations, and in the end he too promised Tisquantum access to all books and periodicals he received from Portugal.

Both of our neighbors, in private conversations with Tisquantum, said, "Did you know that many of us in Northern Portugal are dreaming of our independence from Spain?"

"I have heard such rumors," Tisquantum responded on both occasions.

"I will do what I can," said Diogode. "I might hear a rumor or two worth passing on to you."

"I will do what I can," said José Maria. "My father has many important friends, and he may provide a morsel or two in his letters to me that I can share with you."

CHAPTER FOUR

1584-85
Captain Pike

Our neighbors were miraculously left unscathed during the winter seasons of 1584 and 1585. In fact, the headquarters of both Portuguese plantations were improved beyond recognition with new doors and expanded kitchens and sumptuous bedrooms.

Boxes of Spanish-language newspapers and Spanish-language books were presented to Tisquantum for his pleasure.

It was also true that quantities of letters were exchanged between Captain Pike and Admiral Drake. First to Drake, then a month or two later, a response from Drake. So it was a surprise to many New Founde Landers when Sir Bernard Drake invaded the harbor at St. John's, in late June, 1585, but not a surprise by any means to the owner of Mosquito Cove Plantation. In point of fact, Captain Pike, with his ship and sailors, joined with those ships and sailors of Captain Drake to capture the entire Spanish cod fishing fleet—the sum of which included six hundred Spanish sailors and much of the New Founde Land Portuguese fleet as well. There was no battle, to speak of— merely the sudden strike, a few volleys of cannon, and the clearing of

Spaniards and most Portuguese from the harbors and coves of New Founde Land.

Captain Pike received written orders from the English admiral to help with the removal of fishermen from all the Spanish and most of the Portuguese plantations. Those of Diogode and José Maria were untouched. Nothing was said about the disparity of English justice at our evening gatherings, but our captain was unusually generous in offering his Portuguese neighbors his very best rum and wine.

Captain Pike, however, was disappointed in his aspirations to meet the most famous of all sea dogs. He had both me and Tisquantum and Da sitting in chairs while he paced the floor of his private office, like some deranged moose or brown bear. "Well, now," he said in the manner of a spurned lover, "I certainly understand his need to move quickly, but for the life of me, I cannot comprehend why he couldn't find a spare minute for his friend and confidant." Our captain shrugged his shoulders. "I heard from one of his captains that Admiral Drake means to intercept an enormous shipment of gold."

"There's sure to be another opportunity that will set the matter straight," I said. "A meeting in Bristol, this winter, for instance."

"I was also interested in meeting the famous Englishman," said Tisquantum. "Possibly he will return to St. John's City with a portion of his captured treasure. I'm also certain that there will be another opportunity for us to share our thoughts with him."

"Certainly. Certainly we'll meet with him on another occasion. He and I have intimate contacts with mutual friends from Bristol and also a firm record of mutual correspondence." Pike puffed himself up for our appreciation, but I saw more weakness than strength in his behavior.

Da seemed taken with the same appraisal of Captain Pike. "There are other issues that had the admiral move so quickly from New Founde Land, I suspect," he said.

"Tell me, Da," said Tisquantum.

Da studied the ground before giving a response. "Well, now—first and foremost was to move the admiral on to warmer ports."

"Why is that the case?" said Tisquantum.

"Simple as spice cake," said Da. "For all his braid and bluster, Drake is a rogue and a damn fool who thinks he has no debt to any man or queen alive." Da waited until it was clear that Captain Pike was not going to interrupt his story. "The real facts hold that it is the Bristol gentry that are not beholden to any lord whatsoever. Best of all, the queen knows good and well that her nest is better feathered by the merchants of Bristol than a passing fool like Drake."

"Please excuse me, Da," said Tisquantum. "I can understand that Admiral Drake may have overshot his mark with his invasion of New Founde Land, but I'm at a loss to understand how the queen and the merchants of Bristol might support one another against the admiral."

"Maybe I can help explain the situation," said Captain Pike.

Da and Pike exchanged nods, and Pike continued. "It seems that in ancient times past, Bristol City got lost in the battles between Saxon and Norman. There was never a lord or pope to come around to our lovely city and harbor to build a castle or magnificent cathedral. Even after the invaders settled their boundaries—it was just pure luck, I guess—none of the red-haired lords or black-haired lords made their way to Bristol. Therefore, there were no lords to force their taxes and tithes on the Bristol gentry." Pike smiled at us all, but only Da returned with his grimace. "The Bristol gentry, of course, found methods over the generations to maintain the favorable situation to their advantage, and that is where we stand today."

"I now have a vague understanding of the relationships that exists between Bristol merchants and the queen, but please explain your true meaning to this ignorant savage," said Tisquantum.

"Ignorant, indeed," said Da.

"Please, Master Smyth or Captain Pike, explain your understanding of the current relations between our queen and the Bristol gentry."

Da shook his head. "I give the words of a man with no learning. A man who for most every year of his life has lived with little enough food from one season of hunger to the next."

Tisquantum held his silence but nodded his encouragement to our da.

"It always helps to forget an empty belly with telling stories of the past. Whatever poor folks may do to put bread on their table, it makes no difference to their lives. We are born poor and die the same way. We must please the gentry if there is any chance of obtaining food and shelter for our families. The gentry of Bristol, however, have always survived by their wits. One gentry's family trades with another, and both secure a small profit here and there. The Bristol gentry know that the gentry of London or Paris or Algeria will trade for our salt cod with whatever they have in hand. The Bristol gentry have both wit and full stomachs to give them the time and patience to find like-minded gentry scattered about the seas."

"Well done," said Captain Pike. "We breed shrewd merchants in Bristol Town, wouldn't you say, Master Smyth?"

Da gave his grimace. "More like shrewd smugglers, I'd say, if the truth is required."

Tisquantum joined with a question. "What do these Bristol smugglers exchange for Bristol pots or Bristol fish?"

"There's always wine and grain. Smugglers of every port are always looking for profit, and Bristol salt cod is required by rich and poor," said Pike.

Tisquantum smiled. "Well now, I'd hazard a guess that over the past centuries the ruling queen or king and their lords have also served as customers of the Bristol merchants."

"You'd be right as rain with your guess," said Pike.

Tisquantum's smile was larger now. "I imagine that the lords and kings always receive a significant discount on the normal price. Am I correct in that assumption?"

Pike and Da exchanged their grimace for Tisquantum's large and generous smile.

"The fancy lords get their cheap wine and Bristol merchants get no taxes—that's always been the Bristol way," said Captain Pike. "At least for the ten generations or so that my own family can show."

"Pray tell, Captain Pike—to your knowledge, are there other English cities with the same independence as Bristol?"

"None that I've ever heard tell about," he said.

"Why might this exception to the rule of governance by the English Crown exist?"

"We are smarter than all the rest," said Pike.

"Ahh," said Tisquantum.

CHAPTER FIVE

1588
The Spanish Armada

IN THE LATE SUMMER OF 1588, a ship entered the Port at St. John's to bring the news. "Disaster!" the arriving captain shouted. "There's an invincible Spanish Armada even now attacking the homeland." The English officer sent messengers to all the plantations of English patriots, and very quickly a covey of cod-fishing merchant ships was ready to head east.

Captain Pike called for me and Tisquantum to meet in his office. "The Spanish are attacking my country, and I must leave immediately to help stop them."

My first thought was Da explaining how poor folks always got picked to bleed for the rich. My second was to keep my mouth shut. Tisquantum also kept quiet, and we waited patiently for our orders.

"Blue, you will come with me."

I nodded my head but could produce not a single comment.

"And, Blue, I want you to select six of the smartest Beothic fisherman to join us on our expedition against the Spanish. Tell them that each will receive a musket when we return, plus a full share of anything that we may capture from the Spanish ships."

"How are the shares determined?" I knew Pike could likely be counted for a rogue when it came to shares and the like.

"Half for me, one quarter to our investors from Bristol, and equal shares of the remaining portion for the sailors."

"What if a Beothic warrior is killed during this distant war? Will his family receive some form of restitution for service rendered to the queen?"

"War is war, Blue. No shares for the dead. I'll tell his family that he died for a good cause and to his mates that he died a hero." He stared at the floor. "It's the living that get rewarded, not the dead."

"What about me? What is my status aboard your ship?"

"Mate. You'll be my only officer, and I'll add another full share from my portion to your benefit."

"Mate!" My stomach twisted into a painful knot. "I've never sailed as a mate on a ship of war or peace."

"I'm the captain, and I get to decide who is mate on my ship."

"Sir, you have men and officers who have served you well in the past. You must respect their seniority and loyalty and maintain them in their past positions." I was flummoxed with his belligerent attitude. "I'll continue to serve to the best of my ability, but not as mate on a ship of war."

Captain Pike took a step closer and lowered the tone of his voice. "Here's the only advice I'll give to my new mate: listen to the bosun and do what he says." Pike came a bit closer and spoke at a near whisper. "You will learn your duty from the bosun, and I expect that very quickly you'll be a competent mate. Before we dock at Bristol, you'll be a mate that gives his orders loud and clear for all to hear."

"Who is the bosun?"

"Master Smyth, I call him."

"Da?"

"Bosun Smyth to you and all the crew of my ship."

"Why don't you make Da your mate and leave me to the plantation?"

"This'll be a long war, Blue, and you will learn what I want as a mate before this first voyage is over. You're young and smart, and you can learn what you need to know from Bosun Smyth and the other Bristol sailors." Pike gave a playful push to my shoulder. "Enough with the talk—let's get to work."

A deep voice spoke into my ear. "Shut your yap, matey-boy, or I'll give the back of my hand to you."

I could see in my mind's eye the grimace that Da took for a smile and lowered my head. If Da was in with Pike on this adventure, there was no question about my proper course of action. "Fine," I said, "with the two of you on my back, we should clear St. John's Harbor in a week or two."

"Good," said Captain Pike. "We've got the mate and bosun jobs all straight."

I took a step backward to stand at Bosun Smyth's shoulder, and we listened carefully to what we were told.

"I need to leave good men here on the plantation to finish our cod season. I understand your reservations about my offer, Blue, but you must respect my judgement in managing both ship and shore."

As mate to the captain, I nodded and asked a simple question. "Exactly who will serve as manager of the plantation in your stead, sir?"

"Tisquantum."

"Good, there is none better," I said.

Da nodded. "A fine man for the job, sir."

"Do either of you have any advice that I should hear?"

I was on safe ground now, for no one on the Mosquito Cove plantation had more connections with savages and sailors than me. "Tisquantum is the perfect manager in your absence," I said with some degree of enthusiasm. "However, Captain Pike, there is also the task of training new cod fishermen to replace those chosen as sailors." No comment from Pike. "Also," I continued, "we must anticipate the inevitable uproar your departure will create from the remaining Bristol men and all the Beothic villagers."

When the captain still gave no response, I continued my lecture. "Oubee would serve with great ability to provide assistance to my brother Tisquantum. She can sail a whaleboat to St. John's for supplies, and she can get information from fishermen and savages with equal dexterity." I tried a smile at Captain Pike. "Oubee can speak Bristol English as well as me."

"Better," said Da.

I gave a big smile to my bosun. "Oubee can serve in my place to manage her people of the new village, and she can also keep the Bristol fishermen content with their life."

Pike maintained his neutral expression. "How so?"

I made the effort to speak in a more forceful voice. "If the Beothic continue to develop farms that can supply food for the three plantations around Mosquito Cove, it stands to reason that the fishermen will continue in their appreciation of good food and comfortable cottages."

"So, my young and very inexperienced mate, what does all this yammering about Oubee have to do with the Spanish invasion of England?"

"Well, sir, if you expect to return to a profitable plantation, the Beothic will need the constant support of both Oubee and Tisquantum."

Pike was not paying the least attention to my lecture, so I finished with the feeling I was talking into a stiff breeze. "It is my observation the villagers were reticent to move from their ancient home and that only Oubee can help Tisquantum convince the Beothic to continue in what is a very painful process for them."

Captain Pike turned toward Da. "Do you agree with this fool?"

"Yes sir."

"Then get moving, both of you. Settle all that you need. The bosun and I sail with the morning tide."

We departed St. John's Harbor with eight ships in convoy, but it was Pike's ship alone that entered Bristol Harbor after a mere twenty-seven days. Two of the New Founde Land ships were forced back to St. John's Harbor on the first day, with the sea pouring in through un-caulked timbers. The remaining five saw our wake for a short time, then they disappeared from our sight. The day after the Mosquito anchored in Bristol Harbor, the first of the five ships came alongside and asked for orders from Captain Pike. On the ninth day after our arrival, the last dawdler staggered in to join the New Founde Land fleet.

Bristol! I could hardly contain myself with the thought of seeing Ma and the kids, and of course, Jeremy, the big lug.

Da and I petitioned the captain for a quick visit with Ma and the kids, but he put us off with a firm "No." and then issued a string of orders about getting the ship ready to fight a battle. "I want gun drills twice each day!" Pike gave us a malicious smile. "Then there's the evening gun drill that'll come at a time of my choosing."

The captain departed from his ship at odd times through the day and early evening to purchase supplies and collect rumors floating through one pub or another. He told me and Da that he expected orders to arrive from Admiral Drake at any moment, and that the fate of England might hang on our quick response to such a command. From the first day, before leaving the ship, he stood still on the deck yelling,

"Hear me well and good, my crew." When all were quiet and listening, Pike continued. "Any man that leaves this ship during my absence is a deserter." After a short pause, he added, "England is at war, and deserters are hung from the yardarm."

Later, in his cabin, Captain Pike told me and Da about the taverns around Bristol Harbor, where he begged information about the Spanish Armada and invasion of England. There was little or nothing gleaned from the taverns and no official word from Drake or from any other admiral of the English fleet on what the Bristol captains should do to get ready, or any hint as to when or where we should sail.

All the New Founde Land fishermen spent dawn to dusk each subsequent day with gunnery drills, repairing what we could on ship and sail and loading whatever munitions and supplies each captain could afford. Once again Captain Pike had the advantage of greater wealth and local merchant connections—thus it was that the fastest ship from New Founde Land also became the worthiest ship in Bristol Harbor.

During an early afternoon, five days after our arrival in Bristol, Da and I, with no permission sought or received from Captain Pike, departed our ship to visit with the family.

Our cabin seemed decrepit to my eye. The roof looked battered, and when Da knocked on the door, it slid open on a loose hinge. Ma stood at the half-open door, tears in her eyes.

I pushed past Da to stand before my Ma. "What's wrong?" I asked.

Da crowded my shoulder, and in back of Ma were the kids plus Jeremy and his wife.

"I'm fine," Ma said.

Ma was not fine. She looked frail and near ready to fall on the floor. Jeremy could look neither of us in the eyes. The children old enough to stand I counted in a quick glance. "Where are the young'uns, the rug rats?" I asked.

"Dead," Ma whispered.

Now all the children and Jeremy joined with Ma in weeping big tears.

Da drew a deep breath but kept his voice low and quiet. "Did you get my shares paid from Captain Pike?" was Da's first question to his wife.

Ma was quiet for a moment. "His agent stops by with a bit, now and then."

"That would be Master John Slaney, if I'm correct," said Da.

"Master Slaney it is," replied Ma.

Da was very patient. "We've had above average with the catch both years. Does what John Slaney pay to you compare favorably to when I was last here myself to collect my wage?"

She shook her head. "Not near, my luv. We're hanging from a thin thread, even with help from Jeremy here and the neighbors."

Da stood staring at Ma like some big long-legged bird at a little fish.

"The two youngest died in the past month," Ma whispered.

My stomach pained like I'd been kicked by a horse. Tears popped from my eyes. I heard Da cough into his hands before getting ahold of himself.

"Jeremy," Da finally said, not looking at my brother or me at all. "Go fetch Captain Pike, and don't take a word of back-talk from him."

Jeremy shambled out the cottage door. Da pulled a purse from his pocket and gave it to me. "Take the oldest child and go buy what you can. Hurry along, Son—the best you can."

Sister Ruby took my hand, and off we went at a decent jog. We found a small ham at one stall, and cabbage, potatoes, and wheat at another. "Some sweets, Omrod? Please?" Then back to the cottage at about the same pace, encumbered though we were.

Ruby and Ma set to work with peeling and getting water to boil while the youngsters stood underfoot begging for a heart of cabbage or a pinch of ham. Not a word from them, but big eyes and dour faces got some small reward—from Ruby, in any event.

Just as the cabbage came soft and ready to eat, a one-horse buggy rushed up to the door of our cottage. I watched Captain Pike walk head down into Da's cottage. Jeremy stayed back to care for the horse.

"For the love of God, Mistress Smyth." Pike strangled on his next word and looked hopelessly at the lot of starving children. "What has that damned fool Slaney done to you?"

"Someone has killed two of my children, Captain Pike." Ma hardly ever said a word to gentry, and now her words were ripped and shredded but clear to the ear. "They ate weeds that I could find, but there was not much else to spread among the six of us. I wonder how that sad happening might have befallen my children, Captain Pike."

"I'm not at the root of it, madam." There was no mistaking the captain's misery, for I'd never in the past years seen him show the least concern over the welfare of a person of no consequence. Yet here he was with trembling hands and pity in his voice. He coughed into his hand. "It seems likely that my trusted agent has stolen from both of us and that you have suffered far more that I at his vile behavior." Pike did not look away from Ma. "Words are of no account, I know full well. Two children dead and the rest of you at death's door." Now he looked at Da. "Do you have a safe place to store any coins at hand?"

"Yes sir, we do."

Pike pulled out his purse and emptied it of all coins onto the dining table. One rolled to the floor, and Ruby quickly set it back with the multitude. "Count the lot and then tell me the balance needed to support your family for the next twelve months. Spend the day and night with your family, Master Smyth, and report to the ship by midmorning tomorrow."

"Yes sir," Da said. "We'll settle the difference tomorrow evening, if that is agreeable, sir."

Captain Pike waved a hand at me. "Let's go, Blue—we have work to do and no time to squander."

"Blue?" said Ruby directly to the captain. "How is a mate of your ship called by a color and not his true name?"

I put my arms around my sister's shoulders to whisper into her ear. "It is nothing, Ruby—a nickname given to me by the red savages and taken on by the Bristol men."

"It is a mark of honor, Miss Smyth," said Captain Pike. "An honor recognized as such by all on my plantation."

"I prefer Omrod," said Ruby.

I believe that Da and Pike, and certainly I, were taken by the set of jaw and shoulder that marked both Ruby and Oubee.

Pike nodded to his antagonist. "I'll make it so, young lady. In Bristol it is Omrod who serves as my mate and Blue when we land at Mosquito Cove."

"If you must," said Ruby.

Admiral Drake came by way of a four-horse carriage from Plymouth to Bristol to meet with the New Founde Land cod captains. His fancy coach carried four English sea captains in all, but Drake was the only admiral. There were also a few other merchant ship captains or fish captains, from hither and yon, that had found their way to Bristol and also joined with us from New Founde Land.

Smoke filled the famous Bristol City tavern. I sat at Captain Pike's ear to listen and learn. There was no churning in my stomach over the situation—more likely a peculiar feeling of anger at the lot of ugly admirals.

There was Bristol beer to drink and salt cod to munch while Drake and his captains settled in. They all, at one point or another, had to take a crap in the tavern's miserable privy, and they all subsequently complained about the smell and flies and what all, as if we had a part in making their lives miserable. It came to me that they were not an impressive lot, seeing that lords and admirals had to shit once in a while. They were all five of them short in height and fat through the gut. Even Drake was so inclined.

"Here's the way of it, my lads." Drake stood tall on top of a wooden box supplied by one of his crew. He spoke each word with clear assertion. "Listen to what I have to say, you Bristol men and the others here in attendance. We have better cannon and faster ships than the dons. They will try to land a grapple aboard your ship and pull your small ship to their large galleons." The admiral stopped for a moment to give emphasis to the thoughts that followed.

"Keep your distance from those big, fat ships, or you are doomed. Keep your distance from the Spanish ships, and teach your sharemen how to load, aim, and fire your cannon. You Bristol folks are good Englishmen, and I'm confident that you will defend our queen with honor and bravery."

The Bristol captains and mates beat their beer mugs on the table to verify their loyalty to queen and admiral. "You'd best notice our sharp eyes and accurate cannon, Admiral Drake," said Pike. "You'll find Bristol men are quick to learn their duty, sir."

Drake studied Captain Pike for a long moment. "How many cannon do you carry, sir?"

"Ten cannon and four swivel guns. The cannon I purchased from a Dutch agent, and they all seem well designed for the long-range contests that you require."

"Your name, sir? I'm sure that I've been told in the past, but remind me, if you will."

"Captain Gilbert Pike, sir, of Bristol and my plantation at Mosquito Cove."

"Yes, certainly. Pike it is." The admiral studied Captain Pike for a moment and then said, "Queen Elizabeth will give a speech at Tilbury in six days, and I want you at my side, Captain Pike."

"Yes sir."

Pike sat directly behind Admiral Drake while Da and I were another dozen rows further back from the viewing stand of our queen. She appeared suddenly, a celestial apparition all covered with gold and jewels. We stood to cheer, and some tossed hats into the air. When we had shown the extent of our devotion to the queen for an overlong period of time, she finally raised one hand for our attention and began to speak.

"We have been persuaded by some that are careful of our safety, to take heed how we commit ourselves to armed multitudes for fear of treachery; but I assure you I do not desire to live to distrust my faithful and loving people . . ."

"Mark what she says," hissed Da.

"Quiet, you yokels," those around us whispered.

"Let tyrants fear. I have always so behaved myself that, under God, I have placed my chiefest strength and safeguard in the loyal hearts and good-will of my subjects; and therefore I am come amongst you, as you see, at this time, not for my recreation and disport, but being resolved, in the midst and heat of the battle, to live and die amongst you all; to lay down for my God, and for my kingdom, and my people, my honour and my blood, even in the dust." Her Majesty's voice was calm and clear to my ears, even though she appeared to speak quietly to each man in attendance. "I know I have the body of a weak, feeble woman; but I have the heart and stomach of a king, and of a king of England too, and think foul scorn that Parma or Spain, or any prince of Europe, should dare to invade the borders of my realm; to which rather than any dishonour shall grow by me, I myself will take up arms, I myself will be your general, judge, and rewarder of every one of your virtues in the field." She seemed engorged in brilliant gold, and my mind was dazzled by the sight of her; I shook my head, returning to her words; "...not doubting but by your obedience to my general, by your concord in the camp, and your valour in the field, we shall shortly have a famous victory over these enemies of my God, of my kingdom, and of my people.."

The crowd erupted in cheers and tossing of hats. "Hurrah for our queen," we all yelled and yelled and yelled.

The mates and bosuns had been carried to Tilbury and then back to their ship in a large flat wagon pulled by six horses. There were no seats, just hay scattered on the wood. We made out tolerably well—we were all used to worse, of course. I tried to get Da to answer my single question, but he played deaf as any stone. I repeated, "Is this what you warned me about, Da? About the queen and her very own god-people corralling all the poor folks for their wars and their gain?"

Silence.

"Da?"

Silence.

The storms continued roaring out of the west into late September. After the first three gales had drenched and ripped the fleet of Drake, our admiral told one and all that his fleet would stay put until he had word that the Spanish Armada was clear of the entire northern English coast. After the brief and erratic encounters in the sea channel between

France and England, the Armada sailed with no opposition up the west side of England, over the top of both England and Ireland, and, according to the latest gossip from all taverns, the Spanish Fleet was now sailing south along the western Irish coast toward their home ports.

Captain Pike, Da, and I were in the aft cabin, listening to the constant rain.

"Why, Captain?" I asked. "Why don't we go out to stop the dons? Our ships are faster than theirs and sail closer to the wind."

"As you can see, Blue, we're pretty well set with food and good health on our own ship." Captain Pike shook his head like a sad old dog. "The truth is that most of Drake's fleet is in bad shape."

"I hear there's the plague roaming about the Plymouth docks," said Da. "Some scurvy too."

Pike poured a small dram of rum into our cups. His cabin was small, with a bed, a table with two chairs, and a bench, all crammed into the space. "Drake's got no money to buy food, so I hear," he said.

"Will the dons get back to their home ports with their ships all safe and sound?"

"Can't say, Blue. I believe, from what I hear in the taverns, that when the weather breaks clear, Drake is set on making a short run to head off the Armada from their home ports." He paused to collect his thoughts. "I'd guess Drake will lead the fleet to somewhere off the west coast of Ireland, near the port of Kerry, for instance."

We sipped and meditated for a while.

"I know for a fact that there's lots of Irish rebels to give help to the dons around about Kerry way." Captain Pike paused once again, not anxious to second-guess the admiral. "Yup. Two days of decent wind will get us in position off the southwestern coast of Ireland, and then quick-quick we can pick up what ships offer themselves for battle." He emptied his cup. "I vow there's also a passel of crippled or beached Spanish ships already waiting for the plucking." Now Pike slapped his hands together and leaned toward us, like a merchant delighted with a profitable sale. "Yes sir, Bob, we should find us a way to pick up some gold or whatever; under sail or on the rocks, one is as good as the other to make it worth our time taken from fishing."

I was troubled by the thought of our little merchant craft in a dangerous sea. "Tell me, sir, you'd have us land on a strange beach to pick the bones of a Spanish ship?"

"Blue, my boy, if we don't take the easy pickings, I'm afraid we'll get nothing at all. Drake will be out scavenging with the rest of us, but mark my words—it'll be only a night or two, and the old sea dog will scoot back to Plymouth and leave the dons on their own."

"That would mean Bristol for us," I said. "We could see that Ma and the children are well, and then back to Mosquito Cove before the winter sets in with the ice and all."

"We're too late for that kind of talk, Blue. We'd probably hit ice halfway to home." Pike stood to dismiss us. "I want all of you to stay aboard until I say different." He gave me his evil-eye stare. "We'll get little warning before Drake takes us out for the hunt, so there's no running off for visits without my explicit approval. Mark my words, the two of you."

"Shall I run another drill or two on the cannon?"

"You're the mate, Blue, so you decide. Just remember that I want our Bristol cod fishermen up to Drake's standard of speed to load and to fire each cannon."

"We're getting close to the mark, and that's no fib."

"Get going, then, the both of you."

As we turned to leave the cabin, Pike added a last thought: "And don't go counting on fishing New Founde Land cod for a year or two. The admiral has plans for his Bristol folks."

So, there it was. No visits with Ma and no quick return to Mosquito Cove. I turned to Da for a question, but he up and left the captain's quarters with no word at all. Pike turned his back to me and pretended some business with charts and compass. My fingers felt numb and my throat scratchy. Something was about to happen, but nothing good. No smile from Ma. No roughhouse with Jeremy or teasing by Ruby. Something very bad.

Sure enough, the very next day the rain stopped, and we had orders to weigh anchor and to rendezvous off the Kerry coast. It was rough sledding all the way east to near the Irish coast—no doubt on that fact, with wind and waves that seemed to attack us from every direction. We made a try for a Portuguese merchant ship on the second day from Bristol, but she tucked under the wing of a huge Spanish galleon, and there was no way for us to get near one without the other sending a broadside of thirty cannon at us as welcome.

We watched the tail end of the Spanish Armada as it moved through the cover of fog and brief squalls. Each time an ephemeral vision of a huge galleon or raft of merchant ships made an appearance, they quickly disappeared. Each sighting was always south, a few miles closer to the coast of Spain.

On the fourth day from joining Drake's armada at sea, we received the signal to turn about and scoot back to the harbor of our choice. Bristol Harbor received us on the eighth day after our departure. There was no treasure for any captain of Drake's fleet. Not much food, either—merely a bedraggled mess of ships looking for a quiet spot to rest.

CHAPTER SIX

1589
The English Armada

SOME OF THE MOSQUITO COVE fishermen went sick and died during that futile chase after the dons. There were two Bristol men and three red savages in all, and since the sea was still running high and wicked, we dumped them one by one over the side. All were naked of clothes and deprived of any ceremony whatsoever. The dead men disappeared faster than a blink into the black water, and we fishermen still alive added shameless tears to the ocean. Even Pike stood on the deck, lashed by wind and rain, to mourn the death of our close friends.

The first day back in Bristol Harbor, Captain Pike had a bag of lemons at his feet and his crew of thirty-one staring at him. "Here's the way of it, my lads, so listen close." We were on the aft castle with some of us standing against the rail and others sitting on the deck. "Two things you boys have got to know right now. First is, the admiral says that we beat the damn dons, and those enemy ships that survived are in bad shape."

There were a few coughs and one paltry cheer by our demented Bristol boy.

"Second is, the admiral says that we're going to chase after the bastards to put 'em down for good." When silence was his only response, Captain Pike cleared his throat of phlegm and carried on with his speech. "Also, my lads, Admiral Drake has a mind to capture a fleet of Spanish treasure ships and then split the silver and gold on share and share alike." He tried a big wink of his eye, but the silence of his crew made him look more demented than the Bristol boy.

Da spoke for all of us in the crew. "That what you're telling us, Captain Pike, is all well and good for those that want it, but this crew is mostly fishermen, and it'd be best if we got back to New Founde Land for the cod."

I'm sure Pike knew full well what his crew wanted, and it took but a moment for him to set us straight.

"You boys are the best cod fishermen I've ever seen, and that is no lie." He coughed into his hand to give us some time to think. "The truth is that I don't have a choice between fishing and war because the admiral has set my course with no ifs or buts."

Da kept his chin up in the air. "We've got the plague coming at us from Plymouth way," he said. "Let's weigh anchor and head full sail to the fishing grounds and some clean air."

Captain Pike held both hands toward us. "We'd never make it to the breakwater before the admiral had us all in chains. But wait—let me make another suggestion for us to consider."

Da nodded to the captain. "We're listening, sir. Tell us what we can do."

Pike took a deep breath. "The bosun's correct in saying we've got the scurvy and the damn plague coming down on us from Plymouth way." Pike picked up the bag at his feet. "Bosun, I want you to take the crew—Bristol men and savages both—and parcel them out to families in your end of Bristol. I'll give this bag of lemons to spread around for the scurvy and a bag of coins to buy what food is needed for all—men, women, and children."

There was a sigh from the crew, and Da nodded. "And ourselves, Captain Pike—how do we behave ourselves while living with friends and family, sir?"

"You must keep quiet on everything. There's to be no talking to any strangers who may walk by and no visiting with neighbors not offering comfort to our crew." Pike flipped a large gold coin to his bosun. "Take this and set up your own Mosquito Cove tavern. I'll send a stock of rum and Bristol beer for those who need the drink."

A few men smiled, but most remained silent. I was torn by the desire to be with my Bristol family, and with Oubee and Tisquantum. More likely Captain Pike had the truth about chasing the dons and sucking lemons to stay the scurvy, but the feeling of being trapped with nary an option for us to choose clogged my throat. The damned queen and her admirals would find a way to kill us all, one way or another.

Pike started up again with his orders. "Bosun Smyth, I want you to choose a few women from your neighborhood to do the buying of goods every family will need." Pike gave Da no room for an answer. "I also want you to tell these chosen women to whisper about the markets that our Bristol crew and their savage friends are enjoying a little shore leave until the weather settles."

Da waited a few beats to make sure he could slip in a word or two. "Tell me, Captain Pike—when do we start with this playacting and sitting on our hands with nothing to do?"

"Now. Today. I'll hire some guards to keep thieves from the ship, then Blue and I will go over to Plymouth and meet with Admiral Drake."

"So be it, then," said Da.

I got my best information from a certain second mate in a smoky dockside tavern while drinking a pint or two of piss-tasting Plymouth beer. He said that all the admirals were agreed that the Spanish king had been knocked about in a mighty way. Also—from my friend the second mate, anyway—that the Irish coast was filled with thousands of survivors of Armada shipwrecks, and that most of the Armada sailors had been captured and executed by English soldiers.

Later the same day it was Captain Pike, not the second mate, who assured me that none of the royal dons or haughty captains of the Armada had been jailed or killed, of course, but that five thousand or so sailors and soldiers who were also cast ashore had indeed been shot or beheaded—one or the other. So it was, in fact, that the rich English lords gave comfort to the rich Armada castaways, but the lords of England also ordered the soldiers of their army to kill the soldiers and sailors of the Spanish Armada. Like Da always said: it was the rich who always got richer and the poor who always got buried in a big ditch. Damn sonsabitches.

Pike leaned toward me. "Are you listening to me, Blue, or not?"

"You've got to speak louder through that damn mask of yours for me to hear, sir." If I'd been in a lighter mood, the sight of a tavern full of masked men would have set me to laughing. But even as we sat swilling the rotten beer, a man fell from his chair while his mates departed their table in quick file. None looked back at the fallen comrade, and certainly none returned to help the fallen man back into his chair.

"There's a meeting tomorrow with Admiral Drake and the queen's Privy Council."

"I've heard the same," I replied.

"I shall be in attendance." Pike nodded to me. "And so shall you, my mate."

I could barely understand one bewigged man or the other. They seemed to have honey bees buzzing from between large white teeth for all the gibberish they spouted, but afterward the captain made clear where they ended the discussion.

"Here's the sum of what they said." Pike kept his mask of cotton gauze lifted while he took a long draught of beer, then added, "There were some dozens of Spanish ships wrecked or foundered off the west coast of Ireland, but most of the Armada made it back to ports along the Bay of Biscay."

"Yes sir," I managed through my own mask.

With his lifted mask, Pike ignored for the moment the miasma of plague and scurvy that permeated the tavern. "Our spies tell us that the entire Spanish fleet is in bad shape, and that it is a matter of years, not months, before the Spanish king has a navy of any significance."

"Ahh," I said through my safety net of gauze.

"Further, the largest number of ships under repair are anchored in either the port of Santander or San Sebastian." My captain put his mask back in place to protect mouth and nose.

I asked my question. "What does the Privy Council order as the duty of Admiral Drake?"

"We must make haste and destroy the crippled fleet of the dons." With his mask in place and hands flat on the filthy table, Pike spoke in a loud, clear voice. "First, we must destroy the Spanish fleet in their own nest, and then our Admiral Drake is ordered to intercept the Spanish treasure fleet. Our spies located around the Caribbean Sea tell us that the treasure fleet is just now leaving the island of Puerto Rico."

"And what of our paltry cod ship, sir?"

"We will stay in close attendance to the *Swiftfire*, our commander's very own new ship of war."

Who knew the actual whys and wherefores? Certainly not me and likely not Captain Pike. He and I had discussed the fact that supplies to Drake's fleet dribbled down to his ships in insufficient amounts, and that those meager supplies were conferred here and there with no reason or explanation. Still, the Privy Council's orders remained intact: "Attack with all due speed!"

It was two days before the date given by Admiral Drake for his Armada fleet to sail that Captain Pike had sticks of sulphur burned belowdecks of his own ship. At the same time that any lurking Black Death and scurvy infections, along with hordes of rats and roaches without number, were getting fumigated, the crew of Pike's ship *Mosquito* was safe in our very own Bristol neighborhood tavern. We were drinking watered-down tots of rum and good Bristol beer, all paid for by Captain Pike. As a further indication of his charitable nature, Captain Pike also sent Ma and six other women from our neighborhood, all seven with purses full of coin, to every market to the north of Bristol. The women filled wheelbarrows with barrels of good Bristol beer and whatever fruit, vegetables, and wheat they could find, stored them in corners around our tavern, then returned for another round of shopping for the good ship *Mosquito*.

It was another four days before the first ships actually left Bristol Harbor for the rendezvous with Admiral Drake, and it was then that Pike allowed his crew to board the ship. We, the officers and men, spent the morning clearing the hordes of dead rats and roaches from the ship, and it was well past dark by the time all victuals and munitions were aboard.

At first light the next morning, I put some of the crew to rearranging supplies to make the ship trim, while the rest went to weigh anchor. It was because our ship moved with alacrity and the English fleet moved at the speed of walking turtles that we arrived at the side of Admiral Drake's ship after a mere thirty-six hours at sea. I can honestly say—in retrospect, in any event—that we Bristol fishermen and Beothic savages were pleased with our seamanship skills and with our Captain Pike for his protection of his sailors. Even more to the point—again, I say this with complete honesty—we were excited to go into action against the Spanish enemy. I had a few short dreams of gold in my purse, and I'm certain that, with the possible exception of the demented Bristol boy, the rest of the crew had similar dreams.

There was decent weather for three consecutive days, and Drake managed to arrange his fleet of ships in an acceptable formation. We were tight to the stern of *Swiftfire* and had a white gull's view of messengers as they exchanged one piece of parchment from each ship's captain for another piece of parchment from Admiral Drake. All seemed well; everyone in the fleet was apparently performing his duties with classic English efficiency. What followed, however, was the fault of either a glut of bad intelligence or pure and simple stupidity. Whatever the reasons, the end result was that the bulk of the English armada invaded not Santander or San Sebastian or even Lisbon but instead ended in the port and city of Corona.

There were a few empty hulks and one ship of war at anchor in the Port of Corona. All four were quickly dispatched, and then English soldiers and sailors were landed ashore to conquer the lower city of Corona. Spanish soldiers were killed by the dozen, with many cheers from English soldiers. There were no shots fired at the English troops because the Spanish soldiers had no guns. Most were women and children with no uniforms, carrying sticks or pitchforks as weapons.

The battle was quickly won, and then the victorious Englishmen turned to pillaging all the buildings that surrounded the harbor. Food was the prime goal, and provisions were grabbed for instant consumption by the unruly crowd. Picnics erupted at various points around the Port of Corona, all with large fires to cook meat and boil porridge.

A large barge came alongside our *Mosquito*, and a man with a speaking cone yelled, "Captain Pike, come aboard, sir."

Pike went the rail and shouted, "Why?"

"You must attend the admiral and his captains. They have plans to invade the upper city of Corona."

A line was secured amidships, Pike dropped into the barge, and the crew rowed in ragged fashion toward Drake's flagship.

Since the upper city was protected by an immense and well-designed wall in the port area, a covey of English engineers and artillery officers were called in for consultation by the admiral. At this delicate point in time, with Drake dithering with his fleet captains, and his soldiers and sailors celebrating the absence of hunger in a most unruly fashion, an immense and delicious cache of wine was discovered by a roving pack of sailors. This new and delightful surprise was shared with one and all, and soon the Port of Corona was a huge rollicking carnival of drunken Englishmen.

"Leave the fools alone," yelled Captain Pike. "Quickly now, push the damn tower close against the wall."

Our crew of Bristol fishermen, sober and focused, obeyed the order to secure the large wooden tower and then paused to hear the next order.

"Listen to me, for a moment," said Captain Pike. "I'm giving a reward of triple shares for each man over the wall." The wild look from our captain brought Da to stand nearly nose to nose with his commander. In spite of Da standing in his face, Pike continued with his encouragement of his crew. "A grant of ten acres of my own land to the first man over the wall!"

Da held his left hand in front of Pike's face. "Captain," Da yelled. "Do you promise triple shares for every man here that makes it over the wall?"

"Yes! Triple shares for every man over the wall," yelled Pike.

"Will you make a promise that we return to the cove after this battle?"

"Yes! Agreed, my men of Bristol!" Captain Pike put his right hand toward Da. "Here is my hand, Bosun. Lead the way to your ten acres of prime land."

The tower against the city wall was a rickety patched-together affair, with hemp rope of dubious heritage securing each corner of the battlement. I followed at Da's heels, and the others came as soon as there was room to climb. A high-pitched shriek swelled from the other side of the wall, and as Da breached the top of our tower, I could see that the space below the wall, in the upper city of Corona, was filled with women.

Da took a step from the tower to the top of the wall while I moved another step higher on the tower. Most of the screaming women shook long spears at us, but one near the center of the crowd held a musket at her shoulder. I could see her aim and watched the sudden burst of smoke and fire from the weapon.

Da's head exploded in a red cloud. He fell toward me, and as I held out my arms to catch my da, the tower collapsed to the ground.

Wine dribbled over my face and some into my mouth. I opened my eyes and saw Erdu grab the drunken sailor and throw him out of my sight.

"Da!" I moaned.

Erdu sat me upright and wiped blood from my face. "He's dead. Our bosun is dead," he said.

Captain Pike came into my vision. "Blue," he yelled. "Can you walk?"

"Da is dead," I answered.

"Erdu!" Pike yelled. "Get Blue up and walking—we're going back to the ship." The captain turned to those standing near. "Bristol men, follow me," he yelled.

With one arm over Erdu's shoulder, I was barely conscious as we plowed through the mass of drunken Englishmen. Some of the English invaders could stagger a few paces, but most remained stuck together in small inert blobs of incoherent babblers. A few sergeants and officers held weapons and remained sober, but it was obvious to me that the amorphous mob of Englishmen would yield to no threats from a few killjoys. We eventually made the ship, and I surrendered myself to fall into a deep black hole.

"Blue!" said a voice. "Blue, open your damned eyes."

"Da's dead," I whispered.

"Drake is pulling out of here on the morning tide," the voice said.

I managed one eye and then the next. Pike was kneeling at my side. "We have to bury Da," I said.

"He's buried beneath a pile of English sailors, my mate. There's nothing more we can do for our bosun."

"Da," I said.

"Erdu's my bosun now, so get up and help the red savage get what's left of my Bristol sailors under weigh." He put a hand in front of my face. "No more words. I need both mate and bosun for us to get our share of the Spanish gold."

We managed to stay in formation with Admiral Drake for two days of squalls and fog, but at dawn of the third day we were alone and struggled with all our strength to survive the mighty waves and ferocious winds. On the sixth dawn of our venture to unimaginable wealth, we came about and headed back to Bristol.

CHAPTER SEVEN

1590
Oubee

The surviving seamen of the ship *Mosquito* returned to their Bristol homes. The plague took one of the Bristol cod fishermen and diminished a good part of our Bristol neighborhood, with dozens upon dozens dead of the Black Death. Pike stayed in his manor house and burned enough sulphur to keep his family safe from disease, and in the end his entire household of twenty-eight family members and their retainers suffered the loss of only two servants. The captain sent one of his servant women over to me with a handful of coins each month, but toward the end of winter, not many of the coins were gold. The rations in our cottage were eventually limited to small portions of salt cod, usually immersed in a thin gruel of black beans that Ma and Ruby cooked in a big black iron pot.

Da was a constant reference in conversations at home and throughout the neighborhood. "Remember when Da . . ." was a common beginning for many conversations. I was struck by the numerous references of puns and jokes and innocent humor attributed to my da. Oh, yes! Da's backhand was also frequently noted, but always, the victim of his violence was judged worthy of the blow. Da was missed by all of us in his small cottage, and it was crystal-clear that Da had been loved by all the Bristol cod fishermen. Da, oh, Da, where is your dream of an idyllic New Founde Land? A mythic place where savage and fishermen can laugh at each other's jokes? The home of Oubee and Tisquantum and Erdu? My home, their home, and yours?

Even with the limited information gleaned by the women of our village, it was clear that the Bristol fishermen were surviving the bitter winter weather and the constant threat of the Black Death better than most. The families in our neighborhood made space for the surviving red savages, and the Beothic made room for us. Ma and Erdu became companions at foraging weeds and bark for food or medicine. "This bark of the birch tree relieves aches and pains," my ma said to Erdu.

"Yes! It is the same with us. The same tree and the same medicine." Erdu nodded and whispered to Ma. "The concoction of fine birch-bark powder, lightly mixed with bear grease, is especially effective in alleviating the discomfort women experience during their monthly cycle of bleeding."

"Bear grease, you say?" Ma smiled at her associate in medical matters. "Bacon grease and the birch-bark is my palliative most in demand—here in the land of civilized women, that is."

"Do tell," said Erdu. "Rubbed on the tummy or swallowed with water?"

"Swallowed was always my suggestion, but each woman always worked out what was best for her."

"Civilized women are not always ugly and ignorant," Erdu always said at least once per day.

"Just stay clear of Ruby," Ma always said to Erdu, and more than once per day, I recall.

"Or what?" Erdu said to Ma with his big smile.

"Or I'll have the ghost of Da skin you alive at the least touch of your red paw on that young girl."

Still with his fabulous smile, Erdu continued. "It was the same with my own mother and her neighbors, always telling me what to do for my own good."

Both smiled at the other.

"Pshaw," Ma said, and then asked a question of her own, "Tell me, Erdu—how is it that you and the other two savages are still alive? I thought the plague was quicker with the red savages than with Bristol folks."

"Well, wife of Da, the fishermen of Bristol have traveled to our land for many generations, and they have always been generous in sharing their sins and diseases with the ignorant savages, you know."

Ma was taken aback by Erdu's jesting, and struggled for a proper response. "I do notice some scars on your face—are they from the pox?"

"The other two savages also sport the same scars, you may discover."

"Yes, it is true. The same scars as your own."

"A true gift from our friends from Bristol. So it seems to the elders of the Beothic people—those who manage to survive the invaders' disease, in any event."

"Another question. Are the children of parents who have survived the plague or pox immune to the next wave of the same disease?"

"So it seems," said Erdu.

"Pshaw," said Ma. "It is the same with Bristol folks.

"It seems savage and civilized are not much different in the essential ways of life," said Erdu.

"Show me again that trick with the dice," Ruby said.

"Certainly," said Erdu.

When the snow was mostly gone and the ice entirely melted from Bristol Bay, the messenger woman from Captain Pike gave me the skinniest of all purses and told me that she had an order from my captain.

"What?" I asked.

"Bring me a crew that can carry us to Mosquito Cove," the messenger woman related.

"When?" I asked.

"The master says that he'll leave in four days—with the full moon, that is."

"Can I bring Ma and the family?"

"Captain Pike anticipated that question and said to tell you that, for this trip, only fishermen are allowed."

"Tell Captain Pike that Jeremy will stay in Bristol if he cannot bring Ma and both families."

"The captain is not interested in the details." The gray-haired woman gave me a tiny hint of a smile. "His demand is for you bring him a crew of fishermen, nothing more."

I gave every penny from the final purse to Ma, then I had Jeremy promise me to get his forge started soon, plague or no plague.

"Right as rain," he said. "The gentry still need shoes for their horses." Jeremy looked me in the eye, like when we were young and about to tackle a gang of four rowdy boys of our age. "I'll do some day fishing out in the bay, or hire out by the day for whatever work is available if there's no labor at the forge."

"We'll survive," said Ma. "One way or another."

Ruby whispered over-loud to Erdu. "Stay here in Bristol, Erdu; wait for the next ship to New Founde Land. The ship that takes wives and mothers and children."

"Erdu is our bosun and must leave with me," I said.

"Omrod! Shut your lips or I'll give you my backhand," said Ruby. Tears ran down both sides of her nose. "Damn you both to hell!"

The crew of fifteen Bristol and three Beothic fishermen made do on the voyage. Half rations, at best. The captain gave most of the provisions to the Bristol families who had given protection to the Mosquito fishermen, Englishmen and Beothic both. The dregs we stretched to the end of our voyage, with nary a complaint from a single person. The early March weather was decent, and the pirates were hiding from the plague, I guessed. Four weeks it took from Bristol Harbor to St. John's Harbor—a two-night layover for Pike and us fishermen to conduct what business we could, then another night along the coast, into Conception Bay, and due west to our Mosquito Cove.

Captain Pike let me and Erdu handle the landing at his wharf with no comment, and while I set the men to make us secure and begin with the off-loading of our cargo, Pike made his way off ship and up to his residence. Near noon I told the crew to take a break for a few hours and to return at the sound of our horn. After all had departed, I walked up to see my red brother. I knew that it was Da who crunched through snow and mud behind my back. There was no one else who made such heavy steps.

A trail of gray smoke came from the chimney of the office and residence of the plantation manager. I opened the door without knocking and found Tisquantum sitting in a large chair with a pillow at his back. Captain Pike was sitting in a stiff straight-back chair, almost knee to knee with his plantation manager. Oubee stood at the captain's shoulder.

My brother spoke first. "Blue, welcome back."

"You look like a comfortable plantation owner," I said.

"You look in desperate need of a large osweet liver," Tisquantum said.

"I'll take the first bite of liver raw and frozen and thank you a dozen times."

Tisquantum and Oubee gave tentative smiles for my wit but stopped when Captain Pike stood from his chair. He was in a strange mood—not one of anger but more of lassitude than anything I could imagine.

He waved an arm toward the three of us. "Tisquantum, feed the men what you can. We are all near our death from starvation, as you must clearly see."

The captain exaggerated with the starvation lament, but even so, half rations or worse was certainly wearing on a body. In any event, Oubee moved rapidly toward the kitchen while Tisquantum waved one servant to the storage shed and another to the nearby Beothic village.

"Captain, please return to your chair. We'll have hot tea and smoked salmon for your belly in a moment," said Tisquantum.

"No talk for now, my secretary. Just get the damn food to the crew. I haven't a word for talk until the last sailor calls quits for his full belly."

Tisquantum stood from his comfortable chair. "As you wish, Captain. I'll be ready to talk when you are, sir."

Disturbing it was, this exchange between Pike and his secretary. Food and rest might solve the strain, but still, my stomach roiled from more than the bite of hunger.

The next morning we talked—Captain Pike, Tisquantum, Oubee, Erdu, and I.

"The plantation seems in excellent order." Pike looked down at his cup of warm coffee. He seemed pensive, still exhausted from our ordeal of the plague in Bristol and short rations on the voyage. "Tisquantum, tell me how you fared the past two years."

Tisquantum pushed a small stack of notebooks toward the captain. "We can review the records at our leisure, sir, but for now I'll give a general review of activity here at your plantation." He nodded to Oubee. "I'll ask my whaleboat captain and village manager to add comments as she notes the absence of critical information."

Oubee gave a thin smile to one and all but remained silent. *My*, I thought, *what a lovely young woman we have in our midst! She is even more beautiful than before we left the cove. Oubee, Oubee, my, oh, my.*

"In sum, my lord, the haul of cod the year that you left was average, matched almost exactly with the next two years. I sold the salt cod to whoever sailed into St. John's Harbor—some to English agents but mostly to French and Basque captains who were willing to pay my price." When there was no comment, Tisquantum continued. "On the first full year in my tenure as manager of your plantation, I repeated the sale of salt cod at St. John's with an accrued profit that you will note in the records. The profit in the ledger is supported by the bags of gold coin stored in the safe room you had Master Smyth build."

There was an awkward silence at the mention of Da, but when he felt that we were all ready to listen, Tisquantum continued his discourse. "During this last year, I have retained the cod in storage in the hope that I would be relieved of any decision necessary to sell our sizable stock."

"Very, very good work, my secretary. Unbelievable, in fact."

"Why is that to be true, Captain Pike? Unbelievable, that is." Oubee's voice was not a challenge to the captain—merely a harmless request for information.

Clever and beautiful both, I thought—but managed to suppress even the hint of a smile.

"Well, now." The captain floundered a bit. "Well, now, he is my secretary because he has no peer throughout New Founde Land. The best man in every way." In command, once again, Captain Pike gave a haughty stare at his interrogator. "And you, Miss Oubee. Are your exploits as valuable to me as those of Tisquantum?"

Still his equal, Oubee adjusted herself to face Captain Gilbert Pike. "My first year was a complete failure of your trust in me, sir."

"No, no, sir," Tisquantum injected. "Don't believe such a falsehood. There were some difficulties, certainly, but in the end Oubee established a foundation of knowledge and experience that has established what we now have as a strong and valuable community."

"Well, now," said the captain. "I'm certainly intrigued by the disparity of statements. Tell me your version, Miss Oubee." Now the captain did indeed give a full and genuine smile to the woman of my dreams.

"On the first winter of your absence, I took the whaleboat to St. John's and exchanged two barrels of salt cod for whatever seed I could find from ship captains or plantation owners."

Tisquantum raised his hand and again interrupted Oubee's narrative. "Every transaction has been recorded, Captain Pike—never fear."

Pike nodded and Oubee continued.

"When the warm weather of spring had melted all snow, I worked with the new villagers to plant seeds of maize, squash, potatoes, and beans. It took six days to place every seed into the ground." Oubee let the silence spin for a while before making a hollow cough and continuing. "After three weeks every seed produced a small green plant, and then there were two clear nights that produced a vicious frost. All my foreign plants shriveled into gray goo."

"Listen to what happened next," said Tisquantum.

"There was no seed left in the new village. I asked for and received three hatchets with metal heads from our manager, and one I sent to the ancestral Beothic village near our lake. Another I sent to our nearest Micmac neutral village, and the third I carried to St. John's City. In each case my goal was to secure both a fund of seed and a person to explain to the Beothic farmers of our new village how to bring the invaders' seed successfully to harvest."

"A bit late, weren't you?" The captain didn't seem angry, merely puzzled. "Locking the barn door after the horse has already escaped, you understand. This was the second time of planting with the same conclusion, if I'm not mistaken."

"You are correct, Captain Pike, I thought that we had waited long enough to avoid such a frost, but I was mistaken."

"Again," said the captain.

"Again," Oubee agreed. "And again the women of the village recommended that I should forget the foreign seeds and forget any plants that might provide food to the invaders living in other plantations or other villages scattered about our ancestral land."

Pike nodded but remained silent.

Oubee plodded on with her recitation, untroubled by Pike's attitude. "I was certain that it was too late for planting and for securing a successful harvest that particular year, but within seven days there arrived here at your plantation the Micmac trader of Tisquantum's youth, plus a Beothic warrior who had once spent a couple of years with a neutral Patuxent village far to the south, and a Portuguese farmer from the plantation of your friend Diogode Sousa."

"Ahh," said the captain. "The plot thickens."

Tisquantum smiled at his captain's wit and left Oubee to continue.

"Only the Portugee man had seeds for our gardens, but all participated in the debate of how to engender success. The three wandered back and forth over the land designated as farmland of our new village. They noted the daily line of sunlight, pinched and smelled our soil, and walked those beaches near at hand to pinch and smell the collected seaweed along the high-water mark. In the end they agreed that no seed should be planted until thirty days passed from the last frost. 'Even forty, to be safe,' said the Portegee farmer. All three agreed that the fall season hereabout seems to stay warm for a long spell, so the biggest concern for a farmer is of the sneaky killer frost that often comes upon us in middle to late May."

"I agree," said Captain Pike. "About the time we depart for Bristol each year with our load of salt cod, we enjoy the best weather by far."

"There's no loss going into June with the bean seed, the Micmac trader told me," added Oubee.

None of us had reason to comment on the activities of either Oubee or her experts.

"Come," said Oubee. "It is better to see than hear."

The lot of us walked to the new village and stared briefly at the site of Oubee's initial disaster, then we trudged up a slight uphill to a nearly level bench of land. "Here, my advisors all agreed, there is sun through the day and protection from the north wind.

"The Micmac trader explained that here we must prepare for the seeds with piles of seaweed stirred with the guts of cod from salting tables, and to place our seed potatoes on top of the soil but enmeshed by the seaweed and guts."

"I can't imagine such a task," said Captain Pike.

Oubee continued. "The Beothic told us to keep our piles of fertilizer close in random rows and to plant small families of maize and squash and beans together. It seems that past experience has shown that each plant will support the other to a successful harvest."

Tisquantum smiled at Pike and then at me and Erdu, then finished the report of the manager of his new village. "The three guests of Oubee stayed for another week to help our villagers plant their first crop at Mosquito Cove, and then we celebrated for the next two days and nights."

"What was the cost to me?" the captain asked. He appeared interested in the forthcoming answer, but he was certainly not annoyed or angry, whatever the cost.

"The cost was the final osweet steaks from our storage shed and a dozen seals eaten raw or slightly cooked at the end of sticks."

"Lovely," said Captain Pike. "I'm sorry to have missed such an event."

Tisquantum held up a hand. "And also for our pleasure, and most welcome: the guts and blubber of a good-sized whale."

"A whale!" Captain Pike leaned forward. "A whale from our whaleboats?"

"I was at the tiller of one boat and Oubee captain of the other. It was a great chase with Master Smyth's harpoon a great success." Tisquantum gave another respectful silence and then added, "We had each boat secured to the beast, and our warriors continued to pierce her with spears and arrows until she was dead in the water and we towed her to the nearest beach."

"A cow, was it?" I asked.

"Indeed, a two-for-one conquest, in fact, with a cow and her baby unborn," said Oubee. "The entire village descended upon the beach to help with the harvest, and most of the meat was carried to the storage sheds." Oubee gave us the sweetest of smiles with eyes and lips both.

"The women built a large fire of driftwood on the beach and served slices of the young whale for all to share."

"Wonderful!" said Erdu.

Tisquantum added a small lecture. "The celebration was important enough in the minds of the Beothic people that they now hold the event as a starting point in the history of the new village."

"Did the three experts share in the feast?" I asked.

Now Oubee gave me her attention and a small smile to boot. "Certainly, they did." The smile deepened. "I spent most of my time sitting next to the Micmac trader of Tisquantum's ancient past."

I moved closer to Oubee with a fake whisper. "Tell us how he came to change our friend's name, at that long-ago meeting."

Oubee dropped her smile and moved further apart from me in an abrupt jolt. "Never, ever," she said. "When will you ever learn to mind your own business, you simpleton?"

"Oh!" I said and struggled to find an appropriate response. "I thought that you were joking," I finally managed.

"Ah, Blue, still my simple young nitwit." She gave me the same severe expression from our first days together. "You must think more carefully before speaking. We are no longer children, playacting for each other, so, of all things, you must understand the importance of a promise made."

"Do I detect a lovers' quarrel brewing?" The captain sat back in his chair and shut both eyes. "Finish up with the good news, my secretary. We have many chores at hand."

"The first harvest at our new village was a pale shadow of the second, and your third crop of maize, squash, and beans is the most promising of all." Tisquantum drew a large quantity of air into his lungs. "There are now nearly two hundred residents of the new village. A few dozen tend the crops, while others sail the whaleboats for seal and seabirds, and on the rare days of calm seas, the boats scour the nearby islands for eggs and young birds. All are busy, and most seem satisfied to live near the Mosquito Cove plantation."

The captain sat for a long spell before speaking. "I am indebted to you, Tisquantum, for your rare ability to manage my plantation to such an unbelievable pinnacle." Another long pause. "Here is what I will do next. During the next days we will load my ship with all of the salt cod stored in our sheds. In the evenings, Tisquantum will finish his report to me. I will also tour the new village with Oubee and meet the elders to reward them for their service. As soon as possible I will return to Bristol to set my finances in order and to make sure that the families of my fishermen have adequate funds for their families."

"Da?" I asked.

"The memory of Master Smyth will not go unremarked. I will have a grave indicated with a marble headstone, and also I will give Jeremy Smyth, as an elder of the family, ten pounds in gold coin to spend as he chooses on Master Smyth's grave."

"Da would be pleased," I said.

"I will return the next fall to load the cod from that year and also to take any Bristol men home who want the voyage."

Tisquantum scribbled a memorandum to himself, then spoke to his employer. "I will work with Blue to find a crew for your safe voyage to Bristol."

"Work with Erdu to find the crew," I said. "I'll stay in the cove and work as a fisherman."

Pike held his hand up to stop my talking. "It'll be Blue as my mate—no one else."

"Erdu told me that he's willing to serve as mate on the good ship *Mosquito*." I leaned forward in my chair toward my captain. "I'm finished with the job and will stay here to fish for the cod."

Captain Pike was vexed with me. "What? You will stay at the cove as a fisherman and not serve as my mate for the voyage? That's as near mutiny as anything I've ever heard."

"The cove is my home, and I will serve you better here than aboard ship."

Pike studied me for a while and then for an equal time at Oubee. "Yes, Mister Smyth, I agree with your decision to remain at the cove." His smile was reminiscent of Da's, more downward grimace than upward curl. "Have you any instructions for me concerning your family?"

"Give Ruby a secret fund so that she may buy sweets for the youngsters," I said.

"Granted," said Gilbert Pike.

CHAPTER EIGHT

1602–1614
Letter of Marque

E LIZABETH REMAINED ON HER THRONE and seemed able to live forever. War with Spain continued, and we outlanders of New Founde Land debated every paragraph of London pamphlets whenever delivered. The frequent entry of ships from most of the ports of Europe into St. John's Harbor, and the subsequent entry of their voluble captains into the taverns of St. John's City, also gave much for us to chew upon.

Oubee and I were married by Captain Pike in early February of the year 1602. Oubee's mother and Tisquantum were witnesses at the ceremony; afterwards, the five of us drank two bottles of French wine, and ate a slice of spice cake prepared and baked by Tisquantum. Pike gave us the wedding gift of a vacant fishermen's cabin, which Oubee and I took as a special gift from Da as well.

There was no one more surprised than I over Oubee's final choice for her husband. Every eligible Beothic warrior in the known world stood in line for a kind word from her. I knew she'd had many suitors from the new village, the old village by the lake, and even some warriors who found their way to Mosquito Cove from remote

Labrador and other equally obscure places. Oubee's mother and brother had favorite choices that did not include me, and, as I heard many months later, even Tisquantum counseled his cousin to find a respectable red savage as a mate—any one of the dozens available—but to avoid the perils of marriage to a Bristol fisherman.

"Why me?" I asked on our first night.

A large white owl boomed a challenge into the frigid night. Snow tumbled from a nearby spruce tree.

"I couldn't marry a man who was smarter than me, so I looked around for who was left." She poked me with a smart blow in the belly and then kissed my neck and ear.

"So you picked the dumbest of your suitors to father your children?" I caressed my wife gently on the butt and squiggled down to kiss her breasts and stomach.

"Quiet, Husband—just perform your duties as I require."

I squiggled lower under the warm blankets. "Here?" I whispered.

"A bit lower," Oubee said. "Faster, dummy!"

"Erdu? Ruby? I can't believe such a tale."

Captain Pike, on his first return from Bristol, had pulled me aside and told me of the marriage of Ruby to Erdu, and that they had promised Ma to stay in Bristol Town until Ma died a natural death.

"Nonsense," I said, "just bring them all here to the plantation." I stepped back from the captain and lowered the tone of my voice. "Please, Captain Pike, on your next trip bring Ma, the kids, and Erdu home."

Pike stood quietly for a long moment. "I'm sorry, Blue, I did in fact offer the option of Mosquito Cove this past trip, but none wanted to leave Bristol."

Pike motioned for us to sit down on both sides of his kitchen table. The cook was off to the village for osweet and beans, and the room smelled sweet and clean. "It seems that Erdu met with a gypsy healer, and after a week or so of walking around the edge of Bristol Town and the harbor, and sitting up all hours of the night talking, they teamed up to sell their services as healers and doctors."

"Healers?" I said. "Erdu a doctor to the civilized folks of Bristol?"

"Your ma and Ruby told me in the most emphatic words that everywhere the two travel, to city neighborhoods and close-by villages, many buy medicines from them. They set bones better than any of the fakes and give advice that helps more people than they hurt."

"Ma and Ruby? How do they spend their time at home?"

"They travel with the doctors as nurses, and serve as midwives to boot."

"Da must be spinning in his grave," I said. "Wife and daughter out among the sick; no telling the likes of who might lay a hand on them."

Pike put a hand on mine, for comfort, I imagined. "Listen, Blue, the last words I had from them was talk of building a hospital in Bristol Town. They claimed silver coins were raining down on them from their business and figured they'd build a little hospital to have the sick come to them, rather than the other way round."

I could make no sense of what Pike was telling me about silver coins and hospitals. "Damn!" I said. "Oubee and Ruby are natural chums, and I could hardly wait for them to meet the other."

Pike smiled across the clean table. "If they did agree to moving here to Mosquito Cove, I'd wager that your ma and Ruby would train Oubee as a midwife and Erdu to turn you into a healer."

"I'm a smyth and fisherman, and wish for no other trade. Besides which, there's not a hint in my head that I'd prefer fixing broken bones over fixing broken wheel rims."

The summer cod season was colder than usual, with frequent storms of such violence that no fishing boats could leave the cove for days on end. The final tally of salt cod noted in Tisquantum's ledger was the lowest in the past ten years. Pike was distressed with the world, and the Bristol fishermen were anxious about returning home with skimpy shares from the sale of cod and the fur of seals. I was unconcerned with much other than the well-being of a very pregnant Oubee.

Captain Gilbert Pike, still my patron but not my captain for this particular fall season voyage, was the admiral of a few cod ships in convoy bound for England. I heard all the details of adventure and the humor of it from one fisherman or another, after the ship *Mosquito* returned to Mosquito Cove Plantation in the late spring of 1603.

"What happened?" I asked one of the cod-boat captains on his first night of return.

"We could hardly believe our eyes," he said. "Pike nailed his letter of marque to the door of his cabin with the cove still in sight."

"He's a natural-born pirate, that one," I said. The boat captain was a short, hairy man with whiskers thick on face and when naked to the waist appeared more black bear than human being. His real name was never mentioned, as all knew him as Captain Hairy, of course.

"A penniless Bristol captain, more likely," said Hairy.

"A poor pirate, I'm certain," I said. "But tell me the truth of the matter—was Pike protecting the fishing fleet or what?"

"Well now, we both know that Pike was loaded with a skimpy load of dried cod, and his bundles of fur were a mangy mess." Hairy winked at me." On the third morning at sea—dawn, if you can believe—a single lonely weather-beat ship appeared at our bow, almost within hailing distance. Their stern mast and sail were scrambled on the deck, with a ragged bow sail keeping her under weigh at the pace of a pregnant cow."

"Oh, happy day!" I said. "Were any of the other New Founde Land ships in view?"

"Not a one, so the captain used his old letter of marque to liberate from that beat-up Dutch merchant ship ten barrels of French wine, a large bag of gold and silver coins, and an Irish girl named Shelagh Na Geira."

"Oh, happy days, indeed," I said.

"Best of all, the crew got shares enough to make their trip worthwhile, and the captain married Shelagh."

"No! Married to an Irish woman!"

"You'll meet her, I'm sure, when next they emerge from his cabin," said Captain Hairy.

When Pike brought Shelagh Na Geira back to Mosquito Cove as his wife, it was a simple matter of courtesy for Oubee to make Shelagh feel comfortable in her new home.

Ahh, the two queens. Twins in height and weight. Both with black, black hair. Oubee had black eyes and rufous-colored skin, while Shelagh had the dark blue of deep ocean water in her eyes and skin the color of ewe's milk. I know for an honest fact that a stern expression from either queen could stop any man in his tracks. Together they could send a pack of men or boys or wild wolves running for the woods. Two queens—two savage women who were fierce protectors of their domain.

Pike, gentry though he was, could not diminish the hostility shown to his Roman Catholic wife by the good protectors of the only true religion. I, good craftsman and all, was equally harassed by my marriage to a red savage, also barren of any knowledge of the true religion. Even so, with the constant slights and ugly comments, none could diminish my love for Oubee, nor Pike's love for Shelagh.

"Ignore the buggers," I told Oubee time and again. "They'll be gone in a few weeks, and then we'll have our precious son to ourselves."

"You shall teach him the Smyth business, and I'll take the rest," Oubee said. "Our son will learn of nature and people from his Beothic uncles and aunts, and not from these fools dressed in black clothes and black notions.

"Of course," I said.

There was one occasion when Pike came storming down the wharf to board the *Mosquito* where I was working with three men to off load an awkward three-legged piano—a gift to his wife. He pointed to the least diligent of my crew. "Get me the cat, Blue!" he yelled. "I'll peel the skin from his back, and then I'll walk him to the end of wharf at ten fathoms."

"Now, now," I said. "We'll just send the bastard to St. John's on the next whaleboat."

"Get the cat. He's insulted my wife, and I'll take his slander no more."

"Easy now, Captain. I heard what happened and I've already had a few words with the stupid sod." Pike stood fuming, a helpless expression eroding his face. "I'll take care of the fool, Captain. Just think on the matter for a bit. He and the rest of the white invaders shall be gone in a few weeks, and that's for us to be thankful for."

"A *few* words, my mate?"

"I admit to more than a few, especially when I had his friends laughing and pointing at the fool."

"Could it be, my mate, that you remarked on the poor sod's tool for sex or to his possible inclination for the preference of a boy's butt to a woman's ocean of charms?"

"Both," I said.

"Ahh," said Captain Pike. "I suspect the poor man is either swimming or walking his way to St. John's Harbor before the sun does set."

"Walking, is what I heard. If he's not eaten by bears or savages, he may see St. John's in two weeks or so."

We smiled at the other, mate and captain, the rulers of Mosquito Plantation.

Captain Pike and his bride departed Mosquito Cove in the late summer of 1603, his ship *Mosquito* filled with a bountiful load of fur and salt cod. "We'll spend a few weeks in Bristol," said Shelagh to me and Oubee, just before boarding. "We'll want to spend a little time with Gilbert's mother and his uncle, and a lot of time with Erdu and Ruby and her ma."

"Last word from Ruby was that they will have the new hospital to show and at least one nephew to cuddle," I said.

"According to the latest letter from Erdu," Shelagh said, "we'll sleep in their new Bristol home."

"My, oh my," I said. "Da would never believe the truth of it. His daughter married to a savage, and the both of them living the life of landed gentry."

"And your ma along for the ride," Oubee said.

"I'll give them all big hugs and kisses," said Shelagh.

Oubee made a fake whisper to her best friend. "Between the hugs, get all the juicy gossip from Ma and Ruby." A big smile. "Send the captain with Erdu to study the new hospital, and then share a little brandy with the women, just to get their tongues a little loose."

Shelagh returned Oubee's smile and shrugged. "Maybe we'll spend a few extra days in Bristol, now that it looks to be so much fun."

The women hugged again, and both started with the tears again. Oubee asked another question. "What will follow the visit to Bristol?"

"Gilbert has it all planned, and he claims we'll see Paris in the fall and the south of France during the winter."

"Oh, Shelagh, remember every detail to share with me upon your return to the plantation."

Each hugged the other, kissed the other's young boy, and waved farewell.

Captain Pike walked over and stood at the side of his wife. When it was clear that the women were finished saying their very last words, he turned to me. "Do you have those Welsh builders committed?"

"Yes sir, a week at most, before they start construction on your new home," I said.

Pike turned, with Shelagh on his arm and their son in tow, walked slowly toward the *Mosquito*, and gave a passing wave of departure to one and all.

When Pike and family returned to Mosquito Cove in the late spring of 1604, he left his wife and Oubee hugging and crying each into the shoulder of the other, and marched silently down the wharf and up the hill to inspect his new house. Later, with both families at dinner in the new house and the food prepared by the new French chef, Pike offered the first toast with a glass of champagne. "To the new house," he said. Then he added, after all cups of wine were back on the table, "What good work you've done with my new house, Blue. Shelagh and I are both very pleased."

"I built the house with the expectation of three residents, Captain, so tell me if there's an addition or two for me to handle."

"We're fine, Blue—just fine and dandy." Pike's smile gave truth to his answer.

I pressed my captain a bit. "Those stone masons from Wales are still around St. John's City, and they'd be happy with additional work."

"No, no, we are really very happy with the accommodations that you have managed. Shelagh is especially happy with the kitchen and our bedroom." Again the big smile from our captain and patron. "The two bedrooms for children give us plenty of room in that realm also."

Shelagh matched her husband's smile. "Erdu and his gypsy friend gave me a big tub of grease for the next chick that we hatch."

"Grease to rub or swallow?" Oubee asked.

"We'll just have to figure that problem together, won't we, my luv?"

In my mind, Pike should have been damn well be pleased with his situation because Tisquantum and I had imported a master builder and four assistants from St. John's City to plan and implement the task of building this mansion for Gilbert Pike. The workers were recently from Cardiff and comfortable in working stone from a quarry to fit the dimensions and style that they envisioned. What they had in fact completed was an elegant manor for the likes of Captain Pike, and it was certainly more than adequate for the captain, his Irish wife, and at least a handful of youngsters.

Then there was Oubee, sailing her whaleboat back and forth to St. John's to pick the very best to fill each room and house. All in all, the Pike pile of stone would most certainly satisfy even the wealthiest of Bristol gentry. Two wings off the central core, and two stories high for both wings and core, all mounted on a small hill overlooking Mosquito Cove. A true wonder to behold.

His old cabin, built by my own da, and given to me and Oubee as our home, was enlarged by the Welsh workers to include my very own office, and another bedroom to accommodate our sons. These dwellings of Pike and Smyth were separated by a grove of hardwood trees, mixed with a few very tall spruce, and exactly one hundred and ten paces apart.

Tisquantum, not to be left a beggar, also received a stone dwelling built by the Cardiff crew. His domicile featured a bedroom fit for a lord, a library with shelves—floor to ceiling, on three walls—a thick carpet over a brick floor, and three sturdy chairs backed by small tables holding lanterns that burned only whale oil. The remaining room was an office of organized ledgers, a large desk with an elevated chair, and a large metal safe cemented onto the stone foundation. To cap off the rest of Mosquito Cove Plantation, Da's cabins for fishermen, and his wharf and sheds, were still in prime shape and much appreciated with each new crop of sharemen and their boys.

The buildings and structures remained unchanged from 1604. The years passed quickly. Both women gave birth to an equal number of boys for their father's attention, and I know for a fact that both fathers were suitably proud of their seed. It was also of undeniable fact that the most intimate companion to all four of the boys was named Blue.

"Will you make my eldest a blacksmyth?" Pike queried of me on numerous occasions over the years.

"Only if he stands the tests of time," I always responded.

Queen Elizabeth died in that auspicious year 1603, and she was succeeded by King James I. I speak with complete honesty when I say that all the Bristol captains of New Founde Land plantations were horrified when that damned fool King James I made peace with Spain. When the new king had the audacity to cancel all letters of marque carried by many English captains of the fleet, and then when the fool retired his entire English fleet of ships from service, thousands of English sailors and their officers were suddenly out of work, with none in sight.

I was well aware that Captain Pike was not the only English ship captain enraged by the stupid behavior of King James I, but to Pike's certain credit, he wasn't one of the first of the so-called "erring captains" to fly into action. An erring captain, so named by James and his lackeys, was an English ship captain who went so far as to steal one of the old queen's ships for his own purpose. That purpose, of course, was to attack any ship at sea, including English merchant ships and those of other English erring captains.

With the year of 1613 coming near an end, Pike called a meeting in his own fancy office. A blizzard was running down after dumping a good load of snow all around. A run from one building to another was worth your undivided attention, what with the cold and stiff breeze. "It's a real cock-up out there and getting worse by the month." Captain Pike had the attention of both me and his secretary. We were drinking the captain's brandy instead of his rum, which in itself proclaimed that this was an auspicious occasion.

"We have two years of prime salt cod sitting in storage. We have no income to pay the fishermen or to purchase supplies for the Beothic villages. Standing outside St. John's Harbor and nearly every cove in New Founde Land are shiploads of pirates, mostly English 'erring captains,' but a good many French and Basque pirates as well."

"We savages call the game 'running the gauntlet,'" Tisquantum said.

Pike nodded in agreement. "Well said and true to our situation." He continued, with no smile at this point in the conversation. "Blue, we are going to leave our ladies for a season or two."

"Yes sir." I paused for a moment. "Why?"

"You must trust my judgement in this important matter, Omrod Smyth."

"Your eldest and mine are due for some lessons at my forge."

"They'd rather play savage and invader than pound steel at a hot forge." Pike tried his smile on me. "Give them another year or so with Shelagh and Oubee to ride herd. Let's go sailing, you and me."

"No."

"Why?

"Whatever you have in mind is likely to get one or both of us killed dead." Pike stared first at me than at Tisquantum. "Further, since you asked, I'd hate to imagine what happens to four boys raised by two queens and no kings."

"Nonsense," said Pike. "What I have in mind excludes any chance that harm will come to either of us."

"No," I repeated, with added authority. "You have just noted the fact of pirates at every turn around New Founde Land. The *Mosquito* would never survive the gauntlet set for us."

"Good," said Pike. "I knew that you would volunteer for this exciting venture."

Pike turned to Tisquantum.

"No," said Tisquantum.

"You haven't heard my offer," Pike said.

"Yes or no, it makes no difference." Tisquantum swallowed the dregs of his brandy. "Just tell us what we must do, Captain Pike, for you are indeed our master in all matters, and it is our responsibility to follow your orders, whatever they be."

"Or how stupid they may be," I added.

Pike smiled at both of us, as if we were dutiful full-share Bristol fishermen. "Good, it is settled, and here are your orders."

Unasked, I filled each cup with Pike's expensive brandy, and then led a silent toast to our patron.

"Thank you for your trust and confidence," Pike said. "First of all, I want Tisquantum to assume management responsibilities for the entire plantation."

"Yes sir," said Tisquantum.

"Well now," I said. "If you still trust Tisquantum to run the plantation, I'd trust Oubee to manage the new village again."

"Even with your two young roosters running about?"

"Oubee and her relatives have the boys well in hand," I said. "Indeed, the boys are often off with one uncle or another learning the skills of hunting or gambling, and they can both read with enough skill to understand our tenuous financial situation."

Pike nodded. "Good, everything is in hand. Blue, get us a half-dozen savages ready to join on our trip. I'll poll the Bristol men for their interest in joining my pirate venture. We'll slip the anchor of our trusty *Mosquito* in two days, with the morning tide."

I'd served off and on as mate to Captain Pike from the days when Da was killed. I knew that other than the bedraggled Dutch ship—the ship that had given him Shelagh—the few occasions when the captain made an effort to bring real value to his letter of marque had failed. Erdu told me of one sortie in southern waters that best defined the success of his previous pirate ventures.

"The damn ship appeared upwind of us like an ugly nightmare."

"How so?" I asked.

"My guess is that she was hidden from us in a little cove, so when we passed by, she pounced out of thin air."

"Close?"

"Damn close. A Spanish ship of war—forty guns, I'd say. She was so big and so fast that they never even fired a shot at us." Erdu was talking fast, moving his hands in grand gestures and smiling all at the same time. "There was no doubt in my mind but that they had Pike nearly by the balls."

"What happened?"

"A lovely Caribbean squall arrived just in the nick of time. Rain and wind coming six ways to Sunday, I'll tell you, and when our cover broke clear, the *Mosquito* was all by herself."

"How come I've never heard that story before?"

"Pirates keep their secrets, my friend."

So it was that in the early summer of 1614, my lord and captain called me back into his service as his mate of a pirate ship.

"Here's the way of it." Pike had the twenty of us standing in front of him on the Mosquito Cove wharf. "We'll take our little ship over to St. John's Harbor and swap her for the *Princess*."

The entire crew, including Captain Pike, laughed at the ridiculous claim.

"Listen, you fools." He waited until we settled. "I want my red savages, including Blue, decked out in red ochre, head to toe."

Smiles and a few titters.

"You savages will have knives in your belts and a good stout wooden spear in hand. All six of you, just as I say."

Quiet and serious.

"Bristol boys will look their usual: ugly, dirty, and mean. Pistols in hand, knives in belt."

Dead quiet.

"I've had made a twelve-pound cannon ball wrapped in chain and hooked to a six-foot pole of solid oak. Our Viking from the Port of Grimsby will have this toy to smash a deck or head or whatever gets in our way."

"Jack, Jack!" the crew shouted.

"I've got twelve ropes with knots tied up and down and a fine sharp-pointed grapnel at the end of each." Pike smiled at his silent crew. "We go over the top at first light. We'll sound like the banshees from hell and not stop until the deck is clear and the crew locked below."

Twenty-one smiles all around.

Captain Pike help up his left hand. "I'm sorry to tell this crowd of warriors sitting here, lusting for battle, but to my certain knowledge at least half the crew of our *Princess* is ashore in the taverns of St. John's City."

Very large smiles from one and all, although more leer than smile, in my mind.

The Spanish captain and his Spanish mates of the *Princess* argued and wailed and fell weeping to the deck. Pike laughed at each but drew not a drop of blood from a one.

Jack, our "east coast of England" Viking, had smashed his twelve-pound ball with great vitality and much noise. We red savages added our shouts and sharp spears to the retreat of resident soldiers and sailors into one locked and barred hold or another. We did in fact swap our trusty little merchant ship *Mosquito* for the *Princess,* with the Spanish captain and all his officers, including the mates, taking immediate residence in the smelly hold of the little Bristol cod-fishing ship. Those thirty-six officers swapped their ship of forty large cannon for a ship that was suffering a serious leak somewhere in the stern hold. They relinquished to Captain Gilbert Pike the finest warship in all of New Founde Land.

"Drake designed the likes of her," Captain Pike told me and Erdu.

"Hard to believe," I said. "What with the admiral at sea all the time."

"Well, now," said Pike, "I know for a fact that Drake himself had the best shipwrights in all of England design the likes of her."

"Is that so?" I answered, so as not one to rile my captain in front of the other pirates watching.

"Indeed." Pike stood a little taller. "Drake and his shipwrights called their new breed a 'race ship,' and only twenty-five have ever been built."

I made an act of studying the design of our new race ship. "She's low to the water, that's no lie, and this long prow and little-bitty castles fore and aft—well, that puts every ship I've ever seen out of mind."

"Even better," said Pike. "The damned rigging is set to allow sailing close to the wind." He put one arm behind his back. "I'm told that she skips around like a little sailboat on a lake."

Pike and I stood nodding at each other, like the fools we were, and thought our private thoughts for an overlong stretch of time. I began wondering: if the *Princess* was indeed of English design and build, how came it to be that her captain and officers were all Spanish folks? The crew we had locked below was clearly a mishmash of Basque and French and Portugee—the crew left on board the *Princess*, that is, because the better half were Spanish sailors, ashore and well out of our way.

"Why only Spanish sailors on shore leave?" I asked.

"The others can't be trusted to return." Pike nodded to himself. "The officers probably thought some of those left on board might jump to another ship, set up as farmers or hunters here on New Founde Land."

Pike was full of himself and blind to our obvious difficulties. "Captain, I want you to know that I haven't a single idea about how to serve as a first mate on this magnificent ship of war." Some small part of what I said was to spite Pike's toffee-nosed attitude, but more to the mark was that what I said was true.

Pike didn't hesitate a heartbeat. "Now, now, Blue. The first mate of our *Princess* will merely stand at my side and not say a damn word for the first five days."

"Is 'Yes sir' and 'No sir' acceptable behavior?"

"Now, now, let's not have such flippant talk. I well remember how you learned to serve my little ship by watching and learning. Now you've got to watch and learn what it takes to put the *Princess* into action."

"Captain Pike, I can tell you with no doubt in my mind that it is simply not possible for our little mob to manage this huge ship of war."

"Me too," said Jack the Viking. "Blue is right in the matter of things, so let's talk things out in the open." Jack still had his weapon in hand, and he suddenly swung the chain and ball to strike the deck a loud blow. "Pirates talk before they go into action, not when they are already slogging through deep piles of shit."

"Quiet," Pike said, "the both of you savages."

"Jack's in the right, and I for one will have a one last word if you will, sir," I said.

"What?"

"I'm your designated first mate on this ship, and I cannot even begin to tell my crew how to get under way." I shrugged my shoulders in the French manner. "The *Princess* is a ship of 350 tons, double-decked and three-masted. Some called her a frigate, because she's mounted with forty full-sized cannon and many smaller swivel guns. Then, of course, there are the small guns designed for killing men while not harming the ship under attack and all the men trained to use these diverse weapons." I paused to make sure that Pike was listening. "And that's to say nothing about leading a crew of over one hundred men to keep the *Princess* under way or to attack another ship."

"Now, now, just a little patience is called for, my boys. Just be quiet and attentive for a few days. We'll let those Basque and Portugee boys work things out for us, then we'll ease into control of the whole lot of them."

"That's just what I'm afraid of, Captain Pike. I'll bet that those boys we have buried down in the hold can handle this ship with no help at all from you and me."

"Stop your arguing with me. I'll say again: it is a simple matter for us to just let a few sailors out of each hold in the beginning. Enough to weigh anchor and get under way, that's all. Don't worry so much—just watch and learn."

Pike's pirate ship, still named the *Princess,* had a lovely large cabin in the stern. It had been decked out by the previous captain with rugs, chairs, tables, cabinets, and great lamps that hung on gimbals. In addition, there was a plethora of navigation instruments stored in oak cabinets, and a library. Erdu and I made frequent comments about how much Tisquantum would enjoy life aboard the *Princess*—not that he would have had any part of such a ridiculous venture, but he'd certainly box up the books and head back to his own library. "A pox on you all," he'd likely have yelled, while descending the gangplank of the *Princess* to solid ground. "Come home to where you belong," Tisquantum would certainly have added.

On the first day of our command, with a nice steady wind from the southwest and knee-high waves in the bay, we managed to hang the foresail while still at anchor. That single rag of a sail was enough for the captain to call "Weigh anchor" and for the ship to move out of St. John's Harbor with the speed of a very large and very drunk snail. The mainsail and mizzen sail were unfurled and pulled with no prompting from any pirate officer, but eventually completed with the precision and cooperation expected from a herd of feral cats.

The Bristol boys joined with whatever gang was working one sail or another, and there was more laughter at our combined ineptitude than any other emotion. Through all the confusion and expletives shouted in ten different languages, the captain of this fairy-tale crew found pleasure sitting on the quarterdeck with a book of poetry in hand. Erdu and I had a good laugh at the sight of the lounging Pike, especially when it became clear that he never turned a page.

Jack the Viking was in charge of pulling additional small batches of sailors up from the hold, and Erdu and I, after a fashion, put them to work. The surprising truth was quickly evident. The seamen we'd stolen from their life under a Spanish captain seemed happy to serve Captain Pike. It was obvious to them, if not to us Bristol and savage pirates, that with a ship like the *Princess* and a captain as skilled and affable as Pike seemed to be, that the inevitable shares paid to willing pirates would soon be much more profitable than any previous employment they might have envisioned.

I watched as small groups of sailors discussed this new venture. They asked us questions about shares of profit and where we would ply our trade and what were the rights of pirates on board a pirate ship. It seemed that they saw a golden opportunity to earn enough wealth to purchase such dreams as a piece of land or a tavern. Most of them were uneducated men and assumed that their jobs as English pirates would be easier jobs than those found serving under the command of a Spanish don. In their recent dreams, they were already lords of manors or owners of taverns. It didn't seem to matter—Bristol fisherman or Basque sailor or man from whatever port of origin—they appeared to support the intentions of Captain Pike.

But that damn well didn't diminish the concerns voiced in relentless repetition by me and Erdu to Captain Pike. I was certain that there were likely exceptions to the good-time dreamers on board, but each succeeding batch of sailors released from captivity seemed pleased with their new jobs on Pike's pirate ship.

Those first few days of laughter occurred even with most of the sailors sleeping between decks among the guns, in a space where one could not stand. Hammocks were strung wherever possible, and some even slept on the deck, curled around the foot of a cannon. It made no matter—all were barefoot, of course, and trousers and shirts made of sailcloth had been tarred to make them waterproof. Pike may have appeared to them as a foppish dandy, but most of his new men were willing to accept his foibles as normal pirate behavior. Erdu and I watched and listened and learned as we sailed through the initial disasters.

On the third day at sea, with no land in sight, a small summer squall surprised the third watch, and the main topsail crashed into the sea along with the six good men who were attempting to furl the sail before such a disaster could strike. It took three full days to make things right again, with repaired sail and replaced men, but the loss of all six men and the clear sign of poor leadership turned the crew into small packs of gossipy old women.

It didn't help our situation that the only food offered to officers and crew was prepared by three Greek fellows and a tall, skinny Hindu sailor. The four of them shared some unholy bond and claimed possession of the food pantry. They kept several metal pails at a simmer over the wood-burning cookstove, but the slop, though readily available, was found by us pirates to be unfit for consumption.

There were more than a few sailors from the original batch of Pike's foreign pirates that never bothered to attend to necessary tasks after sunset. Sails flapped, lines swung free, orders were yelled, but most of the pirates found more pressing activities that called for their attention once the sun set and a moon was likely to rise.

There were gambling games up and running in clear sight on the third night at sea. Those active contests above deck were familiar to all the Bristol boys and quickly recognized as opportunities for sudden wealth. Also, in corners scattered here and there below deck, were amusements less familiar to Jack or those from Bristol. All were conducted in words and by devices never imagined by the good Christian sailors. Except the whore quarters, that is, and these were prominent in the dark storage lockers that held boxes full of powder and balls for the twenty cannon also aboard the *Princess*. There were young lads and a few fat women available at two or three pennies per customer. The Greek and Hindu cooks, in recognition of their seldom used simmering pots of slop, peddled potluck food with fish or meat included for a penny a bowl, day or night.

The Bristol fair on a hot summer night was a pale shadow to a night aboard the *Princess*.

Erdu and I moved about the ship to listen and ask questions and determine who would lead the men in an errant direction, or to discover the few who might follow our orders without question. On the seventh morning afloat, Pike called all hands on deck and introduced his "Blue and Erdu" as first and second mate of the deck. Even with no evident support of our commission from our inherited crew, I carried on in the captain's place by bringing forward the third and fourth mates of the deck. These two, of no Bristol connection whatsoever, were received passively by all the sailors, as were the three mates I assigned on each watch for sails and guns and galley.

"We need one hundred fifty men to put this ship into battle," I said.

We three of great discrepancy—gentry, savage, and smyth—were lounging in the captain's regal quarters. Three glasses and a bottle of rum were confined in tight-fitting pits drilled into the large dining table. Pike refilled all glasses. "How many men can we count on for doing their assigned jobs?"

"Hard to say," said Erdu. "I count a hundred and ten bodies, and maybe a quarter that number are willing to report on orders and stand ready to serve."

"If we attack any ship of size, there's both square sails and the large fore-and-aft or lateen sails, plus the guns to manage." I drained half my glass of rum. "It appears to me that there is no solution to solving our problems aboard the *Princess*."

"She's such a sweet ship in any wind," Pike said. "Better at sailing close hauled against the wind than any square-rigged ship on the sea."

"Captain Pike." I kept my voice low and soft, nicely lubricated by smooth Spanish rum. "It was two days past that we had the mainsail disaster and a port-side cannon exploded during an early-evening gunnery practice."

"Killed five sailors and maimed another dozen," Erdu added.

I stared again, and spoke with a slow and soft voice. "Remember our only navigator, that damned fox-faced Portugee fellow? The one who died at your very own feet in a fit of violent spasms this morning?"

Pike stared at the captain's beautiful table.

"There's none to replace the sonnuvabitch," said Erdu.

Pike again filled the three green-colored glasses with rum. "What's on your mind, Blue?"

"We're in over our head, Captain. I'm afraid we'll wake up dead tomorrow morning and never have another chance to hold our wives and children."

Pike took three gulps of Spanish rum and broke the glass on the table. "Erdu?"

"I took some tolerable sightings at sunset and looked about the charts a bit."

"Yes?"

"We can make Nassau in two days of decent weather. I say go to Nassau and trade this damn ark for something red savages and blue Bristol men can manage."

"These Portugee and Basque fellows might not give us even a full day," I said. "They're into the beer and rum locker. The drunks are staggering around waving pistols and muskets. I'm scared enough to shit my pants."

Neither Pike nor Erdu had a word in their mouth, so I kept going. "Everything has changed. There's no more happy Basque and Portugee or Hindu pirates aboard; now most of the crew is talking about giving us Bristol men and their red savages a dinghy with no sail." I let that ugly thought settle for a bit of time. "But more likely, I'd guess, they'll just cut our throats and be done with the matter."

"Have you got the leaders against us spotted?" Pike retrieved another green glass from a cabinet and returned to fill it to the brim with his Spanish rum.

"Doesn't matter," I said. "Just pick one to tell what you want, and the rest will know soon enough."

Erdu spoke. "Make a trade, Captain, here and now. The *Princess* for this crew of crazy drunks and a whaleboat for us."

"Twenty men in a single whaleboat?" The captain was torn between laughing and crying.

"Twenty men and what they can carry aboard," Erdu said.

The Basque contingent carried the day, and on the tenth day from leaving St. John's Harbor, twenty New Founde Landers were set into a decent-sized whaleboat. The pirate vote to kill us died with only a handful of favorable votes. The final proposition, that nearly all the rebels approved, was to let us have a spinnaker sail but no oars for the most decrepit of the whaleboats. They said yes to my small anvil and battered bellows, but no to any guns or other tools at all. No food, no water.

We were set free somewhere south of the Florida peninsula—at least that's what the new captain told us.

"Watch out for sharks," some of the pirates yelled.

"Watch out for pirates," one jester added.

CHAPTER NINE

June 1614
Cistercians

TISQUANTUM SAT BACK IN HIS comfortable chair and smiled. "Life is good," he murmured to the spider—a large brown specimen who was just beginning a new web in the far corner of the room. The fact that the spider's response was either indistinct or absent altogether did not impede their conversation. "Pike, bless his contrary soul, is off to steal gold from the Spanish people, and with any luck at all, Blue and Erdu will keep the gullible man safe for the voyage."

The spider scurried to the far edge of her nascent web but remained silent. Tisquantum peered slowly about his large office as if he were a first-time visitor. There were many books at hand, written in a variety of languages and waiting for a moment of his leisure. Three tables were scattered about the large space and stood ready for a variety of social activities. Large rugs gave comfort to bare feet and subtle colors helped the philosopher spin answers to unasked questions.

"The Portuguese cousins will ride their horses over to Mosquito Cove this evening," he reminded the spider. "I'm sure that we'll have a game or two of chess." Tisquantum felt a bit tired; an afternoon nap seemed an attractive option to consider. The evening meals were always a great joy but tiresome nowadays without the variety of ideas that Blue and Pike always offered for debate. A nap and then a dinner of roasted osweet steak, potatoes, and greens. "Life is good," he murmured.

In the late afternoon a diligent servant took a broom to the web and spider and swept them away. So it was, that on a remarkably warm June evening of the year 1614, Diogode Sousa was able to swallow a mouthful of sweet red wine without sight of the offensive pest. Señor Agonia followed suit with his glass of red wine, smiled and nodded at his affable host, and finally asked, "Tell me, Tisquantum—who is assigned the job of managing the village farm? Now that Oubee is so busy raising both her children and those of the Irish woman?"

"Anares, it is. He will manage the entire farm and also protect the new flock of sheep and goats."

"Ahhh, yes, I've met Anares and talked with him a number of times." José Maria leaned forward toward me. "The man certainly understands the demands of our Merino sheep."

Diogode added, "He could as well have been born in the hills of Portugal for all the wisdom of our sheep that he holds in mind."

Tisquantum shrugged in the Portuguese fashion. "Anares says his job with your stupid sheep is to simply keep the wolves away and let them eat sufficient grass. What else is there?"

We were teasing one another, of course, and my guests nodded in affectionate pleasure at their little project with the new village.

"The women of the village are certainly atwitter with the quality of the wool," I noted. "I'm told that the Merino wool is both fine and strong, with a soft texture. The women predict that it will make a perfect inner layer for the osweet winter jackets."

"The hills of New Founde Land are indeed similar to those of ours in Northern Portugal," said José Maria.

"Our hills also produce lemon trees and warm sun for eight months rather than two," answered Diogode. "Fewer mosquitoes also."

We chuckled at the absurdity of lemons on our three winter-bound plantations and returned to reading our books. Without Pike and Blue around, the competitive energy of card games was gone. Chess was an occasional choice of one pair or another among us, but the truth was that we all enjoyed silence for a comfortable stretch of time. Not one of us seemed anxious to debate an issue or win some point of contention over religion or politics. It was a fact, though, that the interruption of silence was also met with pleasure, as each of us seemed interested to learn something new from a book in the hands of another.

I put a paper marker between the pages and closed the book I was reading. "Tell me, cousins, about your St. Benedict. The little that I have read about him sparks my imagination."

In common chorus from the cousins came the "Ahhhs," then Diogode answered, "There is not an easy description of our beloved St. Benedict, Tisquantum, but let me begin by saying that Benedict was a radical observer of his world. He saw one pope after the next join with this duke or that prince in common purpose. Benedict noted that the rich inevitably grew richer while the poor lived ever closer to the edge of life." Diogode shrugged, as if it were so simple there could be no argument. "It is a fact that the poor survive from the bounty derived from both the land and sea, and when the rich steal that bounty with their taxes and tithes as a matter of divine entitlement, the suffering of the poor increases."

"Master Smyth schooled me on just such a condition," I said. "It was his constant contention that when the god-people and the gentry joined together, the tithes and taxes offered only penury for all the working men."

"Just so," said José Maria. "The myth given in both book and story holds that at some point in his life, Benedict drew around him men who would avoid the secular life. These new monks of Benedict discarded the black robes of common use by monks who were satisfied to be choir monks or servants to one lord or another." José Maria paused to determine if I understood his remarks. I nodded once to move him along, and he continued. "Therefore, since the black robes were marked by those whom he considered ungodly—lackeys of the wealthy lords—Benedict took on the white robes as a mark of charity and self-sustenance."

"What was the alleged cause of his dramatic change? A miracle of some sort?" I asked. "A message from some angel?"

"Who knows or cares?" said Diogode. "What we know for certain is that the white-robed monks of Benedict built their own buildings of worship and either tilled their own fields or paid fair wages to the illiterate serfs who joined with them." Diogode leaned toward me, to better make his point. "These so-called lay brothers—the illiterate ones who labored for the white-robed monks—were also bound by vows of chastity and obedience to the abbot of their flock."

"Indeed? Well, good sirs, I'm very interested in what happened to the white robes over the years. Could they sustain their fine intentions through the generations?"

Now it was José Maria who took the lead. "We know that each of the ancient Cistercian abbeys was self-sufficient and that all the monks of those abbeys seemed dedicated to using only their manual labor in developing their projects. Further, I can tell you, from conversations I've had with my grandfather, that the poor have always seen the white-robed monks as holy monks and that the lords of God and gentry have generally dismissed them as irrelevant."

Diogode waved a finger back and forth in admonition of jumping too quickly to a conclusion. "Slow down, Cousin, for you must know that people are people and monks are monks. Some good, others wanting."

José Maria smiled at his cousin, and then spoke to me. "Diogode wants you to know that black- and white-robed monks survive to this day, and that any man with some shred of learning can choose a life of poverty, obedience, chastity, silence, prayer, and manual labor without looking too far for a Cistercian monastery."

"And a life of ease, debauchery, and loud noise with black robes?" I asked.

"You are a candidate for the white robe, good sir. While I may consider the black, or none at all," said Diogode.

"As you wish, both of you." José Maria snared a piece of spice cake. "In either event of white- or black-robed monks, I will deign to serve as your abbot, pope, and king as long as I am served this marvelous spice cake before the end of each evening."

I smiled, nodded, and said, "So it shall be, my liege: spice cake, red wine, and good books."

"Cheers!" they said.

I found early morning, just before dawn, the best time to masturbate. The colors of my half-awake dreams were brilliant in their lurid tones. Vivid shapes of youthful men and women swirled for my pleasure; a few would eventually separate themselves to give pleasure to my hands and mouth. Always, a deep-purple fog spread through the vision of my closed eyes. Then, as predicted from previous experiences, the flashes of light started piercing through both color and movement, and my erection emerged. I could feel my tight smile along with a need for less languid strokes. A bit more and—

"Pirates!" A piercing yell.

A startling booming noise thundered at my front door, then another: *Boom! Boom!*

"Tisquantum! Pirates are in the cove! Run! Run!"

My feet were barely on the floor when an even deeper, louder crash of cannon vibrated through the entire house. Somehow I rapidly clothed myself and found shoes, and opened the door to find José Maria there.

"I've sent messengers to the new village and to Oubee." José stood before me, nearly naked but with shoes on his feet. "They have landed in our coves as well."

"How many?"

"Two ships and probably a hundred or more pirates." He wrapped his arms around his body. "Many of the pirates have muskets."

My cook and his servant peered over my shoulder.

The first twist of black smoke trickled above the trees between my house and the new village.

"Arturo," I said to the cook, "Go to the manor. Tell the women to bring their children here to me. Run, run, run, and tell them there is no time for clothes or valuable jewels. They must run for the lives of their children."

"Bidisoni, go to our fishermen, quickly. Tell them to get their fishing boats ready and also with eight men ready to pull both whaleboats to the water." My throat and mind were clogged. "Bidisoni, tell all the fishermen to wait for the women and children of Pike and Blue."

"Where will they go, Master?"

"They must sail the whaleboats to St. John's City."

"What about the fishermen and their boats?"

"Have the whaleboats go to St. John's City if wind and waves permit; otherwise, they must go up the coast and find a place to hide until the pirates leave. Let the fishermen make their own decisions on how best to survive."

I was breathing in short bursts. My throat was dry. "The captains of the whaleboats must decide what to do with the women and children. If they can't sail to St. John's, then they must find a hidden shelter on the coast wherever possible."

"Yes sir," the young man said, and ran off toward the cottages of Captain Pike's fishermen.

José Maria was stomping his feet from the cold. "What of you, Tisquantum? What of me?"

"You and Diogode must flee to St. John's in your own whaleboats. Have your fishermen provide escort alongside the whaleboats if they are able. At the very least you must get a good distance up the coast and find a suitable place to hide. Walk to St. John's from wherever you land, if you must."

I walked toward black smoke and chattering muskets. The pirate captain saw me approaching but made no move of recognition. I thought of how Pike or Drake or the queen would behave in such a situation. A squad of pirates held muskets aimed directly at me. I heard screams of terror from our Beothic villagers and made myself stand taller, slowing my pace to a regal amble. The muskets went silent. During the last ten paces I forced a smile on my lips, and when, finally, I stood before the pirate captain, I simply said, "I'm at your service, sir."

He blinked twice and shouted, "Service as my slave, you fool!"

I knew this man from times past in St. John's Harbor. A buffoon. An English weakling. "As you will, Captain Laney."

"You are Pike's pet savage, I'll wager."

"I am called Tisquantum and serve Captain Pike as manager of his Mosquito Cove plantation, sir." With Laney at a loss for words, I continued. "I'm at your service, sir, so perhaps we could have a private conversation in this dwelling." I gestured my hand toward the only uncharred mamateek of the village.

"You are dead, you foolish savage." He simulated his idea of a pirate captain: red eyes, engorged throat, one hand to his sword and the other shaking a long-barreled pistol. "Which do you choose— pistol or sword?"

"I choose, my good sir, to make you a very rich man."

His pistol came to point at the ground. "What do you think that I'm about, fool? I see slaves by the hundred for the taking. There is salt cod by the ton, without doubt." He raised again the pistol. "My share is half—enough to buy land in England and continue my name for generations."

I lowered my voice to a whisper. "I will show you where Pike has buried his gold and where his Irish wife has hidden her jewels."

Captain Laney tucked the pistol behind his belt and handed the sword over to a servant. Captain and servant stared at me with blank eyes, but only Laney followed me into the home of my cousin Wasemook. We settled on the floor of the mamateek, knee to knee.

Laney initiated the negotiations. "Whatever you say to me about gold and jewels, I will still burn every structure in the cove and in this village."

"Yes sir, I understand."

"You and all the red savages I have in my hands are my slaves. You may be the pet to Pike or not, but you and all other savages will be sold in Spain or Portugal."

"I recommend Portugal. Lisbon, to be sure."

Laney stared at me with no words.

"The distance to Lisbon is closer than the Spanish options, and the price per slave in Lisbon is significantly higher than even Seville."

"How do you know this sort of information?"

"Captain Pike also has a letter of marque that dates from the days of the good queen." I let the silence spin until he started coughing and spitting phlegm onto the neat floor. "This spring he assigned me the task of establishing the best market for slaves, and Lisbon was the winner to a handsome degree."

After drawing his hand through his beard a dozen times, Laney emitted a long sigh, like a tall fir tree falling slowly to the ground. "When will you show me the gold and jewels?"

"Today, if that pleases you, sir."

"I'll be pleased or not when I see the truth of your words."

"Yes sir," I said.

Another long silence ensued, and Laney again tried to gain the initiative in our contest. "I know about the fishermen and the whaleboats on all three coves," he said. "We will end their game of escape, and then you will show me the treasure of Captain Pike."

"Let them go," I said.

"Why?"

"If you don't let them escape to St. John's, I will demand my execution at your hands."

"Why?"

"They are all close friends—savage and European alike. They trust me with their lives, and I will not fail them."

Laney pawed his beard and alternatively moved his hands as if washing them in hot water. He finally made a tired shrug of one shoulder. "What else would you have me do, fool?"

"Let me provide food for the trip to Lisbon. Food for both slave and crew. You will dock in Lisbon with a happy crew and slaves worth much more than if they were sacks of skin and bones."

Laney nodded his head up and down for a very long time. "I plan to spend a good deal of my fortune acquiring an estate in Surrey. It'll be bigger and fancier than this pile of rock here on Mosquito Cove, and a little bit warmer in the winter. How would you like to serve as manager of my new property?"

"As your slave, I could not decline the offer. As a free man I would seek other options, sir."

"Slave, then." Captain Laney brushed dirt and ash from the sleeves of his jacket. "What is next, Slave?"

"I will have my cook prepare food for your men while we wait. It may take a few days, but we will wait until I receive word that the families of Pike and Blue—plus all of the people from the Portuguese plantations—are safe in St. John's City."

"You will wait in this hut, damn your hide, and I will secure my slaves from this village and all the salt cod that I find in the three plantations into my ships," said Laney.

"Of course, and I will await the pleasure of your company when my conditions are met," I said.

"Damn your pride, Tisquantum. Just remember, a savage is always a savage and can never beat an Englishman."

"Yes sir," was my only sensible answer.

CHAPTER TEN

June 1614
Eleuthera Island

PIKE HAD THE TILLER, FOR all the good it served. There were no oars. The scrap of canvas was given with a gesture of great benevolence by the Basque captain. "To catch the water," he had explained. "If it rains, catch the water."

The sun remained bright for the first day, the winds capricious. One of the savages drank his own urine with dribbles into his hand, then to mouth, in awkward sequence. The others, savage and Bristol sailor alike, followed suit. There was no dusk; the sun was replaced abruptly by a thin waning moon. Three planets of various hues chased each other across a sky thick with stars.

The dramatic beauty of our evening spectacle did little to diminish my thirst. I dreamed in erratic sequence of Oubee and the boys cavorting through the woods, picking berries, and hiding from me. On the late afternoon of the second day, a lad seated amidships whispered to his companion, "There's an island," and he pointed for all to witness the fact.

"Look there," said Pike. "We've got deep, dark-blue water on the east of the island and pale blue on the west of that point of land." The captain smiled. "So what do you choose, my esteemed first mate?"

"The Atlantic Ocean appears on one side, sir, and what seems to be a comfortable little cove of shallow water on the other," I responded.

"Just so," said Pike. "Listen up, sailors. Those on the ocean side of our pirate ship, row with your hands until I call a halt." He stood with tiller still in hand, to get a better view of the situation, and then yelled, "Row, my lads!"

There was more splash than movement, but eventually, with the little moon as our only light, the captain ordered Erdu and me overboard to sound the depth of our cove, and we yelled with astonished pleasure to find our heads safely above water. "Take the bow line and give us a ride," said Pike.

The water was bathtub warm and the bottom soft rippling sand. In a short while we had six on the bow rope, and, sooner than I expected, we hauled the craft up onto a thin shred of beach. All bailed out of the boat to laugh and scramble in the lovely water.

The first explorer to test the limits beyond the beach quickly screeched, "Thorns!" and wobbled back down to the water, where he moaned and complained while a multitude of sharp splinters were removed from his feet by anxious friends.

"Curl up on the beach, lads," said Pike. "There's no fear of a sharp frost tonight, so we'll see what's what in the morning."

Erdu and I laughed at the humor of our pirate captain. The rest of his crew merely followed his orders, in prompt acceptance of their situation.

"No frost tonight," I repeated.

"No sharp frost, in any event," said Erdu.

"No water to drink either," I said.

"I may have a dribble of pee, if you're interested." We chuckled and silently stared at the stars and at the brilliant Venus as it jumped above the horizon to join the wonderful parade of celestial partners.

Erdu and I, along with the other Beothic savages, spooned together for a decent night of sleep. I heard an owl or two and the soft hiss with the rise and fall of sand all night, but nothing more. All of Pike's pirates came wide awake with the eruption of sunlight, accompanied by the screech of gulls and many birds of strange shape and color.

Pike motioned for me to tend to the crew. "We need water and food. Get your red savages to work on finding us both."

I waved to Erdu and Wasemook, and we sat on the sand to discuss our choices.

"I'll get a few warriors to make wooden spears and try for some fish in this shallow water," Wasemook said.

"Good," said Erdu. "I'll pick a few Bristol boys to hunt for nests with eggs or squab for the taking."

"I'll take Gobidin and hunt for a spring or small stream," I said. "Let's all report back here by noon."

They nodded and turned away from me without another word.

"Here's a path through the pricker-bushes." Gobidin leaned down for close inspection. "We're not the only pirates around here," he said.

I joined to look over his shoulder. "No shoe of any sort."

"Nope." He studied the surrounding bushes and trees and followed the path with his eyes. "Stay here and watch," Gobidin whispered. "I'll check the path and wave you forward if it seems clear."

We moved in that fashion, first with him as my guide and me as the follower. It was not sixty paces before we came to a lovely spring of water.

Gobidin fell facedown in the shallow water to splash and drink. "Ahh," he moaned. "Life is better than death."

I followed his example, and we slithered around the tiny pool like two otters until we sat side by side, with feet still underwater.

"What a beautiful place," Gobidin said. "Sweet, cool water that's shaded by tall trees and blue sky above all. Lovely!"

We drank our fill, slurping from our hands, and then noted the numerous brown shells, broken in fragments, scattered about the area. It was obvious that some bits of shell would serve as handy cups or even small buckets suitable for transporting water back to the beach.

"Look," I said. "Up in the trees around the spring. Do you see those large brown nuts hanging from the top branches?"

"Certainly, and I'll wager Captain Pike can tell us something good about these huge nuts." Gobidin dug his fingernails into the white meat of a fractured nut lying on the ground, tasted a small bit, and smiled. "Sweeter than maple tree sap, and there's also the same pleasant texture of our tiny beech tree nuts."

"You sound like José Maria with his constant running on about a French wine or rice from de Afife."

Gobidin ignored me to stand and look more carefully at the ground around the pool. "Lots of fresh footprints," he noted. "It looks to me like a small family, not a troop of men."

"Yes, three or four prints our size, and the rest from children." I gave one more cursory glance around and gave an order. "Let's get back to the beach. There are others who want to wash the taste of piss out of their mouth."

We brought two small brown-nut buckets of sweet water as a sample of our success and immediately started a relay of three or four pirates to the spring and back. Erdu had a few dozen eggs for us to sample, and Wasemook had about the same number of small fish arranged on top of green fronds from the brown-nut tree.

"Coconut trees, they're called," said Captain Pike. "When you crack one open, take care to save the interior juice from spilling. Both juice and the white meat are refreshing."

One of the Bristol men cracked an egg he'd found into his mouth and immediately spit the contents onto the sand. "Terrible! Like sulphur," he yelled.

"Crack each egg and smell it before eating," said Erdu. "Some will be old and dead; some will satisfy the stomach." He smiled at the offended sailor. "Be careful," he told him.

"This will never do," Captain Pike said. "There's not enough food here for even three of us, to say nothing of seventeen hungry pirates. We'll have to do better. Much, much better."

"We need better spears, or we need to make some nets to get the fish around here." Wasemook held an example of a pathetic little spear. "Nets and hooks and line—that's what we need."

"Me and my mate will look to some hook and line rigs," said a Bristol man.

"I'll work on a net," said our red-haired Viking. "I don't need no help from you Bristol boys, and that's a fact." His dark skin showed the Saxon blood, and his red hair, wild and bushy, testified to the Viking blood. None took issue with his claim as a maker of nets.

I turned to the rest of our crew. "You all know where to find the sweet water now, so let's get to work and find us some food."

All moved away in various directions and showed serious intent with their expressions and posture. Pike waved for me and Erdu to attend him.

"I want you two to take Gobidin and follow those footsteps you saw." He pawed his scraggly black whiskers. "If there's anything that looks like trouble, get back here quick as you can." It was clear from the set of his eyes that Pike wasn't sure that his words counted for much here on this little island, but he blustered on ahead with little pause. "We need friends, not enemies, so if you come upon some people, smile a lot and show your hands with no weapons."

Pike was beginning to wear on me with his simpleminded orders. Even so, I knew that Da would not approve of an impertinent son. "We'll treat any stranger soft and easy, just as any Bristol gentleman would in this situation."

Quick, with no thought, Pike said, "I'm in no mood for mockery from the likes of you, Omrod."

The response was deserved, and only Erdu saved me from an unnecessary tiff. "Let's go, Blue," he said, "The captain needs us on our way."

After twenty paces and into the first row of trees, Gobidin chuckled. "Omrod, the bad boy."

And five paces more: "Blue, the favored son," Erdu added.

We three brothers tittered a bit, but I still felt misused by our captain.

We walked northwest on the hard sand above the high-tide mark of weed and kelp. At each clear indication of a path from the interior to shore, we made short forays to discover additional sources of sweet water and the same family of footprints. As we rounded the northern tip of the island, we could see the deep blue ocean easily, clearly distinct from the light blue of our shallow bay. There was a small island on our left, and the tidal current between the two islands was fearsome to behold. We followed our shore for a few hundred paces, with the current gut always roaring, until we were required to take a sharp right to the northeast along a rocky shore with ocean waves crashing on the beach.

Gobidin stopped to survey the distance from where we started, then traced the shoreline with a stick on the sand. "Our island seems to be shaped like a Bristol hammer—at this end, at any rate."

"The little island is the nail to be hammered," I said.

We traveled further on, with blue water on our left and large waves crashing at our feet until Gobidin held up his hand.

"Wait, look to the far rocks."

There we saw a man, with his back to us, and he was casting a net into the sea beneath his rocky perch. After a short wait, the fisherman pulled at the rope attached to his waist until the net emerged, with the net closed, and then hoisted it up onto the rocks. Still with his back to us, the fisherman transferred fish from his net to a large basket at his side. When the net was empty of the dozen or so fish, he spread the net into a flat circle, secured the edges in his hands, and again cast the tethered net into the sea.

"Have you ever seen such a net?"

My savage brothers shook their heads no, and we watched again with the retrieval and filling of the storage basket.

"What is he doing now?" Erdu whispered.

"Leaving," I said.

"But his net and catch—they've been left behind."

"Maybe he has gone for assistance," I said.

We waited an interminable time. "It will be dark soon," I said.

"The sun disappears around here quick as a wink, light to dark," said Gobidin.

"He left the net and fish for us," said Erdu.

"Us? How so?" I wanted to believe such charity was before us but knew from experience how rare such behavior was seen between strangers.

"I'll go and retrieve the net and basket," said Erdu. "You two wait and yell if you see that danger is near."

"Go," I said. "You must retreat at the least provocation."

"I'll retreat with a smile," said Erdu.

"Yes, a smile and a show of empty hands," said Gobidin.

"Silence, you foolish savages," I said.

When we returned with the net and basket full of small fish, Captain Pike smiled for the first time since the mainsail of the *Princess* crashed into the sea. A small crowd gathered and watched as Gobidin demonstrated over and over how the rock weights were held in the net and how the rope was used to pull the net closed to capture small fish in this ingenious device.

"Has any one of you seen such a fishing net before?"

A few shook their heads; most held their silence.

"We must return a gift tomorrow," I said. "The people of this island must become our friends."

Pike glared at me for a brief moment, then said, "All right now." He yelled in an overly loud voice, "Let's see what we've got that might please the savages of this little island."

An inventory showed two very small knives, my small anvil and bellows, and Captain Pike's spare shoes with leather laces.

Two of the Bristol sailors turned a hardwood stick into a bow with one of the shoelaces, then twirled another hardwood stick on a flat piece of dry driftwood. They placed dry moss and slivers of wood around a small depression in driftwood, and one man sawed his bow in great fury until a small hint of smoke appeared. The other sailor sat on his hands and knees to blow gentle puffs of air until a flame burst forth, to the cheers of his pirate mates.

"Hooray!" a few pirates yelled.

"Cooked fish," the Viking added.

"Cooked squab," Erdu said.

The flame chewed at small pieces of driftwood and then larger and larger pieces of wood until all of us were holding long sticks capped with a single fish or tiny squab over the bonfire. "Best I've ever tasted" was repeated through the second and third fish of the celebration.

The next morning, we dismantled the port gunnel of our whaleboat to dislodge a dozen nails and several long pieces of oak wood. We found rough-grained rocks on the upper part of the beach to serve as grindstones in shaping the angles of whaleboat-oak into long spears. It was a simple matter to set up my anvil near the large fire and turn the whaleboat nails into adequate spear points—some barbed and others straight and sharp.

"We'll give one spear point to our hosts," I said, "and the remaining six to us."

Captain Pike, hands clasped behind his back, gave me a brief nod. "Off you go, Blue, to find our friendly neighbors."

"I'll take Erdu and Gobidin along. They have nice sincere smiles to show the savages."

"Cleaner hands, also," Erdu added.

"Be careful," Pike said.

Two men and a woman met us near the fishing rock of yesterday. Erdu made the presentation of the spear, and all three examined it in great detail and with genuine smiles.

"They look somewhat like the people of Northern Labrador," said Gobidin.

"Similar eyes," said Erdu.

"The same skin as us," said Gobidin.

I'd never seen the savages of Labrador, but the three strangers were certainly handsome to my eye. The white-haired man was not stooped with age but robust in every manner that I could observe. It was the young warrior who exchanged direct stares with me, and though he appeared not more than fifteen years of age, he was my match in the contest. We smiled and dropped our eyes at the same moment.

The morning was spent exchanging names and trying to describe from where we came. Our efforts to describe ice and snow, long days and short, were indecipherable to these people. We did confirm that they called themselves "Taíno" and that we were named "Beothic" or "Bristol." I made every effort to determine what needs the family had that we could possibly fill. There were clear questions in their eyes, but the six of us managed no successful communication that went beyond the names of things.

"We need Tisquantum and his genius at languages," I said.

"But we're stuck with Blue," said Erdu, and he then burst into such a contagious burst of laughter that quickly the Taíno family joined with me and Gobidin in our expressions of joy.

Gobidin looked directly into the eyes of each Taíno. They seemed willing to gamble on our honesty and favor then, before the laughter. The only adult man, an active, vivacious person, was certainly no older than fifty. The boy warrior was probably the son of the fisherman of yesterday, and he was also a handsome character. The fisherman of the net had a larger nose than the rest, pointed not squashed, and slightly slanted eyes always near a smile. All three received Gobidin's smiles and his delicate touching of their hair and shoulders with their own gentle grace.

In his Beothic language, and with facial expression and movement of hands, Gobidin expressed his wish to our hosts. "I want to be your friend," he said.

There was no hesitation as the Taíno elder took Gobidin by his arm and gently pulled him away from where we were standing. The Taíno people, with Gobidin in hand, moved away from us, all the while indicating that the remaining invaders were not welcome to join in their escape. They quickly disappeared within the scrubby forest of bushes and stunted trees.

"What just happened?" I asked.

"Gobidin was kidnapped," answered Erdu.

"It appears that Captain Pike has lost another one of his pirates," I said.

"He was a good gunner's mate," Erdu said.

"A true friend," I said.

We embraced and laughed at the wit of Gobidin, then moved quickly along the path, back to our beach and Captain Pike.

"Kidnapped, you say?"

"We were outnumbered," I said. "There was nothing we could do."

"Nothing," said Erdu.

Pike studied his two most important naval officers; both seemed on the edge of falling to the sand in a fit of tomfoolery. "Well then," he said. "I'm pleased that at least one of my savages had the wisdom to make a peaceful overture to the local natives."

"A brave and wise savage, indeed," I said.

"Away with you, Blue. You seemed to have inherited the same perverted sense of humor as your da."

"I'm always at your service, sir, in the same way as was my da."

We walked off in different directions, but I was most interested in a pile of strange-looking lobsters that one of the sailors had on display. "Where are the claws?" I asked.

"What you see is what I speared." The man seemed as mystified as I was at the desecration of my favorite crustacean.

"You found them here in the bay?"

"No sir. There's this small cove on the ocean side with a big reef to slow the waves." It was Jack again—the quick and nimble Viking. "The ugly beasts were not so deep that I couldn't dive down to spear them, but the cold water and brisk current was something to consider."

"What's your plan to cook these sad-looking creatures?'

"I've been studying the cook fire and waiting for an edge of hot but not red coals to show." He gave up his talking and began placing his dozen dead creatures on the desired coals, and then topped the lot with handfuls of wet seaweed. "There, that'll do the job."

We had nothing better to do, so we sat on our haunches to study the trail of smoke and inhale the increasingly beautiful smell until the Viking took a stick and pulled a lovely red and slightly burned lobster to our side. "Go ahead, Mate," he said. "Tear off the tail and tell me what you think."

It took a while, with burned fingers in jeopardy, but I snapped off the rear fins, split the entire tail from the body, and then pushed the tail meat free of the shell. The first bite was New Founde Land sweet, and I managed to keep my face with a look of disapproval. After the second and third morsel, I announced to the red-haired cook, "Terrible, but what can you expect with those tiny claws and such? Nothing at all like the real thing."

For the second time in the morning I was ignored. The Viking stood and waved an arm at some friends. "Over here," he yelled. "Hot lobster ready to eat!"

It was three days before Gobidin appeared, accompanied by the young man of early teenage years. My Beothic cousin nodded and said, "This is Caonabo, who is son of Yuisa and the fisherman that we met."

Captain Pike and I dutifully bowed in the young man's direction.

"Very happy to meet," said the young man in a very close approximation of Bristol English.

We smiled and bowed once again.

"Caonabo is here to teach us how to survive on his island," said Gobidin. "We have much to learn, and the Taíno request reciprocity for his instructions."

"What do they want, these Taíno people?" the captain asked.

Instead of answering his captain, Gobidin indulged in a conversation with the young man. There was much moving of hands and heads nodding in agreement, and finally Caonabo waved for us to follow him. When we reached a thick grove of coconut trees, we stopped as our guide pointed up to a mass of nuts.

"Don't sit," the Taíno youngster said. "Hit head, dead." He took a few steps, lifted a brown nut from the ground, and threw it at Captain Pike.

The captain barely dodged the missile and held up both hands. "Yes! Yes. Not under tree! Dead!" he yelled.

The boy smiled and we all did the same, although the captain's effort was a bit strained.

Caonabo picked up another nut that was green colored and shook it back and forth. "No good," he said and pointed to a few nuts hanging from a tree that were a combination of green and yellow. The boy shook his hands as if he were holding that out-of-reach green-and-yellow nut. "Good water," he said. "Good water for drink; no white meat for eat."

"Ahhh," we said.

Caonabo pointed toward a mass of dark-brown nuts hanging in the same tree. "No water," he said. "Good meat." He smiled.

We smiled and watched as Caonabo climbed up a large coconut tree until he was an arm's length from the nearest nuts. He reached toward the nuts and made a back-and-forth motion with his right hand. "Saw," he yelled. "Saw."

Pike and I looked to Gobidin for translation.

"Caonabo has told us how dangerous the nuts can be, for they fall at random opportunities, and standing, sitting, walking, or even climbing is a threat to life and limb." Gobidin paused for us to think about what we were being told. "The problem for this small family is how to harvest the particular hanging fruit that can best meet their needs. The nuts already on the ground are subject to rotting and insect infestations that make them very unreliable for consumption. What the Taíno lack, and what they hope to receive in return for the information they have given us, is the gift of a saw to safely harvest the nuts that are needed at any specific time."

"A saw?" said Captain Pike.

"Yes sir. A saw connected to a pole that is as about as long as this lad before us."

"What say, Master Smyth—can you manage such a task?"

"No sir, I can't."

"Why?" asked Gobidin

"I'd need a large piece of metal to work from—as long as the boy, in fact."

Gobidin and Caonabo exchanged words and expressions before Gobidin smiled and said, "Is late tomorrow or early the following day acceptable, Master Smyth?"

"I'll start on a saw as soon as I have my metal hot enough to work."

"Good," said Caonabo.

Pike and I, plus Jack the Viking from Surrey, studied the strip of metal offered by the boy.

"This work was done in a large foundry," I said, "not by any backyard smyth." I tried to bend a corner of the metal with my fingers without a hint of success.

"Spanish?" Pike asked.

"Dutch, maybe, or even English," I said.

"I'd wager the piece was some bow sheathing on a Spanish ship," said Jack. "Probably a top strip from the port side."

"How so?" Pike asked.

"Look for yourself, Captain. See them nail holes along the top and sides?"

Pike peered down at the metal. "I do," he said.

"They'd match the bow on one of those old Spanish caravels, I'd wager."

"It doesn't make much difference where the metal came from," I said. "It'll be a chore to cut and fashion a saw blade with my little anvil and pathetic bellows."

The captain was again annoyed with me. "Your da wouldn't whine about any chore that came his way; he'd just up and get it done."

"Well now, Da was a master smyth with all the proper tools; I have neither his experience nor his tools."

Pike waved a hand at me, as if talking any more would reduce his dignity, then he turned and walked away.

I went to the whaleboat to retrieve my anvil and noticed that Jack kept in my shadow for every step.

"Have you worked a forge before?" I finally asked.

"Here and there," he said.

"Do you have a mind to work with me on contriving a saw for these strange people?"

"I do, First Mate, if you have no objections."

I had offered Red a mate's position twice during our first few days with the big pirate ship. Whatever job he was assigned, I knew that he would do better than most, yet he'd refused my offer as gunner's mate and acted as if any duty that took telling others what to do was an abomination. "First things first," I said. "Let's find as much hardwood as possible and burn it all down to good charcoal. Are you with me?"

"Yes sir. That I am."

It developed that the hardest and heaviest wood readily available to us was also slippery to handle and quick to flame. It held a flame much longer than any other wood we burned, and in the end it gave us such a magnificent pile of charcoal that even my pathetic bellows could blow iron into a white glow.

The Viking and I made a good team with few words but excellent progress on each task. We finished the first metal saw well after the tiny sliver of a moon appeared.

Later that night, clean from scrubbing black dust and sweat from my body, I sat with Gobidin and Erdu on the beach, well away from the rest of our crew.

"How goes the saw?" Erdu asked.

"I'm ready to start on the wooden handle tomorrow. I'd say two to three more days to have it finished."

"Good. Let me know if you need any help," said Erdu.

We sat quiet for a while. The white-faced owl made an over-pass, and the surf was a gentle *hiss-hiss*.

"Gobidin, what can you tell us about the Taíno people?" I moved a little closer to my savage cousins. "It appears that there are only a few people on a very rich island. It doesn't make much sense to me. What do you know?"

"It is a sad story, Blue, for not so long ago there were many Taíno families scattered about this island and on the neighboring islands also."

"What happened?"

"The Spanish came ashore and captured all who couldn't find a place to hide." Gobidin studied the ground and gave a sigh. "Later a few Taíno escaped and were able to return to their islands. They told about a life of whips and pounding rocks located in deep holes."

"Slaves in the Spanish gold mines," I said.

"So it seems. According to the old man and his daughter, most of the Taíno on this island were captured in the time when the old man was an infant."

"Forty years or so," I said.

"The local Taíno live in a large cave down the beach from us and up little hill. It has a sharp-rising cliff on either side and is accessible only at low tide."

"Is there no threat of flooding in the cave at a very high tide?"

"Not that I can see with the hill up a bit." My cousin looked at me with pain in his eyes. "I was told that in the past as many as a dozen families were comfortable in the same cave."

"How many are there now?" Erdu asked.

"There is only one more person that you have not already seen. A young woman," he said.

I could feel a quiver of anxiety in his voice. "This young woman," I said. "Would you say she is as beautiful as Oubee?"

The night birds maintained a constant chatter over the sound of soft waves. The sliver moon had one more night before disappearing altogether. Stars seemed draped on the tall trees of our island. "Yes," said Gobidin.

"As smart?"

"Yes."

"Are you in love with her?

"I think so," said Gobidin.

The required saw was completed with Jack's steady help, and Caonabo demonstrated the value of such a tool. He climbed a coconut tree, then positioned himself so that he held on to the tree with his left hand and reached out with the right to saw a single nut from a clump. It dropped with a hardy thump. "Do you see? I cut and not drop on my head," he told us.

I had made two more saws, one for us and one I gave to the Taíno boy. Gobidin was clearly anxious to leave, as was Caonabo with both saws in hand. They walked south, talking with vigorous enthusiasm, toward their cave.

"He seems very committed to learning the new language," Erdu said.

"Oh, yes, certainly. Gobidin is simply following the captain's orders," I answered.

We smiled and nodded, sensible to the ways of the world.

"He's not the only pirate looking around for the comforts of a woman," said Erdu. "I've noticed that lately Jack is absent from our company a good deal of the time."

"Is there another savage woman of the Taíno cave?"

"The wife of the fisherman is named Yuisa, and they are the parents of Caonabo, our boy with the saw."

Erdu sat to look me in the eyes. "Jack is not set upon Yuisa, is he?"

"Certainly not. Even Vikings try to avoid suicidal love triangles. There is another woman, apparently slightly older than Yuisa, named Kakata, who has attracted the attention of Jack."

"Kakata? A strange name; do you know if it has any meaning in the Taíno language?"

"Jack tells me she is named for a poisonous spider."

"Better Jack than me," said Erdu.

I threw a handful of sand at my friend. "Poor Erdu—first he lost Oubee to me, and now he has lost this unseen sprite of the cave to Gobidin, and the handsome spider woman to the Viking."

"The woman was far too old for me," he retorted. "She's likely the mother of Gobidin's girlfriend. Macu is her name."

"Macu? What is the meaning there?

"A woman of big eyes, according to Jack."

Erdu threw his hands into the air in a fit of gloom. "Spiders and big eyes—what is next with these strange people?" He sat in silence for a moment, then with a small smile showing, said, "Please, oh please, gentle spirits of my own island, let me trust that I will someday return to the sensible land of the Beothic people."

"Now, now," I said. "It doesn't matter where you plant your feet, my friend, you move with alert audacity when in the company of Beothic warriors or red-haired Vikings. Crying in your beer or calling to assorted spirits does not become a mate of the great pirate ship *Mosquito*."

Erdu shook his head while looking at his hands. "My imaginary tears are flowing into an imaginary tankard of Bristol beer and must therefore be allowed by all blue savages in my attendance."

I threw a clump of wet sand in his direction but made no verbal rebuttal to my friend Erdu.

I assigned the remaining members of the pirate crew to various duties, which were intended to keep them busy, more than anything else. Food and water were now easy to find, and we found time to doze on the beach and watch each lovely sunset with genuine awe. After a few weeks in the land of the savage Taíno, the pirates were feeling fit and spending far too much time talking about the merits of a life with women and wine and laughter. They pretended to feel phantom pockets for phantom gold coins to order from a phantom barkeep whatever they wanted. Beer or whiskey, plum duff or Bristol beef— there was no denying thirst or hunger. Again, there was no fiddle, but some managed to whistle and clap while others danced a rough pattern in the sand. "Ahh, for the proper life of a pirate" was a popular sentiment, expressed in droll fashion by savage and fisherman alike.

"The whaleboat is useless," moaned Captain Pike. "Torn apart for the likes of spears and saws and a hot kiln."

"Well now, Captain Pike," I said, "at least we have enough food to eat and sweet water to drink."

"Maybe there are Spanish people on one of the islands close by." Pike was captivated by his thought and continued the new fantasy. "We need to steal a canoe from the Taíno and scout the islands hereabout."

"Maybe we can borrow or buy or learn how to make a canoe of their style," I said.

Pike made himself bigger, just like one of the fish species in the warm-water side of our island. "Then go! Get moving! Act like my first mate, not like some lazy savage with no ideas in his head!"

Two new moons had passed since we pirates had stormed ashore on this beautiful island. We were a sad and hairy lot to see—except for Gobidin and the Viking, that is. In the rare appearances required for meetings called by Captain Pike, their hair was neatly cut on both head and face. Their smiles were more genuine, and they were noted by one and all.

On an early morning, well into the third month of our invasion, Caonabo stood before me, with hands behind his back. "I have another trade for you," he said.

I looked around for Gobidin, but only his student was in sight. "What do you want?"

"An axe," he said.

"For dropping large trees?"

"Yes." The boy stood quietly for a moment, coughed, and said, "Also a large knife with a large handle that can be used to drop small trees and open coconuts with ease."

"Your English lessons are progressing very nicely," I said.

"Gobidin is a demanding teacher," Caonabo said.

"What do you have to trade?" I asked.

The boy stepped forward and brought his hands into my sight. He held a book for my taking.

"Where did you find this?" He could have as easily produced a magical box for making music or possibly some fiendish genie as my slave. I forced myself to slow the movement of blood through my head. I studied the front cover and knew from the writing that it was in the Spanish language. I checked the first few pages and found charts with symbols but few words on any page. There were wonderfully clear charts showing sea lanes from the east coast of Florida, then south through a scattered group of islands. The compass directions were clearly marked, as were points of danger noting a hidden reef or rock. The depth of water near possible landing sites was as clear as any track in the snow. "Caonabo, can you show me where you secured this book?"

"Are you willing to make the trade?" There was a smile on his lips that brought to mind a young sister Ruby and a young Oubee before she agreed to be my wife.

"Yes," I said.

Now the smile was large. "For the trade of this book, I require two axes and a second large knife with a large handle." His eyes joined with the large smile. "For the trade of a trip to show you where I found the book, we must have another talk."

I gave the young Taíno pirate no hint of pleasure with the inevitable question. He had likely been schooled by Gobidin and Jack the Viking. "What else?" I said.

"Ten metal fishhooks and line. Five blankets of my choice from those stored in the remains of the whaleboat." His pause was very brief. "Also the anchor and rope from the whaleboat and the two knives that fold onto themselves."

"Done!" I said. "When do we leave?"

"When all of my demands are met," said the young Taíno savage.

We all went together—Beothic, Bristol fishermen, Taíno savages, and Jack the Viking.

Sea grape vines covered small trees and bushes with large, nearly round leaves, and long skeins of grapes were easily accessible. Whenever red-ripe grapes were seen, the pirates and residents stopped to pick and eat.

"Hurry," Captain Pike admonished.

I matched my captain's pace, and most of the Bristol sailors trotted along, nipping a few grapes along the trail as they went. But my Beothic cousins, the Taíno people, and their red-headed friend stopped at every opportunity for the treat of grapes. "Better than Bristol!" was their war cry.

"Damned right," yelled Jack. "Take the good when you can."

After struggling through difficult beaches for half a day, the Taíno led us over hilly terrain to the ocean-side beaches. The mile or so in distance revealed a striking difference. We were now walking down wide sandy beaches—some a delicate peach color—always exposed to a pleasant offshore wind and large surf.

"Nothing along here where a ship could survive a landing," the captain said.

"There's grapes aplenty," Jack said to his captain. "Eat your fill with the rest of us, if you will."

"Humph!" said Pike.

A loud cry came from the Taíno family, and Caonabo, with Erdu close behind, began sprinting down the hard sand section of the beach.

"What?" shouted Pike.

"Turtles!" Jack responded, then joined in the race led by Caonabo.

They captured one, and six men carried the huge beast up to the grass and stunted trees, where they dropped it upside down.

With little hesitation, Jack, who carried an ax stuck into a sash tied around his waist, quickly sliced the long snakelike head from the carapace of the animal. Blood and guts erupted. Men cheered, and Kakata put savage and sailor alike to gathering wood for a fire.

I waited a bit before walking over to stand next to Erdu. "Who's this woman with Jack?"

"Sister to Yuisa, I'd guess."

"A very handsome woman, to be sure," I said.

"A very beautiful woman, I'd say." Erdu looked me in the eye. "Kakata puts me in mind of those little whales that herd the spring-run of mackerel back home. Fast, strong and beautiful, all in one."

Pike stood mounted on a small mound of sand, hands on hips, and yelled, "Who's in charge of this damn expedition?"

"I'd guess it's Kakata," I answered. "If you want a taste of turtle meat, Captain, I suspect you'd better add your share of wood to her fire."

"Mutiny! That's what I've got on my hands. A blasted mutiny."

"Get the wood, Captain, and don't forget to smile at the savages hereabouts."

The Taíno elders supervised Jack and Erdu as they pulled the offal, and cut bits of liver and heart for those interested in either cooking the tidbit or eating it raw. With the guts finally removed, Jack was directed to place the shell with its tail on the ground and its top against a tree. Then, with two men holding the shell steady against the tree, Jack filled the space recently occupied by head, stomach, and heart with hot coals from the fire. The hiss of burning meat was astonishing, but the smell was delicious. Saliva erupted into my mouth.

Within a short time, although it seemed much longer, the scene became as a swirl of swallows flitting about. A few pirates continued to feed the fire, while other folks begged a piece of turtle meat from Jack or Kakata. Conversation was focused on the turtle and which part of the animal was the most delectable. The liver was especially described in favorable terms, while the heart had a few committed champions. The remaining intestines and kidneys received less favorable responses. After an interval judged suitable by Jack, and with willing help from a few Bristol men, they sawed the carapace from the bottom part of the turtle. Both cooks were then kept busy carving and handing out large pieces of turtle meat and turtle fat to one and all. Many held out hands for second helpings, with a few for third or fourth samples.

The proclamations of appreciation for all parts of the turtle were unanimous. "The meat is similar to that of a tender osweet," was the Beothic consensus. "The fat as sweet as that of any goose," was repeated many times by the Bristol sailors. The Taíno old man and Yuisa smiled at all, as if they were the hosts to an important collection of honored guests.

Just before the sun dropped below the horizon, Jack and Kakata, hand in hand, guided the entire lot of pirates and natives off the beach and to the shelter of a small hill. The two gathered wood and started another fire with iron and flint sparks, while the rest of us watched as if we were the guests at an entertainment.

"I don't want any one of you shitting around here," Jack admonished. "Count to fifty paces toward the ocean before you squat," he added.

Twenty or so "Yes sirs" and "Aye, aye, sirs" came bubbling from the growing darkness, along with accompanying laughter.

Erdu said to me, and loud enough for most to hear, "I thought that the red-haired Viking was too shy to boss any of us around."

"It was Kakata who gave the order, you fool," I said.

"Well, good on her," said Bidisoni. Again, there was pleasant laughter in praise of the disparate couple. Her head was barely to his shoulder, and both beamed steady smiles at their servants.

Good on the both of them, I thought. They might be leading us to a village fair for all the good-humored chatter and smiles, except for Pike.

"What's to eat?" a Bristol man shouted.

"I know that most of you have pockets stuffed with turtle meat, so all you'll need is some sweet water," Jack shouted. "If you fools can follow Caonabo, he'll lead you to a nice spring, just over the hill a bit."

"Damn," mumbled the Bristol men.

"One more caution for all you Bristol boys." Jack was big as a New Founde Land bear in the flickering light. "I want everybody up with the dawn, and no damn complaints about what to eat or where to drink."

Captain Pike spoke into the darkness. "Who in hell is in charge around here?"

"Kakata," I answered, to modest cheers.

"Damned right," Jack said, to loud cheers and whistles from all but one.

By midmorning the offshore reef grew in size, and quickly the surf at our beach was diminished in tepid ripples on a hard sand beach. The chattering and forays for grapes stopped. The beach at this point lay almost directly in a north-south direction, and through the mist to the south, and beneath a steep hill, there was a cove evident. It was mostly hidden from sight until we finally turned the corner, and there for us to behold was an exquisite little harbor, filled with diving birds and scattered knobs of jagged reef. On the far southwest corner of the harbor, at the high-tide mark, was a foundered ship.

"Like I said—a Spanish caravel." Jack lowered a hand from shading his eyes. "Firewood, from what I see from here."

Pike didn't say a word but kept plodding toward the ship.

I found Gobidin and Caonabo walking together. "Tell me," I said to the boy, "how long has the ship been here on the beach?"

He looked to the sky and ticked off on his fingers: "More than five moon, less than six," he said. "There was a huge storm during that time, and we always search this stretch of beach for useful items that are left behind after such an event."

"Is this the first ship driven ashore on the entire island?"

"The old man might have some memory of others, but I can only remember a barrel once and a few odd pieces of wood."

"What was in the barrel?"

"Fish covered with salt. We threw the lot out for the gulls."

"What have you taken from this wreck?"

"The book, the metal you needed, of course, and some knives that we found."

"What of the sailors—what did you find?"

"Three on the beach and two on the ship. All dead from broken bones and crushed heads."

"Were there other people on the island who may have killed the sailors?"

"No, I am certain that only this family has been on the island from the time of my birth. We can ask Yuisa, but that is my memory."

I was anxious to explore the wreck myself and moved quickly to catch Captain Pike. We walked together for the last stretch, and Pike maintained a running commentary of what he saw. "Look there, Blue, the hull seems intact. Not a hole, not even a buckled plank."

"So it seems," I answered.

Pike and I circled the craft twice at a very slow pace while the rest found shade and waited for an order. The fore and aft masts were splintered stubs. The port-side rail, on the sand, was torn, and the hull planks visible above the sand were warped and broken.

"We've got a mess here," said Jack.

"The sand is no problem to move," I said. "We'll know soon enough how far the serious damage goes."

"Let's go aboard," Pike said. "You and Jack, follow me."

It took a while to get my bearings. Everything was scattered about, and with crawling around on hands and knees, it was hard to tell up from down. Two intact skeletons got my attention right off—both bare of all clothes and meat.

"Rats and birds, both," said Jack.

"You two start checking in the bow," Pike said. "Hammer about and see if she's broken to pieces or has enough solid timber to salvage. I'll go astern."

Jack beat a fist on both sides of the bow. "Spanish oak," he said. "An old tub, for certain, but she seems solid enough here at the bow."

"I find it hard to believe." We sat against the hull, looking about. "This ship had to get over or through that big reef just offshore, and the bow, at least from what we can see so far, has little or no damage." I crawled about and cleared away a pile of rope twisted around a set of wooden pulleys and thumped the forward planking. "Can't see or hear a big problem here, either."

We thumped and gawked and burrowed through broken barrels and shattered boxes, but other than some large cracks on the upper port side, we found no serious problems with the bow section of the Spanish caravel. "Hard to believe," I said.

"Blue!" I heard the captain's muffled yell. "Blue, come on over here."

I turned and crawled toward the stern. "Blue! Just you, for now. Leave Jack to give another look in the bow."

Jack smiled and waved me astern. "Captain's found something good, that's for certain," he said.

I shrugged and moved toward Pike's call. It seemed to emanate from a cabin with a door missing and a small bunk nailed to one wall.

The captain was sitting amid the litter, with a chest about two feet by four between his legs.

"Just look at here, Blue."

He dug his hand into the open chest and lifted a pile of coins that he let filter through his fingers back into the chest. "Silver," he whispered. "Two chests for me and two for the crew."

I sat at his side, and we took turns drizzling silver coins through our fingers until the Viking appeared and said, "Well, now, what do you boys have here?"

What followed was beyond any experience I ever had or even dreamed about. Once, during my second year as a Bristol fisherman, Da returned our boat to the Mosquito Cove landing well before noon. We were filled to the brim with huge cod. Happy as larks we were, to sit at our leisure and watch the others arrive near dusk. This silver, of course, brought lingering smiles and huge hugs from one and all, but the larger difference between happy larks and happy pirates came about from the lesson of Kakata: "I'm told by a certain pirate with red hair that you must vote on how the coins are divided," she said.

Every man, woman, and boy was crowded around the chests of silver. "Listen to me," she said.

"Pay attention, you fools," yelled her loyal Viking.

"You sailors most certainly have many days of hard work ahead before you can leave Taíno land for your own wives and children."

Jack repeated what she said in Bristol English, with only slight modifications.

Kakata held a small branch, still holding leaves, at arm's length. "Heavy! Strong! Slippery!" The last with an amorously lewd smile, and she received the expected cackles from all sailors and savages with good humor.

"This wood is for the ship, and the bark from this tree is for those who work hard to repair this ship." Kakata waited until all paid attention. "I will make a tea from the bark, and you will drink my tea and feel strong. When you drink the Taíno tea, all pain from your tired shoulders will disappear." She lowered her voice to barely speak over the sounds of surf and birds. "Drink the tea of the bark and you will smile at one another. Drink the tea and you will piss all the poisons of your blood onto the sand."

The sailors stood to smile and cheer this vibrant woman. A shout or two of a ribald nature brought the Viking to stand for Kakata.

"This is my last word, friends and mates." His smile was strained but steady. "I will work with you to put this old ship into the water, but I will stay here with my wife and her family when you leave." He stared at Gobidin and received an enthusiastic nod of agreement. "That'll be two of us pirates staying on this here island after you leave. Me and Gobidin."

"What about their shares?" one Bristol fisherman shouted.

"All will be paid in full the day we leave this island," Captain Pike answered.

Jack returned Captain Pike's smile and again spoke to the crowd. "For the entire time we work here on the ship, me and Gobidin will have our families over the hill and far away, and I want all of you to keep your distance. I know full well the intentions of a healthy man, and the two of us want to keep your temptations out of sight. Now then, all you boys can use your left hand or right," Jack matched the lewd grin of Kakata, "or your neighbor's butt, as you wish. But never give a thought for our wives and children."

Captain Pike emerged from the crowd and gave Jack a gentle push to move him away. "Just to make what Jack said as clear as the water around here: any fool that makes a salacious move toward their families has me as well to contend with."

I sounded my agreement to the cause, as did the other Beothic warriors.

"Okay, men," said Captain Pike. "Here's the way of it as I see the situation. Blue will have a crew to empty the ship and make an inventory for all to study. Anything of value will be split by the men before we sail back to New Founde Land." No one gave any expression of opposition to Pike's first order.

"I'll have Erdu and his crew pull back the sand from around the hull. Blue will also make us a design for moving this wreck around, so's we can work her out of the sand and down to the water. Jack, I want you to round up who's left and see to what the dons left us by way of tools." Captain Pike spit into the sand. "Tell me when you and Blue have got the pulley system rigged and ready. Once the sand is off the hull and the pulleys are ready, we'll yank the old girl to the surf line."

All cheered the pirate captain.

"Are there votes to be counted on what the captain says?" said Jack.

"Nooo," answered the crew.

"Anyone have a word to say?"

"Nooo."

"Then let's get moving!" said Jack.

"The lot of you," said Gilbert Pike. "Let's get moving."

CHAPTER ELEVEN

September 1614
Portugal

I WATCHED LANEY BURN HIS second pirate craft at the Mosquito Cove wharf. Ship and wharf burned to the saltwater, and bits of both floated away on the tide.

"So, whatta ya think of that, Tisquantum, old boy?" Laney smiled at me with large lips and smoke-smudged face. He looked more a black African than Suffolk sailor.

I maintained my silence and blank expression, and he turned to his next pyrotechnic act. "Over here, my boys," he yelled, and then helped toss pine torches into the next building. When the conflagration was at its highest, he walked the few paces necessary to put both his hands on my shoulders and his nose on mine. I couldn't help the tears running down my cheeks as my books went up in smoke. All that I treasured: chess boards, years of Mosquito Cove records and correspondence. My lovely big bed and warm rugs on every bit of brick floor, now smoke and ash. "That'll learn you to get uppity with me," he said into my face. "Damned ignorant savage is all you are," Laney said.

The vile man burned every structure on Captain Pike's plantation, and on the two Portuguese plantations as well. Captain Laney turned my world into dust and cinders, all to gales of his demented laughter.

After three nights and two days of diligent attention to complete his destruction, Laney weighed anchor on a lovely mid-September dawn. The breeze was as light as could be expected near this northern island, and the sea as gentle as any lake in the world. It was exactly two months after the pirate Captain Pike and his first mate Blue had sailed their own pirate ship from St. John's Harbor. Now the calendar showed September 16, 1614, and the irony of the situation gave me not a jot of pleasure.

I organized wind sails to funnel fresh air into the lower decks where we slaves were confined. The captain agreed to my system of feeding slaves and sailors, and all received fresh water and discarded their body wastes clear of the ship. There was no direct order, but with his tacit permission, I managed to bestow upon Laney and his crew meals that went beyond their fondest dreams. We slaves were orderly in every way, with similar meals as the crew, and quickly some of slaves were recruited to handle the more onerous jobs of a ship at sea. The sailors, Captain Laney, and slaves deferred to my suggestions for managing the slave ship with salubrious satisfaction, and everyone smiled when we sailed into the Lisbon Harbor only twenty-one days after departing Mosquito Cove.

The slave pen was a near-circular fence of twenty-foot diameter. Our prison was an odd collection of wooden sticks, barely knee high and but a few inches thick, tied together with thumb-thick rope. Nothing else marked the separation between slaves and potential customers. Laney made another effort to enlist me as a majordomo of his planned estate, but I refused with a good-natured shrug. The captain returned my shrug. "As you wish, Tisquantum, my lad."

"Do you have any questions to ask of me, or services that I may render to you?" I moved a step backward in the slave pen.

"Well, now"—he moved right to the edge of the pen—"What's your take on the merchant I've found to sell the lot of you to?"

"He seems an honest-enough crook," I said.

"Good, that's my feeling also." Laney turned from me and beckoned to a tall man wearing a red turban. "Señor!" Laney yelled. "Señor, over here for a bit."

I was introduced to Señor Chicharro, the slave merchant, and indeed found him to be an amiable person. The two of us used the Portuguese language, with no comment on how comfortable we were talking of the hot weather and rumors of the Black Death in the ports of southern France. Laney quickly abandoned us to our private tête-à-tête, so I smiled and pitched my voice to reflect a friendly inquiry. "How in heaven's name do you determine the price for each slave?"

His voice was still pleasant, but there was no hint of a smile. "I find that there is never a need for conversation with those who are simply passing visitors—those who enjoy teasing the slaves, for instance."

"Of course," I said.

"However, when there is interest shown by a potential customer for one of my stock, he and I simply discuss possibilities."

"Very interesting," I said.

The smile returned. "I also find that every potential buyer is loath to quote a specific price for his object of interest, and that I must inevitably listen to an extended declaration of his own poverty and the lack of worth so evident in my stock of slaves."

I returned his smile and said, "Of course."

Señor Chicharro retuned my smile with added interest. "It is my rule to never commit to a specific price or argue about the worth of any slave, because a serious customer will eventually throw an absurdly low price on the table."

"Patience is your practice, I see."

"I know what works for me in this business, and I enjoy observing the same sequence occurring with every successful sale of my goods." He paused for a beat of time. "It was the same with selling donkeys or barrels of olive oil, but there is greater profit in selling people than all the other goods that I have offered in the past."

"There is nothing more valuable than practical experience," I noted.

"You are exactly correct," said Señor Chicharro, "and that is why I am the preferred slave merchant in all of Lisbon Harbor."

"What about the rate of interest that you charge as commission for the sale of slaves? Is the commission as well as the price of sale also subject to negotiation?"

"No. I am able to gain the highest price possible for each slave; therefore, my fifteen percent commission from the sale of slaves is a worthy expenditure to those who are interested in selling slaves."

"Has Captain Laney agreed to your required commission?"

"Of course." Chicharro moved close to my shoulder and whispered, "I must feed my family." Closer still to my ear: "Do you have something of interest that I may hear?"

"I have friends here in Portugal," I whispered to Señor Chicharro.

"You speak Portuguese like an educated man," he noted.

"If you could contact my friends, I am certain they will find a way to exceed any commission you might receive for my sale."

"How much of a supplement do you have in mind?" he asked.

"Thirty percent of my potential sale price," I said.

"Who determines what you may be worth? You seem a very valuable commodity."

"You make the estimate, good sir, and the sum is yours to have."

Still no smile, as the final sale was still a distant dream. "Tell me how I might contact these potential customers," said Chicharro.

I gave him a folded paper with the names and address of my friends.

He shook his head in a dismal fashion. "They live in the far north, and it will take at least a week for them to receive your message, and then there is at least another week to sail back to Lisbon."

I retrieved two silver doubloons from my robe and surreptitiously gave them over to Chicharro. He took a quick look and whispered, "I have a friend that owns a small xebec with exceptional sailing ability. Possibly he would consider a trip up to Basque county to find your friends."

"I have two more silver coins for your friend when he delivers my friends to your place of business, and also two additional silver coins to you for your exemplary service."

The slave merchant smiled with pleasant patience. "What would you say to four coins for my friend and four for me if these people from the north are delivered here at my slave pen within the next four days?"

"Done," I said.

Four days later, on the dot, Chicharro handed me a letter. Laney was at his shoulder, and from their mutual expressions of anger, it was obvious that both had read the letter. To spite them, more than anything, I took the letter in hand and read the content aloud to the pair of fools.

To the Most Esteemed and Beloved Tisquantum:

We have arrived at our homes from New Founde Land only two days previous to the arrival of your letter.

Both José Maria and I are in good health, but we are both financially destitute at this current time. The outrageous invasion of our plantations by the Pirate Laney deprived us of our entire salt cod inventory. The pirates also destroyed every structure on both of our plantations and probably have discovered the location of our accumulated store of gold and silver coins.

We are ruined men, and there is no hope of our future investment in New Founde Land.

With apologies and good wishes,

Diogode Sousa

José Maria Agonia

"What now?" said Señor Chicharro.

"Indeed," said Captain Laney, the twisted smile of malevolence back on his face. "What are your plans now, my Beothic slave?"

I could see that both men had discussed my predicament, and they were without irony in posing their question to me. It was as if they expected me to pull a handful of gold from my hat or possibly describe a plan of practical steps that would make them rich beyond belief.

A period of awkward silence descended upon the slave pen of Chicharro. We three stood facing one another, blind to the numerous activities all around us. Pigeons and gulls competed for bits of food. Women shopped for their evening meals in the large marketplace in the harbor of Lisbon. Bells from church steeples rang in clattering splendor.

I pulled a single silver coin from my robe. "This is my last coin. In two days there will be no more food and water for my Beothic people." I gave the coin over to Chicharro. "If you can take us to a nearby tavern that will accept this coin for our meal and beverage, I would like to play the host for an evening of talk. Can you take us to such a place, Señor Chicharro?"

Both men shrugged at each other and then nodded toward me. The slave pen proprietor said, "Follow me. I know just the place for us."

"When we reach the bottom of this tureen of fish soup, it will be filled again and again," said Chicharro. He smiled at each of us. "Our cups of wine also shall be filled whenever the bottom is revealed."

"Good," said Captain Laney. "A fine place to talk and eat."

I took a sip of the rough-edged red wine. "What do either of you know about the Cistercian order of monks?"

Both stopped eating and drinking.

"The queen has forbidden all priests of the Roman church," said Captain Laney. "Even from the time of King Henry, all monasteries in England have been confiscated by the crown."

"Aren't the Cistercians the ones with white robes?" Chicharro looked up into the smoky ceiling. "I believe they have a fine monastery up north near Nazare, a couple days' walk from here."

We tucked into our soup and wine for a decent interval before I started again.

"From what I read and hear tell, the Cistercians hold St. Benedict as their model for appropriate behavior on this earth. They seem to hold that all monks of the order should dedicate their lives today to the same rules that St. Bernard established in his monastery of Molesme in 1098."

My two guests looked at me as if I were a talking ape. Both held mouths agape, dripping a fine fish stew back into their bowls.

Without a pause to allow my guests a word of interruption, I continued with my lecture. "St. Benedict ordered his monks to wear white robes and to follow a life of manual labor and to create a life of self- sufficiency in each and every monastery." I paused again, but this time to give emphasis to what followed. "The Cistercian monks have built churches of great beauty, and they have developed great skills in agriculture, the draining of swamps, and making strong swords and other metal implements."

Chicharro coughed before speaking. "My grandfather was a lay brother of the order," he said.

"Ahh, tell me of your grandfather," I said.

"He was employed as a soldier of the cross by the Cistercian abbot. His job was to protect the monastery from pirates and invading Moors. English pirates were especially dreaded," said Señor Chicharro.

Captain Laney drained his wine cup but made no comment.

"My grandfather made the monastic vows of poverty, chastity, and obedience, plus he accepted the rules of silence, the four days of no sex, and the one hundred *Pater Nosters* daily."

"My goodness!" said Laney.

"There's more. In addition to the simple tasks that I've noted, my grandfather had to sleep in his armor—and full dress it was, including the Cistercian white mantle with the scarlet cross *fleur-de-lys*."

"Good God!" said Laney.

Señor Chicharro regained his famous smile. "I was told, in no uncertain words, that there were no problems with the damn English pirates when my grandfather was on duty."

Laney joined me with a brief chuckle.

"Tell me, sir," I said. "What was the name of the monastery where your grandfather served with such dedication?"

"It was the big one up near Nazare."

"Ahhh," I said. "Gentlemen, now I have a question for the both of you—are you ready?"

They nodded in a manner that expressed little conviction that whatever I asked was likely to have any worth to them.

"Señor Chicharro, answer me yes or no: are you a true Christian with an undying faith in the written word of your Bible?"

"Certainly!" The slave merchant was clearly offended by my question and sat in a stiff upright position. "I attend Mass every Sunday and always seek redemption for my sins with a confession to my favorite priest."

"This confession is daily? Weekly?"

"Whenever needed," said Chicharro.

"I see."

The slave merchant waved an empty wine cup toward a likely servant, but through each separate motion he revealed that my questions unsettled him. Chicharro made an act of pretending that he was still in command of the situation with a loud shout: "Wine for all, dammit!"

Once the wine was poured and both men settled, I asked another question of Chicharro. "Do you believe that the living pope speaks for God, and that the cardinals and priests in the service of the living pope also speak to their parishioners in the name of God?"

Chicharro hesitated with his answer for a long moment, and then said, "Yes," in a low voice.

I turned to Captain Laney, but he started in with his answers before my questions were offered.

"I am, without reservation, of the true faith as ordained by the queen of England, and the current pope of your reference is an agent of the Devil and not a voice of God. Also—"

I held my hand in his face to stop the flood of words. "Listen for a moment," I said. "Both of you good and true Christians, but you must listen to me."

They looked one to the other and then down to their half-empty bowls of cold fish soup.

"Captain Laney, did you find the gold and silver hidden on the two Portuguese plantations before they were burned?"

"Yes, of course. They were both in boxes under the floor in the bedrooms of Sousa and Agonia."

"Of course," I said. "Have you sold the salt cod that was in storage at all three of the plantations that you burned to the ground?"

"Yes," he said.

"Did you receive a fair price for the cod and seal fur and tools that you stole from the three plantations?"

"Fair enough," said Captain Laney.

"Well, then, you must be in a hurry to conduct your business of finding a suitable estate for purchase in England. It was someplace in Surrey, if I remember correctly."

"Yes, Surrey is my first choice to secure an estate that will demonstrate the importance of the Laney name for many generations."

"Good—all this news and information is very good," I said.

Both European guests were silent but prickly in their demeanor.

"I suggest that you both donate your Beothic slaves, including me, to the Cistercian Monastery near Nazare."

Two wooden statues sat in chairs before me. No words from them joined the rumble of a tavern full of satiated men.

I leaned forward to be better heard.

"Listen, Captain Laney. You have riches beyond your best dreams, and the enormous wealth is burning a hole in your pocket. It may take up to three years to find an estate worth your name. You have gold beyond the costs of your beautiful estate that needs investment in profitable ventures—investments that will inevitably lead to the wealth needed to purchase the rank of your choice. Doesn't the salutation Lord Laney strike a pleasant chord?"

"Where on this good earth does this silly donation fit my plans and not yours?"

"A good question, my lord. I suggest you view the donation previously mentioned as a loan to the monastery; a temporary arrangement where you may, at your own pace, return to Nazare and collect one or all of your slaves."

"This is your first mention of loans, you slippery savage."

"The fact of your loan is a contract between us, with Señor Chicharro as the legal witness."

"Slippery indeed," noted the slave merchant. "Where is my profit in your fantasy?"

"Do you ever dream of becoming the mayor of Lisbon?" I gave him a playful wink. "The miracle of rising from the role of simple slave merchant to that of the powerful and wealthy mayor of this grand city. No? Yes?"

"Who are you?"

"I'm a red savage. A magician and the answer to your dreams."

"A magician?" repeated Chicharro.

"You will lead the line of slaves to the monastery of your grandfather. You will hold the line that ties you to a donkey, upon which there sits a young virgin who is carrying an infant in her arms. Following you and the Madonna with child, there is a long line of red savages that you are donating, as a true Christian, to a monastery held in the highest esteem by all people of your faith and blood."

Chicharro would have none of my magic. "All three of us will both be brought before the Inquisition and then burned at the stake."

"Ahh, you are referring to Giodarno Bruno, no doubt. The famous Dominican friar."

Chicharro was red-faced with agitation. "Yes, indeed. The famous friar who had the audacity to deny the Trinity; the famous friar who also denied the divinity of Christ. The stupid fool who also denied the virginity of Mary."

"But you, sir, will soon be famous as the charitable merchant who embraces the Trinity. The famous layman who proclaims to all the divinity of Christ, and, most assuredly, the man who attests to the undeniable virginity of Mary."

Chicharro had consumed more wine than usual, and the soup was moving upward from his stomach, not down. "The mayor of Lisbon, you say?"

"The city of Lisbon for you and an enormous estate in Surrey for Captain Laney."

Laney sat straight in his chair. "Do I hear you accept my offer as secretary of my Laney estate?"

"Yes sir, I am your slave and will accept whatever vocation that you demand of me."

All of the savages were covered with red oakum. The donkey and the girl and the baby held by the girl were also covered in red oakum. I was covered in red oakum and wore a tall red hat as long as my arm that narrowed to a sharp point at the top. An hour after our departure from the Port of Lisbon, a crippled man on two wooden crutches fell in front of the donkey. On cue, the young girl holding the baby sang a song in her sweet Beothic language. When she stopped singing, the crippled man stood, raised his arms, and yelled in his sweet Portuguese language, "It's a miracle! I can walk again."

The crowd attending the parade of red savages increased by twice after the crippled man's testament. A few hours past noon, an old woman stumbled in front of the red donkey. It was obvious to all that the woman was blind, for all could see but a milky-white color where eyes would normally be black or brown or even blue. She crawled over the pavement and, as if by accident, took hold of the left forepaw of the red donkey. Again, on cue, the young girl holding the baby sang a song in her beautiful Beothic language. When she stopped singing, the blind woman stood and stared at the young savage girl covered with red oakum.

The blind woman pointed and yelled, "It is Mary! I can see the Virgin Mary!"

The crowd made an enormous gasp, then went silent as the blind woman turned to face the mass of Portuguese villagers. "There!" She pointed at a person in the crowd. "There is my neighbor." And at another person in the crowd. "There! The merchant who sells oranges!" The blind woman raised both arms. "It is a miracle," she yelled. "I can see."

The crowd attending the parade doubled once again. At dusk, the simple slave merchant who led the parade stopped his red penitents for the evening at a small farmhouse. The crowd settled also here and there, and soon spontaneous fires were built for warmth and to cook what food the spectators had at hand. The girl and her child and the red donkey found respite in a small outbuilding meant to shelter and feed cattle or donkeys.

Soon after Venus appeared, and when the stars were well established overhead, a purple glow erupted in the west, with all quadrants soon showing the same alarming color. The cloud became larger, quickly changing colors from purple to red to orange to yellow and then back to purple. In the space of sixty heartbeats, the multicolored cloud covered the small farm, with Mary holding her child under the vibrant canopy. Then, with twenty additional thumps of excited hearts, the cloud evaporated to nothing, and the stars and Venus returned.

The crowd remained stunned with silence, their vision unimpaired by clouds of any color. They stood in the silence, as if attending a Christmas mass at a large cathedral with all waiting for the first bass note from the organ. The young girl holding the baby sang a song in the beautiful Beothic language, and the other savages, including me, joined with her in a joyful hymn. Those in attendance seemed to understand what we were singing.

"The Red Virgin!" proclaimed the huge crowd. Over and over until the dawn, the proclamation was repeated: "The Red Virgin!" in the beautiful Portuguese language.

On the next day, just past noon, the slave merchant Chicharro led his charges to the Cistercian Monastery near Nazare. The merchant and his red savages were welcomed by a corridor of two hundred white-robed friars. Finally, there at the open gate of the monastery, Abbot Juan-Marie lay flat in the dust, as a supplicant of the girl and her child.

The Beothic slaves kept their eyes on their feet as they followed me past the white-robed friars and their abbot. As we passed through the gate to the monastery grounds, two guards, dressed in armor and carrying long spears, took the lead and very soon brought us to a large barn full of empty stalls and stale hay. When we were in the barn, quiet and waiting for whatever would come next, the guards left the barn, secured the doors with chain and locks, and departed with loud steps down the path just taken.

CHAPTER TWELVE

1614
Hudson River Gold

T HE REPAIR OF THE SPANISH caravel was surprisingly simple. Both the fore and aft masts were solid but merely five-foot stubs, so Viking Jack engineered ten-foot extensions for both and then rigged a mizzen staysail and a lateen foresail. "Ya got yourself a Barbary bastard, for certain," said Jack.

"She'll tack good enough," said Pike.

"She'll swim like a fat cod." Jack cackled. "I'll think about you boys when me and Kakata are cooking up a batch of those pathetic lobsters."

Pike remained in the conversation as an affable participant—certainly a great improvement over his rude disposition over the last few months. "Well, now, my Jack of all trades." Pike even smiled as he spoke. "I'll grant you that the mosquitoes are bigger than the lobster on this island."

Jack smiled in return. "There's the name for your damned pirate ship, Captain."

"*Mosquito?*" said Pike.

"Another damn *Mosquito*," I said.

"Sure enough," said Pike. "Easy to remember, and that's no lie."

It wouldn't do to say out loud that I'd miss the damn Viking. Him and Gobidin both. They were both good men to have at my shoulder during any fight. They were both good men to sit with on a warm night on the beach—or on a cold night in a warm cabin, for that matter. Good people and soon no longer in my life. How could I explain to Oubee that Gobidin would never return to the Beothic people? How could I explain to Oubee and our boys why I remained so long absent from them? I shut my eyes. *Oubee, are you still waiting? Are the boys lively and healthy? Oubee, Oubee, are you there?*

I noticed the silence and opened my eyes to see Jack staring at me. "Never worry about us, Jack," I managed in a scratchy whisper. When he remained silent, I added, "Listen, my Viking friend, every time I eat an osweet steak, it will bump my memory of you and this lovely island."

"So be it," said Jack.

"Look alive," said Pike. "We've got plenty to do before the damn *Mosquito* will float." Our captain seemed to study the horizon for an over-long period before speaking again. "We'll need at least twenty hefty logs to roll the Spanish ship down toward the water, and then with using the same the logs over again, to put the beast afloat."

"There's not a chance of putting the dinghy aboard, captain. The *Mosquito* is more a raft than a ship, and the little craft will tip the balance we need in any rough weather."

"Not aboard, you fool. Tow her at the end of a long line. She'll serve our needs for a run to shore for food and water." Pike was strangely upset.

"She'll slow us down, Captain, and we need to stay trim and free of any drag to have any chance for New Founde Land."

"She's a seaworthy little boat and will serve as our lifeboat if the *Mosquito* founders." Pike waved off any further argument from me or Jack or Kakata. "Get to work, all of you."

The Spanish charts got us north up the Florida Peninsula and north of what was called "The Fort" on the last page of the Spanish book of charts. It was two days further north, in light wind, where we found a cove to hold our pathetic anchor. The barrels we filled with fresh water, and the dinghy proved its worth more than one time. We slept at odd hours and swam in the brackish water for the next four days. I admit to sleeping more than most, but still, we caught our fill of fish, mended sails, and set up to divide the silver hoard and all the other valued trinkets.

"We voted," said the spokesman for the Bristol sailors. "We'll take what's ours to do with what we want."

"In two days a few will have all the silver," Pike said. "The fools will lose everything to the tricks with dice or cards."

"That's our business," the Bristol man said.

"The silver is safe where it's stored," I said. "A storm or a thief will empty your little hidey-holes, and then where will you be?" I knew the spokesman as a man with both trained dice and marked cards. A knave, and no mistake.

"Pirates don't steal from the others," said the knave. "What we do with our money is no business of mates or captain."

Pike stood to assume his prerogative for command. "It's for the entire crew to decide, not just the Bristol sailors. I'll take a show of hands right now to make certain where the silver goes." Pike was not going to back down and made a big show of shouting. "Who is for keeping the silver where it is, safe from accident or theft? Hands up where Blue can take the count."

"I count nine for keeping it safe," I said.

"Tie goes to us," said the knave.

"Captain has two shares and therefore two votes," Pike said, "so forget the dice and cards and let's get to work."

A few carried black clouds over their heads, but most accepted Pike at his word, and we got on with what was needed. On the fifth day, a fair tide and good wind put us heading north and always within sight or smelling distance of the coast.

The brave ship *Mosquito* inched ever northward until increasing wind and tall clouds forced the captain to seek shelter in a large bay. He found a tight little nook to protect the ship from what turned into a vicious three-day blow. The anchor line snapped on the second day during a sharp squall, and once again the Spanish caravel was up on a sandy shore.

Two men ended the storm with broken arms, and most of us were black and blue from head to toe. Still, in all, none were dead and the silver was still safe. Captain Pike and I set the broken arms on small boards and made the slings snug against their chests. Neither of the injured men complained, but they were gray of complexion and not willing to move about for the pain it caused. The rest of the crew found ease under hardwood trees, and mostly they kept dry from the constant rain.

It took four days to repair the hull, and we set some tree branches under the hull as rollers, then winched her from the loose sand back into the water. We'd been under way for half a day, such as we could with a ripped and flapping lateen sail. Pike and I shared time at the tiller, and the crew found their ease in various shady locations near the bow.

"Did you ever meet a fisherman by the name of Henry Hudson?" Pike was in a black, black mood. The mizzen staysail was gone, with no replacement. The hull looked awful, with the port side rail crushed, again. We limped along more than ever like a raft than a ship.

I looked at my captain. "He's a Bristol man?"

"His family has property near a village south of Bristol. Small holdings, of little value, but his father owned a merchant ship that carried Bristol fishermen to New Founde Land each year. Henry followed him aboard and learned the cod fishing trade as a half-share youngster."

"Which plantation did he fish?"

"Fermeuse area, mostly, south from St. John's by a day and a half. The Hudson family never had deed to a plantation and grabbed what they could each year."

"Maybe Da knew him, but not me."

"He's your age, Blue, and captain of a fishing boat at sixteen, just like you."

I was getting irritated with his meaningless ramble and ached for some time to watch the seabirds and dream about Oubee and the boys. "What are you going on about with this Henry Hudson?"

"I met him at a Bristol tavern the last winter I was ashore. He told me that a few Bristol merchants had him scouting for some likely new plantations to the south of New Founde Land."

"He had his own ship?"

"He had a Dutch ship that the Bristol owners gave him to use. It was named *Halve Maen,* as I remember."

"What was the agreement between the owner of a Dutch ship and those Bristol investors?"

"That's the same question I asked, and Hudson said there was some Dutch money together with money from the Bristol folks on a fifty-fifty contract." Pike edged a little closer to my shoulder. "He also told me about two big rivers well south of New Founde Land, both big enough for him to sail north on each one for a week or so in his *Halve Maen*."

"Do tell," I said. The Oubee of my dream smiled at my wit, but Pike kept on with his everlasting drone.

"Yup, Hudson sailed up both rivers with ease, and he told me about hills full of huge trees and valleys prime for farms." Pike was losing his bad mood. "The southern river of the two has a huge harbor and scattered islands all about the harbor."

I moved the tiller a few times, just to pay some attention to the man. "Are you thinking that this place where we just left is the place Hudson went on about?"

Pike shook his head with some conviction. "Nope, not from his description, anyway. I'd say his river with the harbor and islands is somewhat further north."

"What's the plan, Captain?" Now I could see the captain was suffering an itch with some notion of his.

"We need to keep this damn barge afloat and get the lateen sail mended and rigged again." Pike looked over my head to what he saw in his mind. "If we can get another three or four days to the north, I do believe we'd get a look at Hudson's nice big river. That's the best I can imagine for our lovely *Mosquito*."

"What did Hudson say about people there in his harbor? Are there merchants to sell us what we need?"

"He said there were maybe a few dozen families scattered around some islands in the big harbor, and that there were more to follow from the Dutch people, in quick order."

"It sounds to me like we'll get to buy or trade for some eggs and maybe a homespun shirt. Not much more, I'd guess."

"A donkey and our dinghy—that's what I'll be looking for at Hudson's village."

"You just lost me, Captain. Give me some clue as to what in hell you are talking about."

Pike stood but looked forward, not at me.

As he walked away from me he said, "I'll get some men on mending the sail." The black cloud had disappeared from over the captain's head. There was certainly no smile from Pike, but there was a dreamy haze that filled his eyes. A donkey and a dinghy? Just what in hell was our demented captain thinking about doing next? Oubee and Shelagh should be next with our plans, not donkeys and dinghies.

The two men with broken arms turned from gray complexion to deep blue, and both died of sharp pains to their heart during the first night afloat. We put them overboard, and since the lateen sail kept us moving only slightly above walking pace, the bodies remained in sight until noon. On the second day under sail, a mysterious stream of warm water, well-marked by a different shade of blue, picked us up like a magic carpet and doubled our rate of speed. Nut Island was our landfall on the fifth day.

The villagers on the tiny island were Flemish, but a few also spoke French. Pike was handy with the French language, so we quickly knew that we were on Hudson's river.

"His other river is a two days' sail north," said the village spokesman. His ungainly name flew through my ears without a moment's hesitation. "This river we call the Hudson; his other river the Connetcut."

"So this is the river that Henry Hudson explored?" Pike was persistent in understanding that he stood on the correct ground.

"Yes, certainly. We have a family from our village in Holland who are settled on the northern river, and we are in communication a few times each year, what with visits and letters back and forth." The man paused in his monologue. "There is no easy harbor in that northern river, such as we have here, but two days on a small sailboat will usually do the job."

"Why do those folks stay in that Connetcut land if there's no good harbor to receive supplies or to send whatever goods they need to Amsterdam?" Pike baited the garrulous man to provide details.

"Their land in the north is pleasing to farm. Up and down the river there's the same marvelous black dirt, and soon enough a proper harbor will be created."

"Are the savages a problem on either river?" Pike prodded.

"Ahhh." A long pause. "Here on the Hudson River the savages are content to trade their goods with us as long as they receive what they consider a fair bargain." Another long pause. "We have our director-general to deal with in this matter, and he is a man who insists that any contact with Leni Lenape must be made with peaceful intent and with never a show of force."

"You have no guns to protect yourselves?"

"We have guns to hunt wild birds and beasts but never to flaunt with military intent toward the savages." The nameless man smiled. "We buy and sell from each other and give them their asking price for corn or land. I believe that there are no hard feelings on either side. None that I've heard about, in any event."

Pike shook his head in wonder. "Well, now, what other civilized people are there around this New Amsterdam?" he asked.

"The big island just northeast of our tiny Nut Island we call Manna-hata, and over the past few months it has suddenly become crowded with an amazing variety of people. There are folks flaunting strange and unusual religious sects, and there are people arriving from scattered principalities of both Europe and Africa."

"My," I said. "It seems that our New Founde Land and your New Amsterdam have more than a few similarities." When the Nut Island man stared at me for an overlong period, there was nothing for it but to continue. "I speak of the simple fact that both islands, here and there, have many diverse people packed into a small area."

"Ahh, yes, I'm certain that you are correct in that judgement," said the Flemish man. "I've heard the same notion from more than one ship's captain. Still, for Manna-hata Island it is the Germans and Swedes and English in the largest numbers—and the Dutch, of course."

"What's upriver?" Pike gave a large smile of encouragement.

"Beautiful land with many different trees." A large smile in return. "Hardwood of many sorts. Fir trees straight and tall enough for any frigate." The Flemish man paused. "We've got Juan Rodriguez up and about the river looking to collect dried fur from the savages."

"How's he doing?"

"Good enough. Me and a few others on Nut Island are about to do the same. There are beautiful beaver pelts by the dozens from the savages, and they pay a good price for them in Amsterdam."

Pike let the smug expressions hang on the Flemish faces until the first cracks appeared. "Well, now," he said, "if I wanted to have a look up this river, who would there be to grant me the permission?"

"That would be Director-General Minuit," said the fattest of the villagers. "Over on Manna-hata Island."

Pike gathered his pirates around him in the aft cabin. The eighteen of us made a tight fit, but with the four chests on the deck, lids open, they settled to the quiet of mice. "This is the end of our voyage, men. We'll count the shares out here and now, so all can witness the fairness. The trinkets have long since been taken, so now you get your share of the dons' silver."

The knave was first to speak. "What's next, Captain? Are we stuck forever here at the end of the world?"

"Take a walk back to New Founde Land, if you have a mind. Swim if you want." Captain Pike gave his gentry smile to the lot of his crew. "There are jobs here with the Dutch, I'm certain. Good land if you want to farm. Ask around, gentlemen. What you do from here on is your business and not a bit of mine."

The knave gnashed his teeth in an impressive manner but kept his mouth shut.

"Come up to the chests with me," Pike said to the knave. "You and I will count out the shares while Blue writes down the names and their tally."

"Good enough," said the knave, and none of the other pirates made an objection.

The count went on for the daylight hours and finished when the candles were sputtering nubs.

The captain stood and waved my tally sheet. "Are you all satisfied with your shares?" he asked.

No one said a word or looked him in the eye.

The captain turned to a cupboard behind him, opened the small door at the top, and pulled seventeen small leather bags from a shelf. He then turned again to place them on the table in front of the crew. "Here's my parting gift to you for your service to me."

Still not a word or look.

Pike emptied my bag into his hand. "They're all the same: one gold doubloon and seven silver coins. A wage of one year for most of you, if you head back to Bristol Town, that is."

A few smiles cracked hard-frozen lips.

"Blue and I are off tomorrow to see the director-general for New Amsterdam. I invite any who want to use the *Mosquito* as your home for a while to do so. Stay until you have a mind for what direction you want to move in." Pike leaned forward a bit and made his voice the last one they'd hear. "Fair warning," he said. "It may take us a few days or a couple of weeks to settle our business over on Manna-hata Island, but three days or thirty, when next you see me I'll have sold the sturdy *Mosquito* for the highest bid."

"Scrap wood and scrap metal, that's all is left," said the knave.

I felt relieved to be rid of this crew. With just me and the captain to manage our affairs, it seemed an easy reach to find a merchant ship that could be persuaded to deliver us to St. John's Harbor. I could smell Oubee's beautiful scent. I could hear the boys laughing into my ears.

On the very next morning, with Pike at the tiller and me at the sail, the little dinghy took us quickly from Nut Island to Manna-hata Island. We found a tight space to secure our boat to a busy wharf, and after struggling through the crowd of sailors and landsmen, we followed the directions given to us by an Englishman who said he was from London Town. The walk was short, and after we entered his office we noticed Minuit had a wooden leg and that he never showed to smile. His first words, after Pike introduced himself, were, "Do you know Isaac Alleston or Thomas Willet?" We replied no, and the director-general turned red in the face and loud with his voice. "They are thieves and fools, like most of the English we have here in New Holland."

"There's a bad apple in every lot," Pike said.

"The two tried to bribe me to let them land muskets here on this plantation. Guns for the savages and with no payment of taxes! They would bribe the governor of this plantation and then attempt to avoid paying taxes to the owners of this plantation." Minuit was both angry and perplexed. "The bad apples keep rolling down from Plymouth

Town, one after the other. Thieves and self-styled preachers selling their lies to all who will listen."

No one spoke for a spell that seemed longer than it was. I had the unpleasant feeling that Pike was moving toward a goal that was not mine. Finally, Minuit broke the silence with a rude question.

"Tell me, Englishmen. Pirates of little renown, what do you want of me?"

"I'd like to sell the ship we call *Mosquito* to someone here in New Holland."

"Are you referring to the derelict wreck you call *Mosquito?*"

"Good solid Spanish oak and plenty of metal to salvage," said Pike.

Minuit shrugged. "Ask around. There are always fools to make a fool's errand."

"We will pay all the taxes necessary," Pike said.

"Of course you will," said the director-general.

Pike took a step closer to Minuit. "There's something else I would beg of you, sir."

"That you want something from me is no surprise at all," Minuit said in the same dull tone.

"I would like to explore the land north of here, along the west side of Hudson's river."

Minuit stood to attention, wooden leg and all. "We are at peace with all the savages along the river, Englishman, and I'll have no disruption of our relationship with our friends and neighbors."

"Of course," said Pike.

"The tax that you pay will give my permission for your expedition."

"How much?" Pike asked.

"One hundred Spanish silver coins on my desk," said Minuit.

It took a few minutes, but Pike was able to put ten silver coins in ten columns, which the director-general immediately deposited into a stout oak chest.

There was another extended bout of silence before Minuit continued. "I will have you watched at every point that you stop along our river. If there is the least sign of impropriety shown by either of you two Englishmen, I will clap you both into my jail upon your return."

"Of course," said Pike.

"Take a close look at the conditions prisoners suffer in my jail before you leave this island," said Director-General Minuit.

"Of course," said Pike.

On our first night in Manna-hata we found a tavern that allowed us to throw a blanket on the floor after the last customer departed for the night. We walked the streets and studied the fort under construction the next day. A few Englishmen stopped to greet us during our sojourn and without exception recommended that "the best English food and ale is found at Eagle Tavern."

"At what time of the evening shall we find the most convivial company at this tavern?" Pike always asked.

"Sunset and beyond," they answered.

So it came that on the next four nights we met the infamous Alleston and the equally obsequious Willet. These two, together with two preachers of loud voice and little wit and another dozen men who claimed their status as merchants, lately from London, served as sponsors for our visit to the island of Manna-hata. The *Mosquito* we sold for ten guilders to one of the preachers, and Willet nagged us every night with a series of splendid business opportunities that he guaranteed would make our fortunes.

On the sixth morning on Manna-hata Island, we sailed until the wind went against us then rowed the *Mosquito*'s dinghy back to Nut Island.

When I think back on events that occurred during our sojourn from that lovely island in the Caribbean Sea to Nut Island, it now seems clear in my mind that I missed some very important details in the behavior of our ship's captain. For instance, I should have noticed that the dinghy from the *Mosquito* was like a pet spaniel to Captain Pike. It was always in his sight during the trip from the Taínos' island. Also, when the dinghy was loaded aboard, it fit snugly into a special device that had been built by the pervious Spanish captain on the aft rail of our *Mosquito.* Pike could see his dinghy resting dry and secure from his cabin window. When we needed fresh water or information about the passing shoreline, the captain sailed his little craft from one point to another. No one else was allowed at the tiller of his spaniel.

"She was built with special attention," Pike often commented to me during our trip north. "No other person has the skill to manage this frisky little craft."

"I've noticed that the metalwork is special, that's for certain," I said. "Both the stern seat and tiller are secured to the oak hull with six-sided metal screws."

"Have you ever used or seen such metal screws in all your years as a blacksmyth?"

"There'd be no reason for me or Da to ever use this type of screw. It requires a special tool built just to sink or retrieve those screws. Very special," I said.

"I've never seen the like either," Pike said.

Our trip from Manna-hata was short and pleasant. Pike smiled as he nodded for me to ship my oars, then moved the tiller to come about.

The little craft drifted to the Nut Island wharf, gentle and soft for the landing. "She's like a small horse, this little dinghy, full of muscle and grit," Pike said. "The dinghy was not part of my sale of the *Mosquito*, you know."

I made her secure to the wharf cleats, but we remained on our seats.

"I doubt we can sail her to St. John's Harbor," I said.

Pike burst into a course guffaw—not like him at all. "Don't worry your head, Blue. I'll get you back to Oubee as quick as possible."

"Tell me what you do have in mind, Captain."

"Soon, very soon," he said and looked up at the *Mosquito*. Even before boarding her, it was evident that the ship had endured a recent attack. All the bits of exterior metal that could be removed with simple tools had disappeared.

"I expected as much." It was clear that Pike was not upset by the indignity set upon our ship. His eyes squinted as he reviewed the damage. "Poor buggers," he said. "All this work for damn little gain." Now he smiled. "Well, we're finished with that lot of pirates, and we can get on with our own business."

"What is next, Captain?" I leaned toward him. "Maybe we can find a ship heading for New Founde Land, and we can go aboard as either crew or passengers. In a week or so we could be hugging Oubee and Shelagh and watching our boys at play." I felt my eyes puff a little. "I miss my family, Captain. It has been a long time, and we need to make haste with our return."

"Well, Blue, I think that we'll have to delay the pleasure of seeing our families for a bit longer. It is a difficult decision, to be sure, but in the end you will appreciate my decision to purchase a donkey this morning, and then the three of us will set sail with the afternoon wind."

"A donkey?"

"You'll discover the excellent reason for my donkey soon enough," said Pike.

I felt the air leave my stomach. The image of Oubee and the boys evaporated from my mind. "It's likely a fair wind if were headed north," I said.

"So be it," said Captain Pike.

"Is there no option, Captain?"

"None," said Captain Pike.

The dinghy had three ample seats and a bow device to set the little mast. The stern seat was for the man at the tiller, if such was needed. The passenger bench could seat four with some degree of comfort, and the rower's bench gave space for one or two men to pull oars.

We tied a cloth bag over the donkey's head, and with feet tied together, fore and aft, she settled down with little movement or complaint. There was a good-sized windlass built on the Nut Island wharf, so it was no problem to hitch her up and then slowly drop her down into the dinghy. She squealed a few times as we lowered her between the stern seat and the passenger's seat, but there wasn't much fuss at all.

"Now, that wasn't too bad, was it?" Pike reeled the pulley rope back into place and secured the windlass on the wharf without any help from me.

"Two smashed toes is all," I returned. "Two bent toes and a blindfolded donkey as a passenger." I tried a smile but couldn't get a bend to my lips. "Why, Captain? What's the sense of this damn donkey?"

Pike ignored me. "It'll be a short trip, with this wind as it is. We'll stop at the first large stream that comes into Hudson's River from the west."

I surrendered my argument. "That'll be where the savages have their big farms," I said.

"Indeed. I'll drop you off ashore and then go on to the next stream from the west."

"Do I get the donkey for company, or is it just me and the savages?"

"I'll take our four-footed friend, and you will make your acquaintance with the savages."

Pike let out a little more line on the sail to catch additional wind, and we moved away from the Nut Island wharf at a good trot. The dinghy felt solid under my feet. "Tell me what you want me to know, Captain Pike."

With one hand still on the tiller, Pike took his other hand to feel under his seat. After a small struggle, he gave a push to a certain part of the stern board and out popped a little drawer. "A little magic that I learned when we were back on Kanata's island," he said.

Still keeping his course to the north, Pike pulled a metal device from the drawer. "Six sides on this tool," he said.

"What did you find when you made use of that tool?" I asked.

"Under this very seat where I'm sitting, there is a space with custom-built drawers to hold four good-sized bags of gold."

"Gold, not silver?" A foolish question, but nothing else popped into my head.

"Gold."

Pike and his persistent attention to the dinghy suddenly made more sense to my feeble brain. He had sailed the little craft with great affection because she carried four sacks of golden bones. "Why tell me of your secret now? What do you want me to know?"

"After I drop you off with your new friends, I will sail or row to the next substantial stream and unload both donkey and gold. During the next few days my donkey will carry the gold in a special saddle that I've contrived, and when I find a prominent landmark with a companion hiding place, I'll bury my gold."

"Why? Why not take the gold with us to New Founde Land?"

"This amount of gold coin could never remain a secret. Anywhere, anytime, on our trip from Nut Island to New Founde Land, we could be under attack. There is no possible way for the two of us to protect this huge treasure from the inevitable thieves."

"Oh, that much gold, is it?"

"Yes, it is indeed a fabulous treasure of gold."

We sailed on at our steady pace before Pike spoke once again. "This beautiful land alongside this magnificent river is perfect for industrious farmers. The magnificent harbor is worthy of the English merchant fleet and no other." Pike nodded in agreement with his logic. "I'm certain that the Dutch cannot hold such an important place for long, and before much time passes, I believe that the Bristol merchants will usurp the Dutch charter."

"How can you make such a bold prediction?" I was acting the straw man with my weak question.

"Listen, Blue, it is a simple matter. I have this hoard of gold, and I have fools such as Willet to carry my orders. Beyond that, just remember, Blue—I am friends with the powerful people of Bristol, and they will quickly see that there is much for us to share here in New Holland."

"The queen is dead, and her sea dogs are old," I said.

"Still, I know the Bristol merchants, and they are always hungry for sweet prizes. I believe that the transfer of New Holland from the likes of Peg-Leg Minuit will happen within a few years." Pike looked me in the eyes, pleased with himself. "With my Bristol friends in control of New England, no longer New Holland, then I'll dig up my gold and invest in a large plantation with a view of Hudson's river."

"An exciting dream, Captain Pike." I slapped the gunnel of his dinghy by way of getting his attention. "Now tell me, what do you want me to know?"

Pike softened the expression on his face and leaned toward me. "I want you to know that both of our families shall reap a large benefit from this adventure. You and Oubee and your family shall create a lineage that lasts through the centuries. All shall bow to your command and follow your most simple wishes."

"After Willet becomes governor of New England, that is."

"I'll not quibble over details. Just know that you are an important part of my present and future transactions. Your assignment for now is to gain the friendship of those savages who cultivate their excellent farms to benefit the Dutch." Pike gave a sharp slap to the donkey's back and a smile to me. "I'll pick you up in ten days or so."

"What will you have me do if you don't show up?"

Pike looked skyward for a moment and then back to me. "Hire a few likely savages and come tracking my path. If you find me wounded and incapacitated, help me back to my dinghy."

"And if you are dead?"

"Bury me and then go and seek the gold. Do what you want with the bounty, but share generously with Shelagh and my sons."

The entire web of ifs and maybes was too much for my stomach. "Listen to me, Captain Pike. I'll tend to your savages while you are off with your donkey, but when you return, I'll still be satisfied with my share of silver. It will suit Oubee, and the silver at hand is more than sufficient for me."

"Your dreams will change when we put our gold to work," said Pike.

"Just remember that Da was chasing one of your dreams when his blood exploded on my body. I'd rather just head back to Oubee, with your permission."

We continued north, and Pike remained silent as the sun became hot and the wind diminished to half what it was at the beginning of our trip upriver. Finally, he continued with his orders to me. "If I do in fact return and retrieve you from the hands of the savages, you must keep my secret from all, including Oubee."

I raised my white flag of surrender. "Certainly, Captain Pike—you can always trust someone of the Smyth family line with a secret."

"Hummph," mumbled Pike, but still, there was a smile on his lips.

Pike left me on a beach and sailed—or without the proper wind, rowed—ever to the north. At each outflow of streams large and small, he considered their advantages as they entered the Hudson River from the west. It was the twenty-third option up from Nut Island that was his final choice. "The twenty-third," he told me once we got together again. "Big and small streams all counted. If I saw a mere trickle, she counted as a viable stream on my list."

"Why was number twenty-three your final choice?"

"Well, now, it was larger than most I'd seen. Also, there were no significant landmarks on the outflow to attract attention—no large trees or shiny boulders or Mohican farms, for instance. A traveler could blink once and the stream would not exist."

"Nothing special to attract any attention was what you wanted, I guess."

"Right as rain," Pike always answered. Even after twenty times of telling the tale, his choice of stream number twenty-three was "right as rain."

"Matilda and I pulled the dinghy up the beach and into a thicket of scrubby willow trees. That little donkey was as patient as I could ever want. The old girl cropped weeds while I ate salt cod until the sun set."

"Nothing like a good companion on such a trip," I noted. "Why the name?"

"Old Matilda was a treasure to behold from the very first day, and she reminded me of my very first ship, a pleasant old scow named the *Matilda*."

"Makes perfect sense to me, Captain. How did you two fare after the first night?"

"Well, now, from the time dawn came along and until near noon we enjoyed each other's silent company in that willow hideaway. Neither of us saw a single spy from that damned peg-legged governor or from any Nut Island farmer either."

"No savages that you could see?"

"Nary a one. No Mohican trailing along the river in their canoes, and nobody tromping along the edges."

"What was next for you and the donkey?"

"There was a hot sun, I remember, along with a constant swarm of mosquitoes and those damn little gnats. We walked at an easy pace alongside the creek, with nothing but some stunted willow and feeble hardwood to hinder our passage. I did notice, though, that as the stream became smaller, the trees grew taller and thicker."

"Slowed you down a bit?" I asked.

"Well, now, it was Matilda who figured the best course for us was wading in the warm shallow water. Not much faster, but easier to take a drink or escape the mosquitoes with a dip underwater."

"Smart girl," I said. Pike always ignored my comment about his four-footed friend and carried on as if I wasn't there.

"At the top of each rise in terrain, it was clear that I was following the outflow of a stream that had carved a significant valley. Way off to the southwest I could see a flat-topped mountain through the humid haze. Once we got closer, it was easy to see alternate layers of black-and-white rock that appeared at the top of that mountain, like layers on a cake. I counted six discrete seams of black and white and also saw a large beak of jumbled scree that tumbled from the bottom layer down a thousand feet or so and into the valley."

"This mountain is important to the story?" I asked.

"Always remember, first the twenty-three streams and then the six-layered mountain, my friend. Never forget those exact details."

"Most certainly," I said. "Both are etched into my memory. What was next?"

"Well, we plowed through thick brush to get near that flat-topped mountain until it was near dark, then Matilda and I managed our meals, moved our bowels, and fell to sleep with the calls of nighthawks and owls filling the entire valley.

"At dawn I hobbled Matilda in an area where she had easy access to water and forage, slapped her once on the rump, and moved quickly toward my wedding cake mountain. From the very beginning of the climb there was loose dirt and scree that made each step a slippery bugger; therefore, I made a fast retreat to find a stout walking stick. With the stick as a third leg, I was able to move up the steep slope with arduous effort. The faint evidence of a trail took me up and up for about four hundred yards of extreme and difficult gradient, until suddenly the climb became much more manageable. Views of a lovely green valley quickly opened for my appreciation. When I finally achieved the summit, the reward was a view of many mountain peaks to the south and a spectacular panorama of a valley to the southwest. I inched to the edge of an overhanging promontory and observed dramatic cliffs and hills to the north. It was a view that provided a map to my objective."

"Pike," I said, "am I supposed to remember every little detail of this story of yours?"

"If I die and Shelagh dies and my two boys die—all of us, that is—then you and your sons can have a go at retrieving my gold." Pike held my eyes for a long moment. "Do you understand, Blue? If me or any of my kin live, I'll make sure the Smyth family is well taken care of, but if the unlikely happens and all the Pike family dies, then you are welcome to come a-running for where I hid the gold. Do you understand the situation or not?"

"If you live, you get the gold. If you die and Shelagh or your boys live, then I get to show them where the treasure is located. If all the Pike family dies, then the Smyth family gets the gold even if I only want my little pile of silver."

"Good. You understand the situation well, but you must remember exactly what I tell you in my story. If you forget even one small detail, then my gold becomes a game of finders-keepers."

"Talk slower, will you, Captain Pike?"

He smiled and continued at the same rate of words. "As I peered over the edge of that mountain, it was as if a map had appeared in my eye."

Pike paused, more for his need to appreciate the image than to support my need to remember. "I was able to make a clear sighting from my flat mountain into the drainage system of a large river that held close to a southwest bearing. It was clear to me that if I followed a small creek that developed directly below my mountain, that the stream would grow in size and it would eventually join the river. From that juncture of my flat mountain stream with the large river, I simply followed the downstream flow until the very first intersection with a stream from the north. Are you still with me, Master Smyth?"

"I think so, Captain Pike."

"Good, because you must follow the new creek northward to the very end, even if you confront enormous difficulties."

I nodded in confirmation of the apparent final important detail.

Pike settled his bones in a comfortable position to finish his tale of adventure, being the pirate captain that he was and all. "It appeared—from the top of the mountain, in any event—that my forthcoming trip was a mere walk in the park for me and Matilda. Not above twenty miles to a very suitable burial site for our golden burden. Such was the map etched into my mind from the top of Wedding Cake Mountain."

"Ahhh," I said.

"It was dusk when I returned to Matilda. She gave me her usual brief smile, then quickly returned to her evening dessert of clover leaves. I scratched her back for a bit, then whispered into her ear: 'It appears that tomorrow we will make our way to the southwest, my dear.' She shook her head vigorously and turned to stare briefly into my eyes. 'It is a simple downhill walk, nothing more,' I told her."

Pike continued. "It took some time to secure the luggage-saddle to Matilda and load the four casks filled with gold coins. The sun was up and already hot. A pair of vicious stinging flies joined the resident swarm of mosquitoes and midges. After a mere sixty paces, we encountered a thick jungle of vines, barbed bushes, and trees that blocked our downhill trip. I tried here and there to find a manageable passage, but we seemed locked in a green prison. I pulled a hatchet from my pack and hacked away to provide an escape channel, but managed only one or two steps further into the outlandish confinement.

"Matilda started shaking her ears and head in violent fashion. Her cry mimicked that of a terrified infant. I looked at my sweaty arm and saw ticks by the dozen seeking a drop of my blood. The back of my neck and scalp felt swarmed by the incessant movement of ticks. Matilda screamed and bolted into the wall of green. The cords of the saddle were broken, the four casks fell to the ground, and my donkey disappeared."

"Damn!" I said.

Pike continued with no pause. "I left the gold protected by sentries of flies, mosquitoes, and ticks to follow Matilda's trail. She wasn't far—two dozen paces before the prison gates had slammed shut on her. I started again with the hatchet, and we made slow progress until near dusk, when suddenly the way lightened. There, within twenty paces, was a small spring of water leading to an incipient creek and an open view.

"We both rolled in the wet mud and drank the clear water. I pulled ticks from her ears and my arms until the sliver-thin moon jumped above the trees. We curled in a nest of dry leaves and slept until dawn. I retrieved the gold by contriving a sling to carry each cask over my shoulder until the ground was clear enough to roll them toward our little campsite. Matilda rolled in mud and lounged knee-deep in water while I completed the four trips.

"It took another two days before we were rested and clear of ticks to continue with our adventure. We followed the map in my head to the large river, and then the final north-bearing stream did in fact end in a large swamp. We mucked along until dry land was underfoot, then I dropped Matilda's lead rope and walked to a small mound, nearly free of brush and trees, to survey the scene. She followed along to stand at my side.

"From the mound we saw many separate and well-established deer trails that joined as one and eventually disappeared toward another mound. This second high point, not more than two hundred paces away, was filled with ancient oak trees and scattered maple. Matilda, still in good humor, followed after me in a docile fashion.

"It was an amazing sight. Deer by the dozens were gathered in the shade of hardwood trees. Fawns with their does and bucks with antlers of all size blithely relaxed in either standing or reclining positions. As I moved closer, they continued to ignore our imposition, and I became aware of a dramatic lowering of temperature with each step.

"I tied Matilda to a maple tree, well shaded and with ample forage, and proceeded cautiously toward the area that seemed to produce the constant source of cold air. It was surrounded by a redolent brush of some variety or other, but there it was—the mouth of a cave that bellowed forth a constant breath of frigid air."

"A cave?" I said. "A cave blowing cold air?"

"Yes, and that cave was blacker than my most vile nightmare, even a mere four steps into the brush-covered opening."

"What did you do?"

"Well, now, after the four steps I squatted down, and from the feel of feet and hands, I moved forward an inch at a time."

"What did you find?"

"At about twenty paces into the cave, I found that there was a choice of a left or right tunnel. I scooped a handful of pebbles from the floor and threw them toward the right-hand tunnel. Silence. Silence! Then, from a distant place, the soft pecking of pebbles on a hard surface."

"I hate caves," I said.

"Well now, there was no going to the right, so I tried the left-hand option and drew an immediate response of pebbles."

"I'd be out of that damn cave and standing with the damn donkey," I said.

Pike ignored my fear. "I moved with great caution for twenty additional paces before meeting a dead end for this tunnel, and then I returned to find my faithful Matilda."

"What then?"

"Well, my friend, I spent the rest of the day gathering stout pine branches, all slobbered with pine pitch, writing notes in my journal, and smiling."

I was ten full days with the savages. They laughed when I told them that I was called by the name Blue, but very quickly we started to share stories and lies, and I learned a number of useful words. I discovered that Dutch profanities produced much laughter, especially the ones calling for impossible acts of sex. We found a few Micmac words held in common, but none of my Beothic language made sense to my hosts. Their corn was ripe and sweeter than any I'd had in the past. The whitetail deer and other small game were difficult to find near the village, but I joined a pair of hunters who scoured the western hills, and we had some success. I managed the kill of a large buck—and with borrowed bow at that. We three warriors shared the liver of that particular buck over our evening fire and shared common blankets not long after Venus appeared.

Pike and his donkey came ashore on the eleventh day after his departure. He made a short tour of the village and farms, plus suffered through long introductions to the important citizens. On the fifteenth day from leaving Nut Island, the three of us drifted back down the Hudson River in Pike's beautiful little dinghy.

The ship *Nieu Nederlandt* had replaced the *Mosquito* on the Nut Island wharf. The captain of the Dutch ship was a compliant sort of gentleman, and when Pike offered to buy the entire stock of beaver pelts the Dutchman had on board, if only he could make a small detour to New Founde Land, the captain smiled his benign Dutch smile and escorted us to the finest cabin on his ship.

"Thank you," said Captain Pike, and he sipped at his cup of Dutch gin.

"The fare for the two of you and your luggage is three hundred guilder or three hundred gold doubloon," said the Dutch captain with a gentle smile. "I'll keep the beaver pelts to sell to a merchant friend of mine in Amsterdam."

Pike nodded a few times before responding with a smile of surrender. "I shall unpack my bags and pay you the gold coins before we sail," he said.

"Yes, before we sail," said the Dutch captain with no smile at all.

On the second day of our trip toward home, Captain Pike invited me into his spacious cabin. We shared a small bottle of Boston rum and a long comfortable moment of silence. Near the bottom of our bottle, Pike leaned toward me. "In the event that I die in an accident that includes my wife and sons, I leave you with a riddle to solve."

I neither smiled nor frowned but certainly said nary a word to my captain.

"Twenty-three, six-layered cake, and a cave that breathes cold air."

I remained silent. There was nothing new in the little ditty that Pike offered. He'd told the adventures of a donkey and captain to me three times over, but this admonishment was something more. Maybe he'd suffered a sudden premonition of death, or maybe he now felt the pain of choosing to waste time chasing after gold over time spent with family. Maybe the sod wanted me to join him in accepting the theft of time from Shelagh and Oubee and our boys with his version of our mutual gain. There was no telling, for Pike was and always would be an odd duck.

"One more time," said Captain Pike. "Twenty-three, six-layered cake, and a cave that breathes cold air."

CHAPTER THIRTEEN

Fall 1614–1615
The Plague

THE YOUNG WOMAN ON THE donkey—a girl of twelve years, actually—died first. On that second night of our sanctuary in the Cistercian monastery, her chills, fever, and crushing headache started. The next morning her swollen glands turned black, and she was dead before the next sunrise. The baby that the girl had carried on our trip from the Lisbon slave pen to the monastery—a cousin on the mother's side, I was told—followed the same pattern of symptoms and rapid death.

A half-dozen additional Beothic slaves and two Cistercian lay brothers were also taken in rapid order by the Black Death.

I sought help from priests and doctors, but no one listened to my pleas, and all of us were penned into our remote barn with barred doors and armed guards that patrolled around the perimeter of the barn.

"Witches! Witches! The red savages are witches who bring the plague," screamed the milling crowd of villagers and Cistercian monks.

Around and around the perimeter of the barn traveled our guards, villagers, and monks. "Burn the witches," they yelled.

"Torture the witches; discover their allies," they yelled.

"Jews and red savages, together. Witches who deliver the plague." Night and day they yelled.

We were offered a few pails of water for our thirst at each dawn, and the pails were attached to long poles held by men dressed in masks featuring long beaks. These same bird-beaked men lobbed a dozen or so loaves of bread through an open window of our prison before the sun was much above the horizon. In the next two weeks, another dozen of my savage friends died of the plague, and two pails of water and six loaves of bread were delivered each day, without fail.

I had trouble breathing. The pain in my chest became a volcanic eruption of bloody spit and bloody diarrhea. I remember fever and chills in constant syncopation, and then nothing beyond a swirl of black clouds.

"Here, drink this medicine."

I managed to open one eye to see a bird-beaked man sitting on a stool by my head.

"It is wormwood steeped overnight in a pail of ale," the bird-beaked doctor said. "Here, drink what you can."

I gagged on the first dipperful of medicine, but the doctor was persistent, and eventually I managed to swallow an entire wooden dipperful of the vile-tasting concoction.

"You and a few of the other savages may survive this plague," said the doctor.

"Why?" I whispered.

"There are three of you savages that have none of the black buboes," he said.

"I don't understand," I said.

The doctor was patient with me. "There are two distinct forms of plague," he lectured. "Those with the black buboes always die. Those with no black buboes occasionally survive."

"Oh," I managed.

The beak was close to my ear. "There were ninety-three red savages who marched from Lisbon to our monastery nearly one month past. Do you remember?"

"Yes."

"Eighty-six died of the Black Death; seven remain for God's judgement."

"Have the living savages received the benefit of your medicine, doctor?"

"You and two others have managed to swallow at least part of a dipperful of my medicine," he said.

"What is next?" I asked.

"If any of the six live, and they are able to walk a few additional steps each day, the abbot will conduct a trial of those savages who have survived." The bird-beaked man delivered his forecast of our fate, as if the true God always spoke directly into his ear.

"What is the charge against us, good sir?"

"Witchcraft," he answered.

During the next cycle of the moon I could do little more than walk six steps to pee or shit or vomit vile specks on my toes, and then return the six steps to flop my bones onto a pile of straw. There was the pail of water always available but no dipper and no strength to lift the entire pail to my parched lips. There was no food except an occasional crust of bread scattered here and there about the barn. There was no one to help me to the privy or hold a cup of water to my lips or speak to me in one language or another. Even to my muddled way of thinking, it was clear that abbot preferred me dead to the plague than brought to trial on the charge of witchcraft.

Every morning, just after dawn, the bird-beaked doctor returned to make a quick tour of his hospital and give me a count of the survivors. He was without inclination on the subject of my fate in his hands, and on one day he reported: "It is now just you and three others." The next morning, the bird-beak mask was carried under the doctor's left arm. "Now it is you and two others," he said, still with no passion or concern.

"Where is your mask, Doctor? Have you no fear of our contagion?"

"It is no longer needed." He was a handsome man, taller than most from this land, with black hair half mixed with silver. "It has been over a week since a new case of the plague was reported hereabout." He carried a three-legged stool in his right hand and placed it by my side. "You and the other two witches are likely to survive." He sat on his stool and gave me a small smile. "Survive until the trial, in any event."

"What is your name?" I asked.

"Augustine."

"One of my favorite saints," I said. He was about my age, perhaps a little older. Clean shaven, with not even a mustache to distract from his deeply lined face. There was a mass of fascinating scars on his shoulders and neck. "You are truly a doctor?" I asked.

"I'm a plague doctor." His smile increased a bit. "The plague is my common call, but the smallpox and other sudden gifts from the Devil are also within my domain."

"What purpose do you claim for the mask?"

He lowered the mask to my eye level and reached into the beak to pull a handful of weedy dregs for my observation. "Herbs of my choosing," he said. "The lower portion of the beak is fine gauze, and with the herbs between my nose and the vile poisons exuded from my patients, I have survived to the ancient age of thirty-one."

"Congratulations," I said.

We remained in our own thoughts for a long spell. Small brown birds with black stripes about their heads chirped a dull-witted song in a repetitious dirge. Church bells tolled their normal schedule.

"There are two prominent landowners from the north who have made enquiries about your health," he said.

"Yes?"

"Both are from families that are well known for their piety and service to the church," he said.

"Yes?"

"It seems to be a strange fact that your trial as a witch has been deferred until such time as your survival seems inevitable," he said.

I maintained my silence but listened with profound attention to what the doctor might say.

"The abbot of our monastery has spent an exorbitant amount of time and silver on the imposition derived from your invasion of our monastery. A dozen lay brothers have died of the plague, and the village near the abbey has been quarantined by the government in Lisbon."

My mouth was as dry as ashes, but I managed a small whisper. "I apologize for the imposition upon His Worship."

The doctor was silent for a long moment before speaking again. "I am a resident of the isolated village that serves this monastery, and many have died of starvation, not the plague."

"I'm sorry for their troubles," I said.

"There is little food available in my village, and no employment is open to our sailors and fishermen."

"Why are there no jobs for the villagers?"

"All the surrounding towns and villages fear the Black Death and refuse the merest trespass by my friends and neighbors." The doctor coughed into his hands. "You and I are isolated from the world. The plague was carried here by you and the other red savages, and now the innocent and guilty are both condemned to the same fate of inevitable death."

"I beg your forgiveness," I whispered.

"The abbot will make note of your words," said the doctor.

I gave a small flock of small brown birds time to move beyond my hearing before gathering the courage to speak further with the doctor. "Is the excellent abbot considering a strategy to mitigate my damage to your village and his monastery? Is there any action or deed that I could perform that would diminish the difficulties caused by our invasion?" I let the doctor manage his thoughts at whatever pace he considered appropriate.

The bells of the monastery tolled once again before I received an answer to my question. "The two gentlemen of the north—friends of yours, no doubt—have made recent and significant donations of both land and silver to the abbot. They have also made the generous offer of volunteering to supervise the lives of the surviving red savages until their trial is scheduled."

"Indeed?" I said.

"The abbot has accepted their donations as worthy of good Christians."

"Yes?"

The two cousins will arrive today, shortly after the noon bells have rung," he said. "They will take you immediately from this prison."

I stopped breathing for a long moment. My fingers tingled, but my mind remained cluttered with dull thumps of sounds. It was more the roar of heavy surf on a sand beach that I heard rather than a beat of large wooden drums.

The doctor stood at the head of my bed. "You will leave this place before you hear another tolling of the bells."

My fondest memory of my time spent in the lovely country called Portugal was of the enormous fig tree. It was next to the small cottage that José Maria Agonia provided as my sanctuary. During the hottest days, I could sit in the shade of the fig tree and listen to birds forage for fruit or insects. The bright-orange birds that gorged on ripe figs and whistled soft, sweet phrases in constant repetition remained a favorite memory. Then again, the tiny insectivores of many shades and colors that cavorted through the same tree with their busy *chip-chips* and long, rambling serenades ranked next in the list of fond memories.

The headaches diminished. I could walk a short distance over level ground. My urine stopped showing red, and the diarrhea turned into proper stools.

José Maria had sat next to my bed during the early evening for the first few weeks. There were no words exchanged, for I was nearly mute. There was only an occasional "yes" or "no" uttered by my thick tongue, and José was comfortable with our silence.

One day he placed a soft wool blanket over my sheets with the first cool breeze that invaded his land, then stood to give me his sweet smile. "Diogode sends his love to you, Tisquantum, and promises a visit this coming Sunday."

"I look forward to seeing my good friend," I whispered.

"We'll go for a picnic," José Mara said. "A docile mule will pull the cart, and we can talk and eat and drink red wine in a fine shady spot that I have in mind."

"I will dream of your good company and good food," I said.

"We will gather this next Sunday, near noon," José Maria said. "We'll bring a blanket for your shoulders. It is early May, but a passing cloud may hold the sun's heat from your body."

"Thank you, good sir, from the depths of my heart."

"It is nothing, Tisquantum. Nothing at all," he replied.

I shut my eyes and fell into a deep and blissful slumber. There were no dreams—merely a warm purple haze that relaxed every bone in my body.

I opened my eyes to see Captain Jacob Laney and a dour-faced Cistercian friar sitting next to my bed. It was the full light of an early spring morning. The doves were complaining from under the eaves of my cottage. Both men were talking, but thus far not a word of their ramble had surfaced with any meaning for me. There were sharp words—insistent words—combined with belligerent expressions.

"Stop," I said. "I will not say a word to you until José Maria Agonia is at my side."

"It is not his business," said Captain Slaney to me. "You are my slave and therefore my property."

"You have a choice," said the friar. "The abbot of our monastery has decreed that you must appear before a court of monks and answer to the charges of witchcraft." He stared at me with malevolence. "Our abbot also recognizes that Captain Laney holds the legal title to your body; therefore, the abbot has decreed that you must decide on one of two options: you may come with me today and sit at your trial, or you may go with Captain Laney today for your servitude. Today. Make your decision right now!"

CHAPTER FOURTEEN

Fall 1614
Ashes

T HE *NIEU NEDERLANDT* ARRIVED IN St. John's Harbor on September 28, 1614. The blazing-red hardwood trees scattered on the hills of St. John's City gave evidence of a sharp frost in the recent past. The smell of fish and manure brought a smile to Captain Pike's face. "The Dutch captain said that he'd like to have a tour of St. John's City."

"Is this another long delay before we leave for Mosquito Cove?"

"He and his mate are my guests for dinner. After we eat our fill, I'll give them a short tour of our best taverns." A small smile. "It'll be merely a single day of delay before we leave for our rendezvous with the ladies." Another smile. "I promised a rack of osweet ribs for the two Dutchmen."

"I'll send a messenger to warn Tisquantum and the ladies of our arrival tomorrow."

"Good. I wouldn't expect Tisquantum to be here in the city, but ask around and determine the last time he was here or down at the harbor." Pike paused for a thought. "I'll work on the Dutch captain and see if he would consider a regular stop here at St. John's. He may see advantages to finding a market for the fur of New Founde Land as well as those from Hudson's river."

"Fine and dandy." I tried a new phrase I'd heard in Manna-hata, but it felt false in my mouth. "What I'll do this morning is hire a whaleboat to ferry us around to Mosquito Cove as soon as you finish with your business with the Dutchmen."

"Good," said Captain Pike. "Fine and dandy."

"If we can manage to leave tonight, Captain, we'll see our families in the morning."

"Yes! Shelagh and Oubee in the morning!" Captain Pike smiled his old Mosquito Cove smile. "Make it happen, Blue. Get us a whaleboat that's fast and dry."

The *Nieu Nederlandt* was moored at anchor near the wharf that Pike always used to ship our salt cod or to receive supplies from England. The Dutch ship sailors were working efficiently to transfer the paltry load of goods that Captain Pike had purchased in Manna-hata. I waved my arms toward two stevedores standing close by on the wharf. "Hello!" I yelled, and when they returned my wave. I said, "Bring your barge over to the side, and we'll hoist down a few bales."

"Sure enough," the older fellow answered. "You want them put to your storage shed?" he yelled.

"Yes," I said. "I'll come directly to open the doors to the shed."

Both men waved and moved down the wharf toward their small barge.

Pike disappeared in a dinghy that rowed him to shore. There were a few moments of distraction aboard the Dutch ship, yet even with my head stuck deep into the *Nieu Nederlandt's* hold, I heard a woman ashore scream bloody murder.

I looked up from my awkward position to see Shelagh and her two youngsters running down the wharf and waving her arms at me.

"Blue! Blue!" she screamed. "Where is my husband?"

"Stay right where you are, Shelagh. I'll be at your side directly."

I jumped down into the barge standing aside the *Nieu Nederlandt*. "Get me to the damn wharf," I ordered the two men. In a very few minutes I climbed the wood ladder attached to the wharf, and immediately as I stepped off the last rung, Shelagh crashed into my body.

"He is here," I shouted into her ear. "Here, close at hand."

Shelagh pushed me away, a demented look in her eyes. "Where? Lead me to my husband. Quickly!"

We looked around, neither of us ahold of our wits, and just then, with us addled by tears and laughter, Pike came bounding toward us and quickly all was a moving ball of children and the adults that they loved.

"Come," Pike commanded. "There is a tavern nearby where we can sit at ease and talk without crying."

After the very first beer splashed upon our table, I interrupted the reunion with a question of my own. "Oubee? Oubee and my children—where are they?"

"Oh! Blue! What can I say?" Tears once again flowed. "What can I say?"

Pike and I exchanged fearful expressions. "Start from the beginning," Pike said. "We have days and days to listen, so take your time and tell us what has happened in our absence."

Shelagh sipped her beer and passed salt cod to the silent children. "Well, now. The very first event was my pirate husband leaving his family for nearly three years past." She gave her husband and his first mate a look of disdain, a glare worthy of an embittered Irish queen. "It was very early July of 1612, if memory serves."

Pike waved for another round of beer and some dried salmon for the children but said nothing to distract his wife from her story.

"It wasn't a week from your departure before they attacked."

It was quiet at our table, and even through the entire tavern, for all patrons and all employees were committed to hearing each word of the Irish princess and her version of the attack on Mosquito Cove.

"These pirates that invaded our home were English pirates, just like you," she said.

"Who?" asked Pike?

"It was that ill-featured Laney and his gang," said Shelagh.

"Sonsabitches," Pike said.

"It was Tisquantum who sent a runner with instructions for me and Oubee. The messenger said that we mothers and our children must have our fishermen take us to St. John's by boat or foot, whatever it took. 'Hurry, hurry,' the runner cautioned, 'they're burning everything in sight.'"

"Sonsabitches," said Pike.

"Oubee was with you?" I asked.

"Yes, when you two witless pirates left the cove, Oubee and I and our children settled in the new house my husband had recently finished." Once again the harsh glare from Shelagh. "We wanted both families to stay together while our own pirates were out burning and stealing from the dons." Her Irish blood was at a boil, and neither of us said a word.

Shelagh sipped half of a beer before she could look at me. "Oubee said she had to warn the villagers to run as well, so she took her children and disappeared from my sight."

The owner of the tavern filled all steins without a word, at our table and the rest as well. Even those at the bar were kept quiet with additional beer.

"It took us three days of rowing to reach St. John's." The Irish tears returned. "I haven't seen or heard any word from Oubee since that day of the attack by English pirates."

I stood and retreated from the tavern. I took to walking up and down nearly every hill in St. John's City to empty the tears and to list the questions I had yet to ask. It was dark when I returned to the tavern. Pike had taken a room for Shelagh and the children and spent the intervening time interrogating customers and employees of the tavern about what they knew of the pirate raid at Mosquito Cove.

"All buildings were burned," one customer said. "All the cabins, sheds, and wharf, burned to ash." The tavern owner leaned across his bar to Captain Pike. "They took all the barrels of cod Tisquantum had stored, and I was told by Laney himself that they found where you had hidden your gold and silver."

"What about Tisquantum?" Pike asked.

"Him and a bunch of those red savages got took up by Laney and carried off," the tavern owner said.

"Where to?"

"Laney said he'd get his best price for the lot in Portugal."

"Not Spain?

"Laney, the sonofabitch, named Lisbon as his destination."

I tried to get Pike to hire us a boat to sail us immediately over to Mosquito Cove. "I want to find at least one Beothic," I told him. "I'll go up into the hills or over to their lake—up to Labrador, if that's what it takes. I need to find somebody who can tell me about Oubee and the boys."

"Give me a couple of days to make things right with Shelagh."

"That's a good decision for you, but not for me. I'll go alone. Tonight."

"Listen, my friend. You need to get set for a long walk in the woods. Get yourself ready, Blue, and we'll both leave in two days."

I rowed the little sailing dinghy to shore. Captain Pike sat on the stern seat, as still as a wooden statue. His eyes were painted black, and the cords in his neck stood out as thick sticks. It was a long pull to shore, and when we scraped sand I shipped oars, jumped into waist-deep water, and finally handed the captain onto dry land.

We walked a good forty paces before Pike said a single word. "Well, damn the bastards! They made good work of it, I'll admit to that single fact."

"Two winter seasons didn't help," I said. "There's not a single piling left to the wharf, and we've got berry bushes growing where Da had his fine cabins."

"It is amazing how fast the wild returns with our backs turned for a moment."

All that we saw at Mosquito Cove merely replicated what we had been told. An English ship captain, a drunken rogue sonofabitch from Grimsby Harbor or some other bedraggled east-coast English port, had invaded our cove. They had invaded our cove at about the time we were getting voted off our own pirate ship. Everyone in New Founde Land knew that Captain Pike was off to the Caribbean Sea, seeking his share of the Spanish gold, and this pimple on a hog's ass by name of Laney had burned every building on the cove and captured all the Beothics he could catch from the new village. He'd taken Tisquantum, maybe Oubee and our children, and all the villagers who were tilling their crop of squash and maize and even green beans.

"Tisquantum! Oubee!" I yelled. "Sold for slaves in Lisbon. Slaves. Oubee. Tisquantum. My boys."

"Enough!" said Captain Pike. "This is the last time that I will ever set foot on my cove." With not another word, he returned to the skiff, rowed out until there was a decent breeze to set his sail, and then quickly sailed out of my sight.

I brooded for a while, there on the beach, then started searching, step by step through the Mosquito Cove plantation, the new village, the two Portuguese plantations, and at the next dawn through the endless hills and gullies of Beothic land.

On the tenth day of my search, I found Oubee's mother, along with an old man and young boy. They were still in their summer mamateek, even with the sharp frost nearly every night.

"Mother," I whispered.

"Come, my son, sit here in front of me so that I can study your face and eyes." She made a feeble gesture of welcome, then bowed her head until I was settled and quiet. "I knew that you would return," she said. "I knew that you would not abandon my daughter."

"Oubee?" I whispered.

"Forgive me, Blue." She turned to the two who were strangers to me. "The two here in my mamateek are refugees from a village on the south shore of the great river. They are called by their French names: Pierre and his grandson, Nicolas."

I made a brief nod of welcome and back to my mother. "Oubee? Our sons?"

"Soon, my son. Tomorrow or the next day Oubee and Wasemook shall return from their hunt of the osweet." My mother nearly smiled. "We shall celebrate your arrival with a lovely osweet liver for us to eat."

"Oubee, alive!"

"Listen, Blue, your sons are also part of the hunt for the osweet." Now my Beothic mother gave me her gift of an enormous smile. "At least one of your sons may serve the Beothic as a warrior, but the other may have different dreams."

"My sons, alive!"

I could not sit still. My right foot wiggled whenever I sat still for a moment. "Mother, where will you have your winter mamateek built? What can I do to help prepare the family for the dark days of winter?"

"We have room enough here," she said. "Some small improvements will be sufficient."

"Small improvements? You must consider that you will have a delicate Bristol man as a tenant, and he could never survive the dark season in a home built to enjoy the soft months of summer."

"You? Blue? You will stay here with your family?"

"Certainly I'll stay." I gave a small pause, as I knew she expected. "Rest assured, Mother, it is up to you to determine how we spoon together on the coldest nights."

My mother gave me her best teasing smile. The one with the left-side eyetooth barely exposed. "Prepare for the worst, my son."

"No!" I said. "You would put the husband of your daughter with his butt exposed to the frost?"

"Of course," she said. "All the Beothic must learn anew how you acquired your name."

"It is blue for the color of my skin, not blue for my butt!"

"Nonsense," my mother said. "Come now, let us get to work on this draughty dwelling. Why don't you find the ax with the metal head and follow after me."

We heard the hunters returning with enough notice for us to stage our meeting. I had a lovely fire, with hot embers perfect for broiling liver, plus jars of water at hand. Only the old man with the French name was innocent of the incipient meeting.

Oubee was first through the leather door. "Who's been working on—?" A large gasp followed. "Blue!"

A blur for a moment, and then I was buried, first by my wife and then with the addition of my first son, David. We hugged and kissed and stared into eyes of each other until Oubee waved to our younger child. "John, come here to your father."

Oubee and I had agreed upon Bristol names for the boys whenever we lived on the plantation and Beothic names when away from the invaders. "He doesn't remember his name," Oubee said. "He's only four, and you've been gone for most of his life."

"Come here, Son," I said with my kindest voice. There was still no recognition of me or of any willingness to leave the side of his uncle.

I stood and walked over to my brother. Wasemook showed the same reticence toward me as did my son, but I put my hands gently on his shoulders. "I'm sorry, Brother. I'm sorry for what the invaders have done to the people, and I'm sorry that I was not at your side to help protect my Beothic family."

Wasemook tried to remain aloof from me, but eventually and with obvious reluctance he broke his silence. "I have some liver outside, Blue." He glanced briefly into my eyes. "Let me retrieve it for your excellent fire."

"Good," Oubee said. "It is a large liver, and we are all very hungry."

During the next passing moon, the first heavy storm deposited a great deal of snow over a period of four days and nights. Next, we endured an interminable spell of clear skies and very cold weather. We had worked hard to make our home tolerably comfortable; still, there was never sufficient warmth in the patched-together summer mamateek to give a moment of pleasure to our daily chores. Layer upon layer of clothes merely made every movement more cumbersome, a little relief from the bone-chilling cold. Much of the day was spent under blankets, spooned together near the fire and whispering into the nearest ear. The old man with the French name was last in line, with his grandson next to last. With each small break in the cold days, we hunters added another six osweet to the winter storage shed. The grouse population was abundant, and along with rabbit caught in snares, we managed a varied and tasty diet. Wasemook remained distant from the family and twice disappeared for unannounced sojourns of ten days or so.

It was after the week when little or no sun appeared above the horizon that Wasemook was back in the mamateek. I took my snowshoes and snow goggles and a basket of necessary items and prepared to leave my family again.

"I must tell Captain Pike what has happened, but I will return before we see the soft-mud days of spring."

"So you say," said son David.

Wasemook said nothing.

Oubee bowed her head and cried.

CHAPTER FIFTEEN

1620
Plymouth

"HERE'S THE WAY OF IT," said Laney.

The Port of Lisbon was still in sight on this first day at sea. The two of us sat in his mean little cabin of a shabby little merchant ship. I sat on a three-legged stool and stared across a tiny table at the ugly sight of Captain Jacob Laney. An occasional spit of rain rattled the deck, as if to emphasize the dismal atmosphere. A sharp northeast wind made for an uncomfortable chop to the ocean, and I felt my gorge rise to the limit.

"I'll tell you the truth, Tisquantum—my entire life is invested in New England Company shares. Nothing else is mine—not even this miserable little ship."

The smallpox pits were most prevalent on the left side of Laney's face, and the configuration of pits and his twisted nose gave him an air of dementia tinged with wickedness. I tried to hate the man but found little energy to support the effort. "Do you mean that all the gold that you stole from Mosquito Cove is gone from your hands?"

"Long gone," murmured Laney. "Spent with no return of pleasure or joy." His pitted face was further humiliated by a sheen of sweat that filled every orifice. "Pike's gold and the Portugee gold is all disappeared in a blink of my eye," he whispered.

For some undefined reason, I felt better with my own mood through Laney's confession. I was certainly less bilious and more interested in surviving my long battle with the plague—for another day or so, in any event. "Explain yourself, Captain Laney. Do you mean that the entire fortune you gained as a pirate has disappeared? All the gold you took from New Founde Land was in turn stolen from you?"

"Even more—also the possible gain from my slaves has disappeared." Laney poured a tot of rum into his cup of coffee. "The slaves are dead—except for you, of course—but my gold, my wonderful boxes and boxes of gold and silver, were taken from me by thieves of great cunning." He sipped his coffee but managed to never look at me. "My gut says I'm near the end of my life." Laney's hands quivered, and a tear oozed from the left eye. "You are my only possible hope for some small degree of comfort." The fool, the weakling, seemed to melt into his chair. "There is only the damn beaver trade with the damn Massachusetts savages that hold any hope for me."

I felt no need to give a response. The chop of waves continued unabated, and the remaining pains derived from the plague still bothered every part of my body.

When the silence had continued through the consumption of an additional cup of rum, Laney coughed a lungful of phlegm onto the cabin deck, then continued his confession to me. "This New England Company has a few plantations stuck here and there along the coast of Massachusetts, and all of the plantations are stuck in the middle of a bloody war with the local savages." Laney fell silent for a few moments, exhausted from all his talking. "I need for you to talk with the savages, Tisquantum. I need you to convince them to trade their beaver pelts with me and to stop killing the English settlers who want only some small part of their land."

"Laney, you know full well that I'm still sick with the plague." I paused to make certain that he was listening to me. "I can barely stand or think a serious thought, and there seems no end in sight from the nightmare."

Laney said nothing and made no movement of his body.

"There's nothing I can do to help solve any problems that you may have. Indeed, there's nothing I can do to solve my own problems of health and mind."

Laney shook his head. "Tisquantum, you are my slave and must listen to me. It'll be a month before we make the coast of Massachusetts. Get some rest, eat some salt cod, and your mind will be ready soon enough. We must move quickly to bring peace for all three of the English plantations."

"Take me to Mosquito Cove first. I need to see Blue and Oubee and to eat some proper Beothic food. Give me at least a season's respite for the recovery of my plague, and then maybe I'll be ready to help with your plantations that are under siege."

Laney finally looked me in the eye. "There is no Mosquito Cove plantation. Your Captain Pike has abandoned the ashes that I left for him, and he has moved to St. John's City."

"What of Blue and Oubee?"

"No word of either. There is talk of a plague among the Beothic."

"You must put me ashore among the ashes of the cove. I'll find the truth of my brother and his wife."

"Not a chance, Tisquantum. My share of the New England Company has value only if you are able to do the work required of you. Our first landing will occur in the northern reach of Massachusetts."

The rain stopped with a sudden plunge into silence. Both wind and ocean chop diminished. "Laney?" I said.

"What now, Slave?"

"How did you lose your enormous hoard of gold? What happened to you?"

"Do you want a tot of rum?"

"Just a drop in a full cup of water," I said. "Medicine for the plague, if nothing else."

Laney sat over his cup of rum as if asleep, moving his bones for an occasional sip and subsequent belch before returning to his somnambulant pose. The rum was eventually finished, and the captain stirred on his chair, as if scratching an itch.

"Do you know the name Henry Howard—the Earl of Surrey?"

"Whig, I'd guess. Does he represent a seat from Sussex in Parliament?" I scanned my memory of articles from the *Times* of London. "Arundel, if I recall correctly."

"That's him—my mentor."

"Yes, I have him now: gentry class, of course, and claims everyone for a friend. He's a man who lives without prejudice to religion or class, so I've read in the *London Times*, in any event."

"I met Lord Surrey during my search for land in the east of England." Laney sat more or less erect in his chair. "It turns out that the gentleman had extensive holdings in both Suffolk and Norfolk, and it was one of his managers of a property in Suffolk that introduced us." Laney gazed at the ceiling of his cabin. "This was early in 1614, with snow in the hills but none in the valleys or along the shore of either county."

"I'm curious about an awkward problem that you must have encountered."

"What's that?" Laney asked.

"During this search for your estate, and with your travels hither and yon, how did you manage the care of all the gold that you had acquired?"

"What else could I do?" Captain Laney leaned toward me. "There's no bank I'd trust, so I hired two strong men to guard me and the gold both."

"How many boxes for the coins?" I asked.

"After I traded all the silver coins for gold, it got down to eight boxes, each the size that two strong men could carry."

"My, what an enormous chore. How did you manage the details of daily life?"

Laney gave me a hint of a smile. "I was a rich man, so I bought a stout wagon and four horses to carry the gold and hired two men to drive and care for the horses."

"Plus the two strong men already mentioned?"

"Of course, my retinue usually included four men and a young woman to care for my personal needs."

"Ahh, now then, did the two strong men sleep in the same room as you and the young woman and the gold?"

"No! Certainly not." Laney set me right with some degree of indignation. "I'd certainly never trust those two hoodlums not to steal my gold as I slept. They were strong of limb, for certain, but dodgy-mined as you'd expect of such characters." Laney managed a wink of his left eye. "I always had one to stay awake outside the locked door of my sleeping quarters."

"I see," I said.

"Maybe not, Tisquantum. Maybe you do not really see the true situation, that is."

"Then explain yourself, Captain Laney. Tell me what I may be missing."

"Rich men never need to sleep rough, so I always found the largest and most expensive inn where I could spend my evenings. I always asked around to find those that provided excellent meals and wholesome entertainment." Laney leaned toward me. "Best of all, these establishments of fine repute always had a safe place to store my gold. Usually a steel vault cemented to the floor and constant surveillance by their own staff of guards."

"Marvelous," I said. When it was apparent that Laney was waiting for an additional response from me, I queried, "This Norfolk gentleman of high status—did he have some ideas for your money?"

"Lord Surrey, I was told, was both a gentleman and secretary at war and treasurer of the British Navy. All at the same time, in fact." Laney was pleased with the memory of his intended neighbor.

"Ahh, yes, plus an honest Whig into the bargain," I said. "Strange, I have no recollection of any Lord Surrey as the British secretary of war."

"The plague must have addled your brain," said Laney. "No man can remember everything he hears or learns from reading."

"Most assuredly Lord Surrey was a knowledgeable gentleman of the world. Especially since he was a gentleman with the intimate knowledge of both English naval requirements and the power of English gold."

"Mmm," said Laney.

"Now, Captain Laney, exactly what suggestions did Lord Surrey give you for investing your awkward pile of gold, may I ask?"

Laney was pleased to answer the question. "Shortly after our first meeting I was able to put most of my gold with the Bank of London."

"And how did you manage such a difficult task?"

"Lord Surrey told me that his family had used the same institution for holding their funds safe for many generations." There was a quick sip of rum by Laney. "He told me that nothing on earth could be safer for my fortune than the Bank of London—nothing at all."

Laney stood from his chair, took two large steps, and opened his cabin door and yelled, "Bring me some rum, you fool." He took two steps back and waited in his chair until a frightened servant entered. The man put a full bottle of rum in front of Laney, turned, and retreated through the door without a word.

"I put my fortune in the Bank of London, and they paid me two percent of the total that very day they received my gold. I had cash money in my pocket, and the president of the Bank of London himself told me I was free to purchase anything I wanted on the word of his bank."

"My, what a charming arrangement for you."

"Easy as wiping my ass with a soft cloth. Write my name on a scrap of paper and have the bank take care of any details."

"Heaven on earth," I said.

"Best of all, I got rid of those two likely thieves and the two inept drivers in the bargain."

"Good work," I said.

"Well, I'm proud to say that it was Lord Surrey's very own secretary who introduced me to the president of the Bank of London."

"My, my."

"You must understand that Lord Surrey took me in hand, so to say, and invited me to table at his favorite tavern in London a mere week after the deposit of my gold. And on more than that one occasion he gave the same courtesy to me at different taverns. More than a few times I sat and talked with Lord Surrey." Laney smiled with fond memory.

"Taverns, you say. Not to his private clubs, I assume."

"That's correct—taverns of very good quality, they were."

"Did he pay the fare each time?"

"Of course he did! Lord Surrey was always a true gentleman." Laney paused for a moment. "Mostly we talked about possible estates in Suffolk or Norfolk that I could consider for purchase and of the many responsibilities that evolve from ownership of a fine home on a magnificent estate."

"Also, he spoke of them as a very expensive venture, I gather."

"I never imagined the many demands that accumulated upon a landed gentleman."

"Of course you didn't." I felt only slightly uncomfortable with goading the poor fool. "I suspect that he urged you to never forget that there are dances that must be held and that the hunting for fox is expected." I paused, giving him a chance to say something of support or denial of my recital, but Laney remained a silent bump on his chair, and therefore I continued my act. "There are servants for servants to hire for the many events held or planned, and then the neighbors with their retinue to accommodate during their lengthy visits of great purpose. All very expensive, I'd wager."

"That's not the half of it," said Laney. "I could go on and on—beyond the life of this bottle of rum, for certain—in an effort to tell you what it takes to run an estate such as I had in mind."

"Tell me about the investment Lord Surrey arranged for you."

"He narrowed down the options to the very best available. In point of fact, Lord Surrey himself, and many members of Parliament, he said, were already invested, and they all had positive expectations for enormous profit."

"Tell me the name of this particular investment, Captain Laney."

"Lord Surrey recommended that I purchase shares in the South Brazil Company."

"Tell me," I said.

"First of all, you must understand that in the late fall of 1614, Lord Surrey and his friends in Parliament authorized the South Brazil Company to assume a portion of the national debt."

"Stop, stop, stop!" I was staggered by the concept. "Can this be true? Norfolk and his friends managed to create a private stock company and then authorized this private company to pay for and be responsible for a portion of public debt?"

Laney shrugged and swallowed some rum. "That is my understanding of what happened. Something along those lines, in any event."

"Did you in fact purchase shares of this company on the recommendation of Lord Surrey?"

"Oh no, certainly not. He told me that the price was much too high and I should keep my fortune in a safe place."

"What was the initial price for a share of Parliament's invention?"

"I was told by Norfolk's personal secretary that it was a little under 130 pounds for each South Brazil Company share. That was early January of 1615, of course."

"You have a good memory for important details," I said.

"Lord Surrey told me his very own self that the company already had plantations in Brazil and also on some very rich Caribbean islands."

"Is that so?"

"In February of 1615, the price of each share was 175 pounds."

"My, a substantial profit for those who made the investment, indeed."

"Lord Surrey said that I could double the price of any investment that I could make in the South Brazil Company, and that the profit would accrue within a very short period of time."

"How much did you invest?"

"Not much—a few hundred pounds—and in early March the shares sold for about 330 pounds."

"Ahh, a wonderful profit on your investment. Bravo!"

"Lord Surrey himself told me that an even greater profit could be made that very day, and he strongly suggested a more serious investment, in the same level as other Suffolk County gentlemen were making."

"How much this time?"

"Half my entire fortune!"

"My goodness gracious."

"Then, if you can believe, in May of 1615, each share of the South Brazil Company sold for 550 pounds! I was rich beyond anything I could imagine. My mind put into rank order the possible estates of Suffolk and Norfolk I'd viewed and dreamed of choosing, to purchase the two most expensive of the lot."

"What happened next?"

"Lord Surrey sent his secretary and also his accountant to help me understand the extent of my wealth. The two esteemed gentlemen told me that I could be assured of another doubling of the price for stock shares, and for the sake of my potential title—to that of duke or something equally grand—and also in consideration of my likely progeny, I should now invest all my original gold, plus the already accrued profit, in shares of the South Brazil Company."

"You followed their advice?"

"Of course. They were merely telling me what Lord Surrey knew for certain."

"I'm afraid to ask, but tell me what happened next."

"In June of 1615, the price per share exceeded one thousand pounds, and on the advice of Lord Surrey's secretary, I hired a four-horse coach to carry me and a lady that was referred to me by Lord Surrey for a tour of my potential estates."

"A lady?"

"She was a maid to a Norfolk lady, and she was educated to a very high degree."

"Could she read the poetry of Shakespeare and play the lute?"

"She did indeed read some poetry aloud to me while we were traveling in the coach, and then there was one evening where she both sang to me and played what she named a lute."

"Did you enjoy your tour of the estates?"

"It so happened that after visiting the second estate that I had in mind to purchase, Lady Jane Musgrave agreed to take my hand as my wife."

"What a happy event," I said.

"We agreed on a late fall wedding, which would give us time to take possession of the larger of the two Suffolk estates, and thereby we would be guaranteed a fine home with ample servants from the very beginning of our marriage."

"What a remarkable story, Captain Laney." I looked around at the current accommodations of my owner. "What happened to your lovely plans for a happy marriage?"

Now Captain Laney's ugly face assumed a somber visage. "When Lady Jane and I returned to London in early September, the price per share for the South Brazil Company was under two hundred pounds, and Norfolk's secretary and accountant both advised me to stay the course. They reasoned that the South Brazil Company was sending a large shipment of nutmeg or marjoram or some important spice or other from a plantation in Brazil, and within a fortnight the share price would again exceed one thousand pounds."

"What happened?"

"There was no nutmeg, nothing at all, and the shares of stock lost all value. They were as worthless as a wooden nickel." Laney drank his cup dry and struggled with how to tell his story. "It was the accountant to Lord Surrey who explained it to me, in words that I couldn't fathom but I took to be true."

I tried to get Laney back telling some facts. "Captain, slow down a moment. When did this conversation with Norfolk's accountant take place?"

"The middle of February, 1616. A Monday it was."

"Didn't your Lord Surrey also lose all of his wealth?"

Laney nodded his head a few times. "I heard mention that there was an investigation into the widespread deceit and corruption concerning the South Brazil Company and that many members of Parliament were likely to be prosecuted."

"Not Norfolk?"

"No, certainly not Lord Surrey; he was an honest and good man." Laney emptied the bottle of rum. "Lord Surrey did send a note to apologize to me for my loss, and then, as a mark of his generosity, he gave me some shares of the New England Company as compensation for my losses."

"This is the company that buys and sells beaver skins?"

"Yes, Tisquantum, and it is you who will make my next fortune."

CHAPTER SIXTEEN

1622
Lord Baltimore

I FELT ITCHY. DIRTY, WITH oily skin from the smoke of St. John's chimneys. I missed the clean silence of Beothic life and I missed my family for the first time in seven years. Instead of setting traps with my boys and kissing the left ear of Oubee as the log turned to ash, I was eating salt cod and drinking St. John's beer. "This better be damned important, Captain Pike, dragging me down to this infernal place."

"You got my letter, I guess."

"Oubee read the letter aloud to the entire family maybe ten, twelve, times."

"Well, then, what do you think of my proposal to you and Oubee?"

"What? No time for a little idle chitchat? Maybe a 'How be you?' before we're off and running?"

"Time's a wasting," Pike said. No smile, no pat on the back. "Do you know anything at all about Lord Baltimore?"

"I know that Lord Baltimore is or was a papist. From what Tisquantum told me at one time or another, back in the old days,

Baltimore and Cromwell was friends." I was under full sail now. "In point of fact, Captain Pike, this admitted papist was given a New Founde Land plantation by the damn pointy-head Protestants."

"Pretty good, for a blue savage, at any rate." Pike gave me a feeble round of applause with two claps of his hands. "What do you know about his plantation?"

"Not much. A nice little harbor, I hear. Deep and protected by 'arms' on three sides—hills that are steep and rocky." I was stumped for any more facts or rumors. "What do you know about the man or his plantation?"

"Well now, I know it was years and years before Lord Baltimore finally brought his family to live in the place that he called Ferryland, and that in preparation for their arrival, he recruited a crew of Bristol-area farmers to plant fields of wheat, barley, oats, beans, peas, radishes, turnip, cabbage, and kale on his plantation. He also hired a crew of Welsh builders and a French engineer to build a magnificent solid stone mansion for his residence."

"Do tell," I said.

"Yup, and there were fortifications built around the harbor, plus a forge, saltworks, a brew house, and some comfortable dwellings for those doing all the work in the new village of Ferryland."

I looked around the bar we were in, as if I was some newcomer from Bristol. It was nice enough, called the Cod, like a dozen others around about St. John's City and Harbor. "Anything else I need to know before I finish my salt cod and beer and go back home?"

"Well, now, I also know that when they finally arrived in Ferryland that the man's wife complained constantly of the cold and wind and mosquitoes."

"Can't say that was very friendly of her," I said.

Pike didn't blink. "Do you know what else that papist fool did?"

"I can't begin to imagine."

Pike looked me in the eyes for the first time of this visit, abruptly changing the subject. "What name might you be using nowadays? Blue or Omrod?"

"My wife and children prefer Omrod."

"So be it. I'm not inclined to be upsetting the likes of Oubee, now."

I finished my beer and thumped the tankard on the pinewood table. "There's the other problem, sir. My wife prefers the name of Laura for all to call her."

The barkeep, who had been quietly eavesdropping on our conversation, nodded his head a few times before taking our empty tankards, filling them full, and thumping both back on the table. "That'll be on the house, Omrod," the barkeep said. The man was nearly a dwarf with his twisted back, stumpy legs, and crooked smile that had not a shred of affection in it. "So, Omrod, you must forgive me for being so far behind times with calling you Blue for so many years and serving you with the rest of my customers, even though you up and married an Indian squaw with a savage name of Oubee. All in the old days, of course."

I drank the foam and the top swallows of beer, all to let my head clear. "Good beer," I said. There was no gain to confronting the man or reminding him of long-past days when he and Oubee shared quips and jokes and distant memories.

"Only the best St. John's beer for St. John's fishermen," he said.

About halfway down the tankard, I gave a smile to the barkeep. He was leaning with his backside on the bar, not two paces from our table. "Listen, old friend, might you have a story to share about this Lord Baltimore fellow?"

He straightened a bit and came even closer to our table. "You won't believe it, Omrod, but what I do have to say came directly from an honest Welshman who worked for the fool."

"Go ahead—tell me and Captain Pike what you know."

"The damn papist lord had silver coins made with 'Spina Sanctus' printed on one side and 'Avalon' on the other."

"Ever seen one of those coins?"

"Naw, but that's only the beginning. He declared that his entire peninsula of land, including both St. John's Harbor and Ferryland Harbor, would be known as Avalon." The barkeep paused for a brief moment, indignation filling his tortured body.

"Ah, well," I said. "We're shut of him now, aren't we?"

"Mark it down," the barkeep said, "the papist Lord Baltimore left us with no word of warning. He abandoned Ferryland to a few Welshmen and moved his family way down south to start a Virginia plantation. The damn fool."

"It's been a long time since I've been here in this bar of yours, my friend. Hell, seven years since I've been in St. John's, I'd guess."

Now the barkeep gave me a pleasant smile. "I remember like it was yesterday, Blue—Omrod. It was you and the captain here who came in for a St. John's beer. Back from Hudson's river and with you busting to see Oubee and for Pike to hold his papist wife."

"You've a good memory, sir." I let my smile soften to let him know we could still be friends, in spite of his rant about savage names and such. "My old da always warned me to watch for the Bible-thumpers to get between friends. I hope you and me and Oubee can still sit here and have your company sometime soon. What about you, good sir—are you of a similar mind?"

"My good memory and St. John's beer is why I'm still in business after all these years." The little man waved his tankard of beer at me in a toast. "Tell you what, Blue, next time you and Oubee take a stool here in this bar, the beer is on my tab."

Now I could smile at the little man. "Da was always a one get straight on a matter. He said that friends can have some differences along the way, but in the end a good beer always settled the mind."

"A good man, your da," said the dwarf with the twisted back.

"I also remembered the day we returned from the Island of Eleuthera, true and well. Every single detail."

Pike stood from his chair. "We're finished here, Omrod. Let's go up to my home and see an old friend of yours."

We exchanged a friendly nod with the barkeep, then stepped away from our table. That was the way of it, nowadays. Hot and cold, friendly and evil, all from the same man in the space of a few tankards of beer. The little man was a god-man now, most of the time, anyway; and mostly he'd feel obligated to show the evil ways of us non-theists. Yet he was a man of the old New Founde Land days, and could still remember friends and hopeful times. I guess the barkeep was a man with a confused mind, much as was the case with the rest of us on this blighted island.

"Blue!" Shelagh hugged me with her warm Irish blood. "Blue," she repeated three more times. "Tell me of Oubee. Tell me of my only true friend."

"She is well," I whispered into her ear. "Also the boys and our daughter—they are strong and healthy, one and all.

Shelagh put me at arm's length. "Bring them back to us, Blue. I miss her terribly, and my boys keep asking about their friends John and David."

I dropped my arms. "As soon as I finish my report to Captain Pike, I will return to my Beothic home."

"Of course," she interjected, "you must return to your beautiful lake. But then, after you've talked and listened to Oubee, I hope upon hope that you will bring your entire family to St. John's City as quickly as possible." Shelagh gave me her green-eyed smile. "You will bring my friend Oubee back to me, won't you, Blue?"

"Still the queen of all you survey, I see."

"Not merely what I see, my lowly vassal. You must hear what I say and do exactly what I say."

"Or suffer what consequence, Queen Shelagh?"

"I will hug you and kiss you and repeat my wish into your ear in until you finally succumb to my royal pleasure."

"Please consider a truce, my queen. Your attack is too ferocious for any mortal to withstand."

Shelagh draped her arms and head on my shoulders. "Do what you must, my friend," she whispered. "Kiss Oubee and the children for me, and tell them how much I miss them."

"Oubee has a message for you, Shelagh."

"Tell me."

"My wife and I invite you and your family to visit us in our home near a beautiful lake that is surrounded by hills full of trees and animals. We would like to share with you the peaceful quiet and to appreciate the fact that there is never a single person dressed in black within sight or sound."

"Ahh, Blue, so you know of our problems with the god-people?"

"Yes."

"Your lake and hills sound very attractive, I must admit."

"I will hear from your husband this morning, and after a very short visit, I will leave to report everything that I am told to Oubee and to our mother."

"I miss you and Oubee," said Shelagh.

Captain Pike escorted me to the tavern favored by the gentry of New Founde Land. There was Bristol beer, of course, and likely a barkeep with straight back and no memory of the old days. A fancy man with wire glasses on his nose came to lead us through the large ornate dining hall and into a small room with a table and four chairs. It was a simple room, clearly designed for the gentry of St. John's City to conduct their important business, drink a decent beer, and consume food that was unknown to all but their class of people.

"Two beers and a plate of pickled eggs," Pike ordered.

The fancy man disappeared and we sat down.

I was first to begin the conversation. "Your wife is after me to move to this civilized town, and I don't like the idea one bit."

"Be quiet for a while and listen to what I have to say."

"You're still my captain," I said.

A serving man entered our room, placed the beer and eggs near the center of the table, turned, and left us.

Pike consumed two eggs and half a pint of beer before asking, "What do you know of Ferryland as it stands today?"

"Nothing. Are there elves as well as fairies at Ferryland?"

Pike smiled. "Well, now, the place is named after some Frenchman or other, and Bristol folk say Ferryland is the best translation of an impossible name."

"Well and good sir, and even though I'm nothing but a trumped-up red savage, I do in fact know that the papist Lord Baltimore built a fort and town around a neat little harbor and that he and his wife got tired of the long, dark, cold nights and deserted their town for his Virginia plantation."

Pike nodded. "You remember a tad from yesterday's time at the Cod Tavern, I see."

"I can also remember that Da always advised me to avoid all papists as dangerous to my well-being, so I haven't given much thought to the adventures of Lord Baltimore or his magical land."

"After Baltimore went south, Cromwell had all the cannon taken from the Ferryland fort and then turned the little town into rubble."

"Da also warned me about the likes of Cromwell and his pointy-headed priests. They are worse than the papists, he always said."

"Why's that?" Pike seemed genuinely interested in what Da thought of Cromwell and Baltimore and all their various god-people.

"Well, now, it seems that the pointy-headed protesters believe that their god and the man telling about the god are one and the same." I ate my first egg and then finished my beer. "The papists, on the other hand, say the same thing about their god-people."

"That's it! From your Da?" Pike had a big smile on his face.

"Well now, he also said that the papists keep a little or no distance between their required pledges to their god and to the king's taxes, but that the pointy-heads fill both hands with taxes to Cromwell plus the god pledges twice over."

"They are called 'round' heads, not pointy."

"Why?"

"Cromwell has his boys cut their hair short all around their head, while the papists have long ringlets or wigs."

"Da would have a pox on both—round or pointy."

"I'm getting ready to take a lease on all of Ferryland," said Pike.

"Why?"

"I'm married to a papist, and you are married to a red savage. The two women seek solace from the other, and you and I need a safe refuge for our families."

"I have lived with my family for fourteen years in a safe refuge. My boys are now warriors, and I have some gray hairs in my head. Why don't you and your family come to live with my Beothic family?" I waited through his silence before adding: "Our mamateeks are much warmer than your mansion and much more comfortable than your pile of stone, and if one is turned into ash, another is built within a few days."

Pike rang a little bell that he picked up from the table. Almost immediately the serving man appeared. "A bottle of wine and beef steaks," Pike ordered.

The red wine was decanted, and we sipped quietly until the meat was delivered.

"The world is a mess." Pike shook his carving knife at me. "The plague is everywhere, and every prince and pope is at war with one another. France is again on the attack and seeks to take New Founde Land from the English. Refugees the world over are seeking a place to rest."

"It is quiet and restful in the far hills, and near a large lake. I think it is safer for our families with the red savages than with the fairies and elves and mean-spirited gods."

We finished the meat and emptied the bottle.

"Listen, Blue. Return to your family. Talk with them and listen to the wisdom of their stories. Work with your savage neighbors and play with your sons. Hunt for answers as you will, my friend. It will take a year or so to clean the mess of Ferryland and to recruit workers and craftsmen to live in our village. I'll send a messenger to you at this time next year. When you see him, please tell him what you and Oubee have decided about moving to Ferryland."

"Where does the gold of Hudson's river play into this story of yours?"

"I'm in contact with a few important merchants of Bristol." Pike leaned forward across the table to whisper. "My lease at Ferryland will end at about the time that England chases the Dutch from New Amsterdam."

"Two years? Ten years? What is your best guess?"

"We'll be moving from Ferryland when our boys are mature men and ready to begin their own plantations along the beautiful river of Hudson. Eight to ten years, I imagine."

I sat with this information until the servant delivered another bottle of wine and disappeared. "I'll have at least two years with my family to make a decision?"

"Earlier, if you and Oubee so choose," said Pike.

I filled and drained my cup of red wine. "Listen, Captain, I'll agree to talking with Oubee and the boys, but I'll make no commitment to come live with your fairies."

"So be it," said Pike.

The French soldiers and their pet savages came to our village by the beautiful lake a few months after leaving Pike and Shelagh. The officer screamed words I could not understand, and suddenly three savages killed the old man with the French name and took his grandson as a slave. They pushed the rest of us out into the snow, and while two savages and a French soldier stood guard, the rest of the invaders stole my gun and all our food. In rapid order, the sonsabitches burned all the village mamateeks and our storage sheds, then disappeared into the early dusk.

Ours was the only dwelling remaining in the village, and the dozen survivors moaned and cried. There was no food for anyone, no weapons for defense or hunting, merely the omnipresent cold. At dawn Oubee's brother and a few others headed for a Micmac village to the west. Oubee's mother and two other women headed southeast in an effort to find a small village of relatives along Placentia Bay. I guided my Smyth family on the long walk to St. John's City.

Oubee said little, and the children followed as silent refugees to a dismal goal. There was a persistent buzzing in my head that prevented any comments from my family to sink into my mind. So it was that beyond my call to stop for rest and the setting of snares or to prepare for an evening meal, I tolerated no conversation as we traveled each step away from our home.

Shelagh and Oubee held each other for long spells and cried off and on with such regularity that the boys of both families took to leaving the Pike mansion during daylight hours for adventures that were not shared with any parent at all. Pike and I spent time in his office and walking the streets in constant discussion over how we would manage Ferryland. It was six weeks after our arrival in St. John's City, the early fall of 1622, that the Smyth family and the Pike family took residence in their Ferryland homes. It was an easy sail from St. John's, south to Ferryland—eight to ten hours by sail, or a hard six days by oxcart or sleigh, in decent weather.

During the spring of 1623, I had Da's old anvil delivered by oxcart from St. John's City to Ferryland. Pike had an order for supplies he wanted delivered from Bristol Town, and I was able to add two bellows, three pair of vise-grips, and hammers of six different weights to the same load delivered at our new Ferryland wharf.

Soon enough I had a rough stock of black iron ore stacked in back of my forge shed, and set to work making runners for the huge sleds we used to haul wood during the dark season. I also made skates for the children in Ferryland who could not afford them. I put a fancy curl on the front of the few skates that I actually sold each year. Of course

I welded and fit the hub rings for wagon tires, put the shoes on nearly every horse that trod the Ferryland shore, and I tried and tried to train my boys to be smithies. David stuck with the craft but showed little passion for the hard work. He reluctantly promised to continue the Smyth line when his own sons were of age. John was twitchy with his attention to the forge and was more often out with the fishermen or cutting trees in the woods. Both were good boys, and I loved them almost as much as I loved our daughter, Suzanne.

Oubee could sew my aprons with strong stitches and cook caribou in the same manner as her mother, but when Pike and Shelagh and their children, and grandchildren came for a visit in our small cottage, Oubee would, more often than not, cook a fresh cod in the many varieties of *Robalo con Algas*. Always with a side dish of *Arroz Doce de Afife*, of course. Even my son John smiled when he joined us at our meals with the Pike family.

Out of thin air, David asked a question of the gathering. "What was his name? The smart one that could speak any language on earth?"

"Tisquantum," said Oubee. "My cousin and true friend."

"What have you heard of the fellow of late?" Pike asked.

"Is he not in Portugal still?" I asked.

"I heard he was in England, slave to that bastard Laney," Pike said.

"Can you not ask a friend or relative in Bristol to find the poor man?" said Shelagh.

Pike finished his glass of red wine. "Yes, certainly. I'll write to my uncle and have him put someone on the job."

"Maybe we could buy his freedom," said Oubee.

"Certainly," said Pike. "Certainly."

"It's not a bad life," Oubee whispered into my ear. She snuggled against my chest in a perfect spoon, my left hand on her breast.

"If we'd stayed at our home at the lake," I said, "the French would have made us good papists by now."

"Or dead savages," she mumbled. "It's not always bad here."

I whispered into her ear, "We'll move to where they don't call us bad names soon enough."

"Suzanne has her eyes on a boy, so I suspect later rather than sooner is the better choice." My lovely Laura kissed my arm and made a huge sigh from deep in her stomach. "She's near sixteen now, and thinks of naught but boys."

"Not like you, at all," I said. "You were a whaleboat captain and my constant enemy at sixteen."

"Not enemy!" Laura turned her body in my arms and chewed on my ear for a bit. "More like a teacher of a very ignorant child." She tickled my ribs and whispered, "Now you are nearly the perfect husband."

"You were the perfect teacher," I answered. "No exceptions at all."

"I said you are *nearly* the perfect husband, my dear oaf."

"What is left for me to learn, my love?"

"Less talk and more action," she said.

I moved to hold one breast in my hand and kiss her on the neck. "Better?"

"Will you please shut up, my ignorant child?"

Later, much later—early morning, in fact—Laura moved her head from my stomach to my upper chest. She was warm and soft and still sleepy. "Do the boys both know the story by rote?" she whispered into my ear.

I sat up in our bed, to better watch the expression on Laura's face. "Well, David has everything in order, but John only on his civilized days," I said.

"Twenty-three, seven-tiered cake, and cold air from the ground," she whispered.

"What?" I said, "I remember the cake with an even number of tiers. Six or eight."

"Seven, for certain," she said.

I tried to retrieve our old ditty, but thoughts of the past night kept intruding into my mind. Laura continued. "John was wondering a while back if the twenty-three was from Nut Island or from where you waited with the Leni Lapa."

"From Nut Island," I said.

"Are you certain of your facts?"

"Damn," I said. "We'll go over the entire story next time both boys are here and together."

Oubee nodded. "I'll take their wives and children to find some eggs from the seabirds while you get the story straight in their heads."

"Good. With those two, no distractions are necessary."

"Two weekends from now, Suzanne has her birthday party. That'll be a good time for storytelling."

"Two weeks, then. Good."

"Twenty-three, eight layers, and a cave that spews cold air," said Laura Smyth.

"Right as rain," said Omrod Smyth.

CHAPTER SEVENTEEN

1622
Squantum

"TELL ME, MY SLAVE, WHAT did you find with all that looking around?" Laney stared at me over the aft rail of his miserable little ship. "Any English alive?"

The dinghy clapped sharp little taps against the ship's hull, and it was all I could manage to hold tight to the ship. "Secure this line to that cleat by your feet, Captain Laney." The poor man moved in slow arthritic movements to complete the simple task. I kept my own voice as steady as possible. "Now give me your hand and pull me aboard, then we'll talk."

Climbing aboard was difficult for me in the extreme, especially with the ship coming about and wind whipping me with spirited force. When I was finally able to roll over the aft rail onto the deck, a short rest was required before I could move again.

"Any English at all?" he repeated, staring down at me with blank comprehension in his eyes.

"There were only Passamaquoddy people ashore," I said.

The fool shook his head. "Why must those damn savages have such awkward names?" He was such a dumb, ingenuous fool, and my master in this world. "Let's go to my quarters," he said. "The wind has shifted, and we're getting under way. He bent at the waist and leered at me. "When you can manage to walk the great distance, that is," he added.

"In a moment," I said.

I stayed in my prone position to rest my body and clear my head. Then again, I thought, maybe he is the genius between us and me the fool. More likely, we were both fools and deserved the other as a fitting companion. Eventually I managed to lift myself upright and did indeed manage the long walk to my master's cabin and to sit at his table.

He stared at me for a long moment and eventually shoved a cup across the table. "Rum," he said.

"There were no English alive that I could find," I said.

"Your friends with the strange name—what do they say about the English settlement?"

"They told me that two years past a small batch of white invaders had been dropped ashore from a large ship and left to spend a long, dark winter."

"No survivors?"

"None."

"Is there any interest on the part of your Quoddy friends in selling beaver pelts to us next spring? After the sea is free of ice, of course."

"None."

Laney drained his own cup and stood to encourage my departure. "Get out of my sight, my worthless slave. We'll try down near Cape Cod next."

I stood to leave. "Cape Cod? That's Wampanoag Confederation territory, I believe."

"Nogs and Quaddys, what can be next?"

"Who are they?" I squinted into the sharp winter sun. They appeared to my weak eyes as black ants, scurrying about their nest.

Laney leaned close to my ear. "I'll have a couple of my boys row the dinghy over for a parley. You go with them and find out what they're about. You know what I mean by parley, don't you?" Laney squinted back at me. "None of your fancy talk, now. Just get on and off their damned ship with answers to my questions."

"Me Squantum. Me help all English people."

"Good. Perfect. Get going," said Captain Laney.

I watched as the ship people lined at the rail to stare at me. I'd added a little red oakum here and there and even found an old turkey feather to stick in my gray hair. "Me friend!" I called across the water. "Friend," I repeated.

They hauled me up over the stern rail, and I stood surrounded by black-robed men, women in black dresses, and children in black rags. All were sunken-eyed, clearly suffering the last stages of starvation. "Help us," an old woman whispered. "Have you food aboard your ship?"

"We'll pay everything we have for food." This said in a loud voice from a tall man.

"I've noticed that you have been shuttling back and forth, ship to shore, this last day," I said. "What is your plan with all this movement?"

"You speak our language as an educated man," said the now-alarmed old woman.

"Who are you?" said the tall man.

"You may call me Squantum for short discussions or Tisquantum in more formal conversations."

"Tell me, where did you receive your education, Tisquantum?" The tall man took a step closer to me.

"At a Cistercian monastery in Portugal, my good sir."

"Praise to God! I'm very impressed with your erudition, sir, I hope to have a long conversation with you in the near future." The tall man actually bowed his head toward me.

"Squantum," said the old woman. "What about food for us?"

"Tisquantum," said the tall man. "We are indeed in desperate straits, and God will reward you with any help that you may be able to provide his starving penitents."

The smell was equal to the plague-prison perfume created by the Cistercian Order of Holy Monks. The same smell enveloped the entire ship. My memory of the aroma spread from dead red savages matched those of the dead English people. Cistercian or Puritan—was there even a mite of difference between them? Both were confident in the benevolence of their own god, and both generated the same perfume of death in equal parts.

I walked over to the aft rail and called down to the dinghy. "Listen to me, Sailors. Tell Captain Laney to send us a few barrels of beer and as much salt cod as he can afford. Bring the food back here to this ship called the *Mayflower*."

One sailor called, "Aye," shipped the oars, and started back to Captain Laney's ship.

After watching the dinghy depart, I returned to the Pilgrims and their crew. "I am here as a representative of the New England Company," I said, and when no one responded to my declaration, I continued. "I am here to help you build a successful plantation in this Colony of Massachusetts."

"We are starving to death," said the old woman. "All are of us are starving, and some of us have already died."

"Did you hear me order beer and salt cod for the *Mayflower*?"

They remained silent in contemplation of the old woman's statement of their problem and my answer to her. Finally, I spoke in a soft, compassionate voice. "The people who have lived here in this land that we see to the horizon are called by others the Nauset."

"If others call them the Nauset, then what do they call themselves?" asked the tall man.

"The People. They call themselves the People and declare themselves to be the best loved by the spirits and therefore the most important people in all creation."

The tall man was flummoxed by my information. "Where are these 'best-loved people,' Tisquantum? We have remained at anchor in this bay for nearly two months, and no one has preceded you, good sir, with any word of help."

"The Black Death has devastated the Nauset and their neighbors of the Wampanoag Confederation. Entire villages are empty of residents. The elders who remember the old stories are dead. The youngsters who were to take the place of the elders are dead."

The tall man digested my story with tolerable sympathy. He nodded and shook his head in morose appreciation for the difficulties encountered by others, savage people or not. "From what you say, Tisquantum, it is clear that the true God of the universe has likely prepared the way for our arrival by killing the savages who would stand in our way of implementing the grand design envisioned by the true God, whose son is Jesus Christ—"

I held my hand to stop the flow of well-remembered clichés. "Tell me, sir, who is named the person in charge of this mission to the New World?"

"It is I," said the tall man.

"What may I call you, sir?"

"Edward Winslow is my name. I am the elder for the Plymouth Church."

Tall and quiet was Edward Winslow, with soft brown eyes and a manner of listening that I found most pleasant. We could work together, the two of us. "Pastor Winslow," I said. "All of you must evacuate this ship as soon as possible. The smell of death must be cleared from your nostrils if any of you hope to survive much longer."

He stood stock-still, but his eyes showed an obvious comprehension of the health problems suffocating his congregation. "We are building homes ashore as quickly as possible, Tisquantum. Do you have thoughts of other options for us?"

"Come with me—you and three others who are held accountable by the survivors of this pilgrimage. Quickly, now. Over the side of your *Mayflower* to your own ship's dinghy, for the tide is in our favor."

I had Winslow set the sail and I managed the tiller, with my four passengers on the two benches facing me. "How many were in your congregation when you departed England?" I asked.

With no hesitation Winslow said, "One hundred and two— seventy-three males and twenty-nine females."

"And now, good sir?"

"What with the scurvy and winter cold, about three-quarters of the total are still alive."

"Are fewer dying now that you are safely at anchor or not?"

"Starvation and severe cold add to the previous deprivations, Tisquantum, and the rate of our misery is clearly increasing day by day."

"So I would guess," I answered.

We maintained our silence for the rest of our short journey, and soon the dinghy was sledding through shallow water. The man named Standish was first out of the dinghy, and he took the bow to guide and pull the craft to shore. He was also the first to lead the way to his chosen site for the insipient town of New Plymouth.

Standish was a head shorter than all the rest, and with his constant chirping voice, he put me in mind of a particular wren that was partial to muddy, marshy land. "We spent two weeks looking high and low, and without any reservation at all we determined that this spot is far superior to any of the other options considered." Standish preened for a moment. "Here." He pointed to the foundation of a possible building at the very first stage of construction. "Here is our meeting house and"—he gave a casual wave of his arm—"there you see the beginning of Plymouth Town."

Indeed, and a very fragile beginning it was. In one instance there was a partial wall of small logs, to the height of a dwarf such as Miles Standish. The logs were held upright with smaller posts pounded into the mud on both sides to hold them in place. Another similar effort was complemented with daubs of mud mixed with moss that were plugged into the most grievous holes showing between the twisted logs.

"Forgive me, gentlemen of Plymouth Town, but I must interrupt this interesting tour of what will certainly become a substantial community."

Standish held a hand to my face. "We've come a long way before your mysterious appearance, Squanto, so listen to your masters to their completion before you impose another interruption of any sort."

"How many Pilgrims have died since the *Mayflower* dropped anchor here in this bay?" I spoke with my Queen Elizabeth's voice and looked at the tiny man with her full quota of disdain.

"Nearly half the congregation, plus a few of the sailors," said John Carver, the duly elected governor of Plymouth Colony.

"The total, as of this morning, is six of my crew dead," said Captain Christopher Jones, master and owner of the *Mayflower*.

With my voice remaining at the tone and strength of imperial dignity, I said, "How would you characterize the health of the remaining Pilgrims and crew? By that I mean those who sleep every single night in the fetid confines of a ship that has held them prisoner for a time exceeding four months. How do they fare, these visitors from England?"

"All are near death," said John Carver. "Only Captain Standish has the vitality of a healthy man, and he has been a true Christian with his constant help of all aboard the *Mayflower.*"

"True enough," said Captain Jones. "All my men are down with one problem or another, and Captain Standish has been a great help to all, including yours truly."

"We must remove all the occupants of the *Mayflower* and bring them to shore," I said.

"Nonsense!" said Miles Standish. "It'll be six to eight weeks before we have adequate shelter for the citizens of our town. Nonsense, indeed!"

"The ice is still on all the freshwater lakes and ponds," said Governor Carver. "We'll have another blizzard or two before the weather breaks to the spring season." He drew a deep breath. "None of us could survive the harsh winter of this place without adequate shelter."

"Follow me," I said, and without confirming the fact, I led the Puritans of Plymouth to their eventual survival.

In point of fact, it happened that when my manager of foul deeds, Captain Laney, dropped me ashore on Cape Cod, he introduced me to another of his employees—an Abenaki warrior named Samoset. After the miserable Laney disappeared back to his miserable ship, Samoset in turn introduced me to Massasoit, a sachem of the Pokanoket people.

The three of us savages spent a fortnight together, gnashing our teeth and disclaiming one villain or another before finally designing a scheme that might diminish the intrusion of the Pilgrims upon the loose confederation of villages that surrounded their self-declared Plymouth Town. All the savage villages of the Cape Cod area had suffered from a recent raging plague. Every village had been severely ravaged, but the immediate neighborhood of Plymouth Town had been completely destroyed of all citizens.

"These wigwams hold no evidence of the plague," I said.

"How do you know such things?" Standish chirped. "A savage is still a savage and always an alien to the love of our Almighty God."

"Did you and sixteen others stand in this very dwelling not two weeks past?" I gave no time for interruption. "And did you not order these sixteen Pilgrims to forage in and about this home of the previous residents? Did you not in fact encourage your men to steal their tools and their food?"

"All is according to God's grand design," proclaimed Standish. "It was the Lord God who ravaged these savages, and it was he who made available to his children their remnants. The mere dregs left by those savages are of no consequence to a true Christian."

"Still, Captain Standish, two weeks or more have passed since you rooted around in the homes of the departed savages, and I notice with my two eyes that you have survived your conquest of the plague-killed villagers, with no harm from the plague to you or to the other sixteen visitors."

"Such is God's will," said Standish.

Carver and Jones smiled through their fuzzy beards, and Mr. Winslow, with his gentle voice, said, "Tell us, Tisquantum, what do you recommend that we do at this point in our lives?"

"We must repair the wigwams and fill them with Pilgrims and crewmen. Quickly! A few families today and the rest within another day or two. We must get everyone out of the cesspool they have created on board the *Mayflower*. No exceptions! All must evacuate the ship or die of their own constant bile and their own insufferable bloody flux."

"Pshaw!" said Standish. "They'll freeze to death on the first night spent in these flimsy tents."

"Today, you and I, Captain Standish, will repair this dwelling, and tonight we two will spend the night. If we survive, we will then teach all the rest what they need to know in order to survive in the Colony of Massachusetts."

The little man squared his shoulders and nodded. "We'll see what we see," he said.

The *Mayflower* was empty and the former Nauset village full within six days. Every home had a stash of salt cod and at least one bucket of Bristol beer. Captain Standish was a whirlwind of activity, helping with the digging of privies and wells and organizing hunters and fishermen to feed the starving lot of Pilgrims.

Pastor Edward Winslow walked across a muddy field to join with me and Standish. "God's blessings," he said. There was no strength in his voice, and gray skin covered his face. "We now sleep better at night, thanks to you two gentlemen."

It was obvious that the pastor had more to say but needed our patience to order his thoughts. We both remained silent.

"Two more of our Pilgrims are now sitting in the arms of God." Another stretch of silence. "We need more food to live, good sirs. Is there hope of charity from our savage neighbors?"

"No," I said. "They are in much the same predicament as you are—and dying as quickly."

"My prayers seem unanswered," said Pastor Winslow.

Captain Standish and I remained silent.

Winslow looked directly at me. "Help us, Tisquantum. Please help this sorry lot of God's children."

"There is one chance that I see, but it seems an unlikely possibility."

"Tell us," said Standish.

"Please, in the name of the Lord Jesus Christ, give us some hope," said the pastor.

"Follow me," I said.

"The people whose homes you are now using call this brook Agawam," I said. "Please note that at low tide you can traverse the brook with water to your knees." Winslow and Standish studied the moving water but made no comment. "At high tide the water will reach the chin of a very tall man."

"Do I see a cloud of small fish passing in front of me?" asked Standish.

"The Bristol people call them alewives or smelt."

"Yes, certainly," said Winslow. "Together with dandelion leaves and salted water, the small fish make a hearty soup."

"Indeed," said Standish.

"We are near low tide, and you can clearly see a large battery of sticks stuck upright in the mud."

"Yes, I see them," said Standish. "They are arrayed in a manner that would funnel fish carried by a flood tide to a small confined area." The captain smiled. "It is a fishing weir! I've seen them used on the coast of France."

"This fishing weir of the Nauset people is currently in disrepair, but in one day, with everyone able to walk at hand, we could replace the missing sticks and interweave both ends of the weir with brush strands."

"One day?" asked Standish. "This old weir can be made into an effective fish trap in one day?"

"One day, in freezing-cold water," I said.

Pastor Winslow nodded in our direction. "What benefit would we Pilgrims gain from this venture?"

"Fifty barrels of fish per day," I said.

I worked with God's children on that long day. From dawn to dusk I was often up to my neck in water that was derived from recently melted snow. I joined a good number of God's children with their first taste of hot alewife chowder that very next evening. I joined a dozen pilgrims and two crewmen in spending the next week shivering under a pile of blankets. The old woman seemed to take a special pleasure in feeding me hot soup—once at dawn and again at dusk. Her smile was a constant solace to me from the first sip to the last.

The remains of my bout with the plague combined with the day submerged in cold water decimated my energy and turned me into an invalid. The old woman fed me bowls and bowls of hot soup, along with constant prayers offered to the true God in heaven for my recovery. I slept both day and night with little thought of any god. There were no dreams—only a constant black cloud in my mind.

I could walk a bit with the aid of a stout stick after two weeks as a shielded invalid, and it became apparent that Standish needed my help in placating the local village leaders. "The foolish savages are arguing over nothing," he moaned. "Come, you and I need to talk sense with our neighbors."

"I can barely walk a few paces," I said. "My head is filled with wool threads, and my tongue is a burnt stick."

"Now, now. Let me help you up and on our way. It'll be good for you to be up and about. Come now, Tisquantum, off we go."

It took nearly five days, and I have little memory of what passed during that time. A treaty was finally written, and it seemed that all the participants agreed that the document included the essential thoughts from one and all, and it was signed by all the village sachem and by Captain Miles Standish.

"Good work, Squanto," he whispered into my ear. "I'd never have managed the treaty without your help."

Four soldiers of Captain Standish's army carried me back to the Nauset village on a litter made of wooden poles and army coats. I stopped drinking the alewife soup, and the old woman cried into her hands. I pulled the wool blankets over my head.

The tremors stopped within a day, and my dreams became warm and in full color over the next few nights. My true brother, Blue, smiled at me, and we talked about the old days and the wonderful man we both called Da and how it was that Da, we both agreed, had been the smartest man in our lives. Oubee also appeared, smiled at the two of us old men, and disappeared. Then there was black mist that replaced the red sky. Black silence enshrouded every particle of my being. Finally, there was nothing.

CHAPTER EIGHTEEN

1634
Providence Plantation

W HEN CAPTAIN PIKE AND SHELAGH and their two boys decided
they'd move to Ireland, I was just plain dumbfounded. Here it
was Pike's idea for the Smyth family to move to Ferryland, and then
off he jumps to Ireland.

"Why?" I said.

"To buy an estate near Galway," Pike said to me and Oubee.

"What about Hudson's river and that big plantation plan of
yours?" I was more than irritated; I was scared to my bones. It was the
protection provided by his wealth and the reputation of his family that
allowed Oubee and me to survive on the island of New Founde Land.
Insults called to Shelagh as a "Catholic whore" were one thing, but
rocks hurled at Laura was another thing altogether.

"It'll be much safer at our home near Kerry than for us than here
at Ferryland."

Pike seemed unable to hear my words or understand the dilemma
of the Smyth family. He kept staring at the ground.

"Captain Pike," I said. "What about the gold?"

"The gold will stay where it is until the times are right." He looked at my belt buckle, but his eyes kept blinking. "Come and visit us in Kerry, if you have a mind."

I knew, of course, that it was the constant terror of words that pushed Pike and Shelagh from Ferryland. In fact, I knew that they were constantly threatened by the miserable likes of one Puritan minister or another. All of those miserable cowards stood around one place or another, like black crows over a dead cow, chattering on and on about Catholics killing Christ or some other idiotic nonsense. Erasmus Stourton wasn't the only devil dressed in black, nor the only one with a packet of vile words in his mouth, but he was always the first with rousing his flock of pinched-faced Protestants to make life miserable for Shelagh and her family.

"We'll try Ireland for a change," said Shelagh. "I'll miss you, Laura, more than either of us can imagine." She took a deep breath and squinted her eyes. "But we cannot take the words of those vulture-neck bastardy sonsabitches another day."

Shelagh and Laura cried on each other's shoulder for weeks and weeks until the Pike family actually boarded the French merchant ship in the early spring of 1634 and waved good-bye to the Smyth family. The fog was thick offshore, so as soon as their ship left St. John's Harbor, it disappeared.

It seemed, from what I heard from the fishermen in and around St. John's Harbor, that the French ship had probably been sucked into the tail end of a hurricane and sunk. Others, more familiar with the ways of commerce than navigation, claimed that the ship was lost simply because the French captain and crew were ignorant and not suitably aware of the hidden rocks scattered off the shore of New Founde Land. A few barrels of wine came ashore on a small beach near Capelin Bay. Pieces of wreckage large and small were noted by sailors and those that walked deserted beaches in search of treasure, but nothing more.

When Laura first heard the news, she dropped to the floor of our house, and tucked herself into a ball for the best part of a morning. She cried and screamed and pulled her hair until noon when she stood, wiped the tears and snot from her face, and prepared our noon-time meal. No one talked at the table, and only the boys ate anything at all. Suzanne cleared the table and washed the dishes while the rest of the Smyth family found quiet corners to think and brood and let small tears ease from one eye or the other.

The black crows of all the Puritan congregations flapped about with fiendish grins and loud voices, all crowing that the Roman Catholic captain and crew had received a smite or two from the true God. "We have been given an example of God's good judgement," Stourton told his parishioners. "Praise our Lord, for he loves us above all others on his earth."

"I fear for our lives," Oubee said. We sat in a circle, sons and daughter, to discuss our options, now that Pike and his entire family were proclaimed dead. "Tell us, my husband and father of my children, what shall we do to survive?"

I had been back to the name Omrod for more than ten years now. Oubee was Ma Smyth or Laura, when asked by some neighbor or other. "No more with the Blue and Oubee," I told the boys and Suzanne. "If some busybody asks, just say your Da is a Bristol fisherman named Omrod and your ma was a Portugee washerwoman named Laura. Other than that, you've not got a memory for any bit of our family history."

"Yes sir," they answered.

"Aren't the Portugee as Roman as the Irish?" David asked.

"That's exactly what I'm warning you about, David. The smartass comments that get you and the family into more trouble than life is worth." I gave him the threat of my backhand, and here he was a grown man at thirty-three years of age and as strong as any horse in Avalon. "Do you understand my meaning, my son?"

"Yes sir, Da, I do."

I gave a brief nod to show I expected a more than a simple yes or no.

David sat straight in his chair. "It stands to reason, Da, that with Stourton's gang of pious thugs able to chase a gentry's family to hell or worse, then you can bet the family fortune that the Smyth family's name will now and forever stand defamed at every Sunday service in Ferryland."

Now I sat straight in my chair. "Tisquantum certainly gave you a mouthful of words to chew on, didn't he?"

David had a lovely smile. "I do miss the old bugger. It's been years and years since he last took me in hand."

"That'll be 1614 since he took you in hand, and that 'old bugger' is the same age as your Da." I gave David the grimace we both knew for a smile. "What do you have in mind for the Smyth family, son David?"

"That box under your bed with a few silver coins rattling about— is that the extent of our fortune?"

"Just those silver coins," I said. "We're down to a precious few, and that's no lie."

"Da, tell us—is there anything else we should know? Me and Robert, that is."

I smiled with no teeth showing. "Your ma and I have decided to head down to Providence Plantation."

"Is that a fact." David said.

"It is, indeed, and soon as I can find a ship to take my labor in exchange for our passage, we'll be on our way."

"You'd go aboard as a deckhand?"

"A week or so of some idiot yelling orders at me seems a fair exchange for the ride."

Robert looked up from the store of rocks he was studying. "Does Laura, our ma, get to wash the captain's undies for her passage?"

"Robert, Robert, my boy, you'd better come along with your ma and da because that mouth of yours is worse than David's and will be your certain death in the very near future if you stay here in New Founde Land."

Robert held a shiny stone up for our examination. "Here's a beauty, for certain."

"What's the use of cluttering the house with a bunch of dusty rocks?" Ma was curious, not angry, at her younger son.

"Some are just pretty to see, but a few are powerful in a special way."

"How so?" asked Ma.

Robert made that fuzzy-eyed look of his—the one that showed whenever he was staring at his damn collection of rocks. "Don't be surprised, Ma, but I'm finding that some of my stones are good to help in finding something special."

"Like what?" I said, with the same tone of voice that I often gave to Robert: a spate of impatience tinged with anger.

"The stones vary, one to the other." Robert was certainly never reduced in words by my tone of voice or any feeling in my gut. "One stone might show where to dig a well for water, while another stone might help find some lost gold. A woman's ring or man's coin, for instance."

I was afraid that I looked at Robert with a very worrisome stare. "Gold coin, you say."

"Well, now, truth be told, Da, I've nothing in this pile of stones to tell me where to find gold or water, either one, but I'll keep looking for the one that tells me of special magic powers."

"Now, Robert, I thought you were shutting down on this magic stone business." I was more begging than telling. "Here you are a married man and thirty years of age. You've got to settle down and get some honest and steady work."

"I'm thirty-one, Da, and the wife whose name you never use is called Rachel." Robert always figured it was best to attack than take any guff from me.

Ma intervened. "I understand that Rachel is with child—can that be true?"

"Indeed she is with child—a male child whose name shall be Asael Smith." Robert smiled in his phony sweet way. "That'll be S-M-I-T-H Smith. No more with the name for a man who pounds horseshoes into shape."

"It'll be one of your stones telling if Rachel will deliver a son, will it not?" David displayed his real smile to his pretentious brother.

Robert in turn flashed a stone with bright red colors to the entire family. It was marked with a vivid green streak down the middle. "I can charge two silver coins to tell any woman if her child will be born living, and another silver coin to tell if it is a boy or girl."

"We'll have to board a ship to Providence straightaway," I said. "Before the good Reverend Stourton catches on to Robert's shenanigans, that is." I had to give Robert a serious notion to chew on. "Do you not know for a fact that the Reverend Stourton'll name you a witch with such shenanigans with pretty rocks and have your butt on a big toasty fire before you can say a word?"

Robert held both hands in mock surrender toward me. "Oh, woe is me, dear father. I hereby promise to sew my mouth shut till we reach Providence Town."

I held both my hands up as a sign for family peace. "Listen, Robert, to your father for a change. You may want to consider that a sharp needle through your lips may also save the lives of our entire family."

Robert signaled his true surrender to the family. "I'm sorry, Da. You'll have no more back talk from me."

David smiled his best older-brother smile. "Da, tell us what you want from us," he said. "Now that we have such family harmony, that is."

I settled into my chair. "What could you be wanting, my boys? Name what you have in your very own mind."

Robert was first off the mark. "I'll tell you, Da, I would appreciate your telling us some of the old-time family stories as we travel along the way to Providence Town." He had the audacity to wink an eye at me. "I want to hear the stories you've never told before."

"Well now, if you're buying the pints, my boy, then I'll be telling the stories."

Robert was steadfast with his request. "New stories, Da, new stories. No more of the old Blue and Tisquantum adventures. No more of you and Ma and the Beothic people. Never-told stories is what I want to hear."

"Son, I've got stories that'll cross your eyes."

"Like, for example, Da—what will I get for each pint of bitters?"

"Stories of pirates and buried gold—that's what I have in mind."

"I'm packed and ready," Robert said. "What about you and Ma?"

Ma gave us the favor of an old-time Oubee smile. "Just give me a week to sell what I can, then we're off to Providence Town."

"And north of there, I vow," said Robert. "My red and black stones say the Smith family will follow the rivers of Henry Hudson to the north. North, always north."

"Do you see a six-layered cake for a mountain?" Suzanne grinned. "Or maybe a north-flowing stream and a cave that spews cold air as well?"

"Not from the stones at hand," said Robert, "but soon enough, I'll wager."

www.ingramcontent.com/pod-product-compliance
Lightning Source LLC
Chambersburg PA
CBHW030319200626
46816CB00006BA/1857